the perfect block

(a jessie hunt psychological suspense—book 2)

blake pierce

ISBN: 978-1-64029-697-8

BOOKS BY BLAKE PIERCE

A JESSIE HUNT PSYCHOLOGICAL SUSPENSE SERIES
THE PERFECT WIFE (Book #1)
THE PERFECT BLOCK (Book #2)
THE PERFECT HOUSE (Book #3)

CHLOE FINE PSYCHOLOGICAL SUSPENSE SERIES
NEXT DOOR (Book #1)
A NEIGHBOR'S LIE (Book #2)
CUL DE SAC (Book #3)

KATE WISE MYSTERY SERIES
IF SHE KNEW (Book #1)
IF SHE SAW (Book #2)
IF SHE RAN (Book #3)

THE MAKING OF RILEY PAIGE SERIES
WATCHING (Book #1)
WAITING (Book #2)
LURING (Book #3)

RILEY PAIGE MYSTERY SERIES
ONCE GONE (Book #1)
ONCE TAKEN (Book #2)
ONCE CRAVED (Book #3)
ONCE LURED (Book #4)
ONCE HUNTED (Book #5)
ONCE PINED (Book #6)
ONCE FORSAKEN (Book #7)
ONCE COLD (Book #8)
ONCE STALKED (Book #9)
ONCE LOST (Book #10)
ONCE BURIED (Book #11)
ONCE BOUND (Book #12)
ONCE TRAPPED (Book #13)
ONCE DORMANT (book #14)
ONCE SHUNNED (Book #15)

MACKENZIE WHITE MYSTERY SERIES
BEFORE HE KILLS (Book #1)
BEFORE HE SEES (Book #2)

BEFORE HE COVETS (Book #3)
BEFORE HE TAKES (Book #4)
BEFORE HE NEEDS (Book #5)
BEFORE HE FEELS (Book #6)
BEFORE HE SINS (Book #7)
BEFORE HE HUNTS (Book #8)
BEFORE HE PREYS (Book #9)
BEFORE HE LONGS (Book #10)
BEFORE HE LAPSES (Book #11)

AVERY BLACK MYSTERY SERIES
CAUSE TO KILL (Book #1)
CAUSE TO RUN (Book #2)
CAUSE TO HIDE (Book #3)
CAUSE TO FEAR (Book #4)
CAUSE TO SAVE (Book #5)
CAUSE TO DREAD (Book #6)

KERI LOCKE MYSTERY SERIES
A TRACE OF DEATH (Book #1)
A TRACE OF MUDER (Book #2)
A TRACE OF VICE (Book #3)
A TRACE OF CRIME (Book #4)
A TRACE OF HOPE (Book #5)

Recap of Book 1 in the Jessie Hunt series

In "The Perfect Wife," masters candidate in forensic psychology Jessie Hunt and her investment banker husband, Kyle Voss, leave their downtown Los Angeles apartment for a McMansion in the Orange County community of Westport Beach after he gets transferred and promoted.

While Kyle is thrilled about their new life, Jessie had misgivings and feels uncomfortable among the entitled elite. Nonetheless, she tries to embrace their new life, making friends in the neighborhood and joining the local yacht club with its secret, seemingly sinister rituals.

In class, Jessie impresses visiting lecturer LAPD detective Ryan Hernandez by solving a complicated case study. To complete her field work, she manages to get assigned to a nearby state mental hospital where notorious serial killer Bolton Crutchfield is incarcerated.

Crutchfield's crimes remind her of a man called the Ozarks Executioner, who abducted and killed dozens of people when she was a child in Missouri. Those abducted included Jessie and her mother, who was murdered in front of her. Jessie sees Dr. Janice Lemmon regularly to deal with the trauma.

In interviews, Crutchfield reveals that he is an admirer of the Ozarks Executioner, who was never caught, and that they've somehow communicated. He also suggests, based purely on observing and talking to Jessie, that her suspicions about her new wealthy, lifestyle are legitimate.

As her criminal profiling skills improve, a now-pregnant Jessie discovers the yacht club is actually a front for a high-end prostitution ring. She also uncovers the dark truth about her husband: Kyle is a sociopath who killed a club worker he'd been sleeping with and has tried to frame Jessie for it. Jessie has a miscarriage, a result of being drugged by Kyle. Only Jessie's quick thinking prevents Kyle from killing her, as well as two neighbors. She is injured but Kyle is arrested.

Jessie returns to her old neighborhood in downtown L.A. to rebuild her life. Not long after, the mental hospital's head of security, Kat Gentry, visits Jessie and passes along a message from Crutchfield: The Ozarks Executioner is looking for her.

Jessie reveals to Kat her deepest secret: the reason The Ozarks Executioner is pursuing her is because he is her father.

Jessie Hunt is a soon-to-be divorced aspiring criminal profiler.

Kyle Voss is her sociopathic, now jailed, estranged husband.

Bolton Crutchfield is a brilliant serial killer who idolizes Jessie's murderous father.

Kat Gentry is the head of security at the mental hospital where Crutchfield is incarcerated.

Dr. Janice Lemmon is Jessie's psychiatrist and a former profiler herself

Lacy Cartwright is Jessie's college friend, with whom she's staying for now.

Ryan Hernandez is the LAPD detective who lectured in Jessie's class.

The Ozarks Executioner is a notorious, never-caught serial killer—and Jessie's father.

CHAPTER ONE

Splinters from the wooden arms of the chair dug into Jessica Thurman's forearms, which were tied to the chair by a coarse rope. The skin on her arms was raw and bleeding in several places from her constant attempts to yank herself free.

Jessica was strong for a six-year-old. But not strong enough to break free of the ropes her captor had strapped to her. She could do nothing but sit there with her eyelids taped open as she watched her own mother stand helplessly before her, her arms manacled to the wooden ceiling beams of the isolated Ozarks cabin where they were both being held.

She could hear the whispers of their abductor, standing behind her, instructing her to watch, softly calling her "Junebug." She knew the voice well,

After all, it belonged to her father.

Suddenly, with an unexpected strength she didn't think possible, little Jessica flung her body sideways, sending the chair—and her along with it—toppling to the ground. She didn't feel the thud of hitting the floor, which she found odd.

She looked up and saw that she was no longer lying in the cabin. Instead, she was on the hallway floor of an impressive, modern mansion. And she was no longer six-year-old Jessica Thurman. She was now twenty-eight-year-old Jessie Hunt, lying on the floor of her own home, staring up at a man holding a fireplace poker above his head, about to bring it down on her. But the man was no longer her father.

Instead, it was her husband, Kyle.

His eyes blazed with frenzied intensity as he thrust the poker down toward her face.

She brought her arms up to defend herself but knew it was too late.

*

Jessie woke up with a gasp. Her hands were still raised above her head as if to block an attack. But she was alone in the apartment bedroom. She pushed herself forward in bed so that she was sitting upright. Her body along with the bed sheets were covered in sweat. Her heart was nearly beating out of her chest.

1

She swung her legs off the bed and placed her feet on the floor as she bent over, resting her elbows on her thighs and her head in her palms. After giving her body a few seconds to acclimate to her real surroundings—the downtown Los Angeles apartment of her friend Lacy—she glanced at the bedside clock. It was 3:54 a.m.

As she felt the sweat start to dry on her skin, she reassured herself.

I am no longer in that cabin. I am no longer in that house. I am safe. These are just nightmares. Those men can't hurt me anymore.

But of course only half of that was true. While her soon-to-be-ex-husband, Kyle, was locked up in jail awaiting trial for various crimes, including attempting to murder her, her father had never been captured.

He still haunted her dreams regularly. Worse, she had recently learned that even though she had been placed into Witness Protection as a child, given a new home and a new name, he was still out there looking for her.

Jessie stood up and headed for the shower. There was no point in trying to go back to sleep. She knew it would be useless.

Besides, an idea was circling in her head, one that she wanted to cultivate. Maybe it was time she stopped accepting that these nightmares were inevitable. Maybe she needed to stop fearing the day her father found her.

Maybe it was time to hunt him.

CHAPTER TWO

By the time her old college friend and current roommate Lacy Cartwright came out to the breakfast room, Jessie had been awake for over three hours. She had brewed a fresh pot of coffee and poured a cup for Lacy, who walked over and took it gratefully as she offered a sympathetic smile.

"Another bad dream?" she asked.

Jessie nodded. In the six weeks that Jessie had been living in Lacy's apartment, trying to rebuild her life, her friend had gotten used to the semi-regular middle-of the-night screams and early morning wakeups. It had happened occasionally in college, so it wasn't a total surprise. But the frequency had increased dramatically since her husband had tried to kill her.

"Was I loud?" Jessie asked apologetically.

"A little," Lacy acknowledged. "But you stopped yelling after a couple of seconds. I went right back to sleep."

"I'm really sorry, Lace. Maybe I should buy you better earplugs until I move out, or a louder noise-canceling machine. I swear it won't be much longer."

"Don't worry about it. You're handling things much better than I would be," Lacy insisted as she tied her long hair in a ponytail.

"That's nice of you to say."

"I'm not just being polite, girl. Think about it. In the last two months, your husband murdered a woman, tried to frame you for it, and then attempted to kill you when you figured it out. That doesn't include your miscarriage."

Jessie nodded but didn't say anything. Lacy's list of horribles didn't include her serial killer father because Lacy didn't know about him; almost no one did. Jessie preferred it that way—for her own safety and for theirs. Lacy continued.

"If it was me, I'd still be curled up in the fetal position. The fact that you're almost done with physical therapy and about to enter a special FBI training program makes me wonder if you're some kind of cyborg."

Jessie had to admit that when things were laid out like that, it was pretty impressive that she was so functional. Her hand involuntarily moved to the spot on the left side of her abdomen

3

where Kyle had plunged the fireplace poker. The doctors had told her she was lucky it had missed her internal organs.

She had an ugly scar. It made for an unsightly addition to go with the one from childhood that cut across her collarbone. She still felt a sharp twinge in her gut every now and then. But mostly she felt okay. She'd been given permission to ditch the walking cane a week ago and her physical therapist had only scheduled one more rehab session, which was today. After that, she was supposed to do the required exercises on her own. As to the mental and emotional rehab required after learning her husband was a sociopathic murderer, she was far from getting an all-clear.

"I guess things aren't that bad," she finally replied unconvincingly as she watched her friend finish getting dressed.

Lacy slid on her three-inch heels, turning her from a tall woman into a full-on Amazon. All long legs and cheekbones, she looked more like a runway model than an aspiring fashion designer. Her hair was tied back in a high ponytail that revealed her neck. She was meticulously decked out in an outfit of her own design. She might be a buyer for a high-end boutique right now. But she had plans to have her own design firm before thirty and be the highest-profile lesbian African-American fashion designer in the country soon after that.

"I don't get you, Jessie," she said as she threw on her coat. "You get accepted into a prestigious FBI program at Quantico for promising criminal profilers and you seem to be lukewarm to the idea. I'd think you'd jump at the chance to change your surroundings for a bit. Besides, it's only ten weeks. It's not like you have to move there."

"You're right," Jessie agreed as she downed the last of her third cup of coffee. "It's just that there's so much going on right now, I'm not sure the time is right. The divorce from Kyle isn't final yet. I still have to lock down the sale of the house in Westport Beach. I'm not a hundred percent physically. And I wake up screaming most nights. I don't know that I'm up for the rigors of the FBI's behavior analysis training program just yet."

"Well, you better decide quickly," Lacy said as she moved to the front door. "Don't you have to give them an answer by the end of the week?"

"I do."

"Well, let me know what you decide. Also, can you open the window to your bedroom before you head out? No offense but it smells a bit like a gym in there."

She was gone before Jessie could reply, though she wasn't sure what to say to that. Lacy was a great friend who could always be counted on to give her honest opinion. But tact wasn't her strong suit.

Jessie got up and headed to her room to change. She caught a glimpse of herself in the full-length mirror on the back of the door and didn't immediately recognize herself. On the surface, she still looked the same, with her shoulder-length brown hair, her green eyes, her tall, five-foot-ten frame.

But the eyes were red-rimmed with exhaustion, and the hair was stringy and greasy, so much so that she decided to put it in a ponytail and wear a cap. And she felt permanently hunched, a result of the ever-present worry that her abdomen might unexpectedly pulse in pain.

Will I ever get back to who I was? Does that person even still exist?

She shook the thought away, forcing the self-pity to take a backseat, at least for a while. She was too busy to cater to it right now.

It was time to get ready for her physical therapy session, her meeting with the apartment broker, her appointment with her psychiatrist, and then one with her OB-GYN. It was going to be a full day of pretending to be a functional human being.

*

The apartment broker, a petite whirling dervish in a pantsuit named Bridget, was showing her the third apartment of the morning when Jessie started getting the urge to jump off a balcony.

Everything was fine at first. She was on a bit of a high from her final physical therapy session, which had ended with the pronouncement that she was "reasonably equipped for the tasks of daily living." Bridget had kept things moving as they looked at the first two apartments, focusing on unit details, pricing, and amenities. It was only when they got to the third option, the only one Jessie was intrigued by so far, that the personal questions began.

"Are you sure you're only interested in one-bedrooms?" Bridget asked. "I can tell you like this one. But there's a two-bedroom one floor up with virtually the same floor plan. It's only thirty thousand dollars more and it would have greater resale value. Plus, you never know what your situation might be a couple of years from now."

"That's true," Jessie acknowledged, mentally noting that only two months ago she was married, pregnant, and living in a mansion in Orange County. Now she was separated from an admitted killer, she'd lost her unborn child, and she was bunking with a friend from school. "But I'm fine with a one-bedroom."

"Of course," Bridget said in a tone that suggested she wasn't about to let it lie. "Do you mind if I ask what your circumstances are? It might better help me target your preferences. I can't help but notice the skin on your finger is white where a wedding ring might recently have been. I could gear location choices based on whether you're looking to aggressively move on or... hunker down."

"We're in the right area," Jessie said, her voice tightening involuntarily. "I just want to see one-bedrooms around here. That's the only information you need right now, Bridget."

"Of course. I'm sorry," Bridget said, chastened.

"I need to borrow the restroom for a moment," Jessie said, the tightness in her throat now expanding to her chest. She wasn't sure what was happening to her. "Is that okay?"

"No problem," Bridget said. "You remember where it is, down the hall?"

Jessie nodded and walked there as quickly as she could without actually running. By the time she got in and locked the door, she feared she might pass out. It felt like a panic attack coming on.

What the hell is happening to me?

She splashed her face with cold water, then rested her palms on the counter as she ordered herself to take slow, deep breaths.

Images flashed through her head without rhyme or reason: cuddling on the couch with Kyle, shivering in an isolated cabin deep in the Ozark Mountains, looking at the ultrasound of her unborn and never-to-be-born child, reading a bedtime story in a rocking chair with her adoptive father, watching as her husband dumped a body from a yacht in the waters off the coast, the sound of her father whispering "Junebug" in her ear.

Why Bridget's mostly innocuous question about her circumstances and references to hunkering down had set her off, Jessie didn't know. But they had and now she was in a cold sweat, shaking involuntarily, staring back in the mirror at a person she barely recognized.

It was a good thing her next stop was to see her therapist. The thought calmed Jessie slightly and she took a few more deep breaths before leaving the bathroom and heading down the hall to the front door.

"I'll be in touch," she called out to Bridget as she closed the door behind her. But she wasn't sure she would be. Right now she wasn't sure of anything.

CHAPTER THREE

Dr. Janice Lemmon's office was only a few blocks from the apartment building Jessie was leaving and she was glad for the chance to walk and clear her head. As she walked down Figueroa, she almost welcomed the sharp, cutting wind making her eyes water and immediately dry up. The bracing cold pushed most thoughts other than moving fast from her head.

She zipped her coat up to the neck and put her head down as she passed a coffee shop, then a diner filled to near overflowing. It was mid-December in Los Angeles and local businesses were doing their best to make their storefronts look holiday festive in a town where snow was almost an abstract concept.

But in the wind tunnels created by downtown skyscrapers, cold was ever-present. It was almost 11 a.m. but the sky was gray and the temperature was in the low fifties. Tonight it would drop close to forty. For L.A., that was bone-chilling. Of course, Jessie had been through far more frigid weather.

As a child in rural Missouri, before everything fell apart, she would play in the tiny front yard of her mom's mobile home in the trailer park, her fingers and face half-numb, fashioning unimpressive but happy-faced snowmen while her mom watched protectively from the window. Jessie remembered wondering why her mother never took her eyes off her. Looking back now, it was clear.

A few years later, in the suburbs of Las Cruces, New Mexico, where she'd lived with her adoptive family after going into Witness Protection, she would go skiing on the bunny slopes of the nearby mountains with her second father, an FBI agent who projected calm professionalism, no matter the situation. He was always there to help her up when she fell. And she could usually count on a hot chocolate when they got off the barren, windswept hills and went back to the lodge.

Those chilly memories warmed her as she rounded the final block to Dr. Lemmon's office. She meticulously chose not to think about the less pleasant memories that inevitably intertwined with the good ones.

8

She checked in and peeled off her layers as she waited to be called into the doctor's office. It didn't take long. Right at 11 a.m., her therapist opened the door and welcomed her inside.

Dr. Janice Lemmon was in her mid-sixties but didn't look it. She was in great shape and her eyes, behind thick glasses, were sharp and focused. Her curly blonde ringlets bounced when she walked and she had a coiled intensity that couldn't be masked.

They sat down in plush chairs across from each other. Dr. Lemmon gave her a few moments to settle in before speaking.

"How are you?" she asked in that open-ended way that always made Jessie genuinely ponder the question more seriously than she did in her daily life.

"I've been better," she admitted.

"Why is that?"

Jessie recounted her panic attack in the apartment and the subsequent flashbacks.

"I don't know what set me off," she said in conclusion.

"I think you do," Dr. Lemmon prodded.

"Care to give me a hint?" Jessie countered.

"Well, I'm wondering if you lost your cool in the presence of a near stranger because you don't feel like you have any other place to release your anxiety. Let me ask you this—do you have any stressful events or decisions coming up?"

"You mean other than an OB-GYN appointment in two hours to see if I'm recovered from my miscarriage, finalizing a divorce from the man who tried to murder me, selling the house we shared together, processing the fact that my serial killer father is looking for me, deciding whether or not to go to Virginia for two and a half months to have FBI instructors laugh at me, and having to move out of my friend's apartment so she can get a decent night's sleep? Besides those things, I'd say I'm cool."

"That does sound like quite a bit," Dr. Lemmon replied, ignoring Jessie's sarcasm. "Why don't we start with the immediate concerns and work outward from there, okay?"

"You're the boss," Jessie muttered.

"Actually, I'm not. But tell me about your upcoming appointment. Why does that have you concerned?"

"It's not so much that I'm concerned," Jessie said. "The doctor already told me that it looks like I don't have any permanent damage and will be able to conceive in the future.

It's more that I know going there will remind of what I lost and how I lost it."

"You're talking about how your husband drugged you so he could frame you for murdering Natalia Urgova? And how the drug he used induced your miscarriage?"

"Yes," Jessie said drily. "That's what I'm talking about."

"Well, I'll be surprised if anyone there brings that up," Dr. Lemmon said, a gentle smile playing at her lips.

"So you're saying I'm creating stress for myself about a situation that need not be stressful?"

"I'm saying that if you deal with the emotions ahead of time, it might not be so overwhelming when you're actually in the room."

"Easier said than done," Jessie said.

"Everything is easier said than done," Dr. Lemmon replied. "Let's table that for now and move on to your pending divorce. How are things going on that front?"

"The house is in escrow. So I'm hoping that gets finished without complications. My attorney says that my request for an expedited divorce was approved and that it should be final before the end of year. There is a bonus on that front—because California is a community property state, I get half the assets of my murdering spouse. He gets half of mine too, despite going on trial for nine major felonies early next year. But considering I was a student until a few weeks ago, that doesn't amount to much."

"Okay, how do you feel about all that?"

"I feel good about the money. I'd say I more than earned it. Did you know I used the health insurance from his job to pay for the injury I got from him stabbing me with a fireplace poker? There's something poetic about that. Otherwise, I'll be glad when it's all over. I mostly just want to move on and try to forget that I spent nearly a decade of my life with a sociopath and never realized it."

"You think you should have known?" Dr. Lemmon asked.

"I am trying to become a professional criminal profiler, Doctor. How good can I be when I didn't notice the criminal behavior of my own husband?"

"We've talked about this, Jessie. It's often difficult for even the best profilers to identify illicit behavior in those close to them. Often professional distance is required to see what's really going on."

"I gather you speak from personal experience?" Jessie asked.

Janice Lemmon, in addition to being a behavioral therapist, was a highly regarded criminal consultant who used to work full time for the LAPD. She still offered her services on occasion.

Lemmon had used her considerable string-pulling influence to get Jessie permission to visit the state hospital in Norwalk so she could interview serial killer Bolton Crutchfield as part of her graduate work. And Jessie suspected that the doctor had also played an integral part in her being accepted to the FBI's vaunted National Academy program, which typically only took seasoned local investigators, not recent graduates with almost no practical experience.

"I do," Dr. Lemmon said. "But we can save that for another time. Would you like to discuss how you feel about being played by your husband?"

"I wouldn't say I was *totally* played. After all, because of me, he's in prison and three people who would otherwise be dead, including myself, are walking around. Don't I get any credit for that? After all, I did *eventually* figure it out. I don't think the cops ever would have."

"That's a fair point. I assume from your snark that you'd rather move on. Shall we discuss your father?"

"Really?" Jessie asked, incredulous. "Do we have to go there next? Can't we just talk about my apartment troubles?"

"I gather they're related. After all, isn't the reason your roommate can't get any sleep because you have scream-inducing nightmares?"

"You don't play fair, Doctor."

"I'm only working from things you tell me, Jessie. If you didn't want me to know, you wouldn't have mentioned it. Can I assume the dreams are related to your mother's murder at the hands of your father?"

"Yep," Jessie answered, keeping her tone overly jaunty. "The Ozarks Executioner may have gone underground but he's still got one victim very much in his clutches."

"Have the nightmares gotten worse since we last met?" Dr. Lemmon asked.

"I wouldn't say worse," Jessie corrected. "They've been pretty much at the same level of terrifyingly awful."

"But they got dramatically more frequent and intense once you got the message, correct?"

"I assume we're talking about the message Bolton Crutchfield passed along to me revealing that he's been in contact with my father, who would very much like to find me."

"That's the message we're talking about."

"Then yes, that's around the time they got worse," Jessie answered.

"Setting aside the dreams for a moment," Dr. Lemmon said, "I wanted to reiterate what I I've told you previously."

"Yes, Doctor, I haven't forgotten. In your capacity as an advisor to the Department of State Hospitals, Non-Rehabilitative Division, you've consulted with the security team at the hospital to ensure that Bolton Crutchfield doesn't have access to any unauthorized outside personnel. There is no way for him to communicate with my father to let him know my new identity."

"How many times have I said that?" Dr. Lemmon asked. "It must have been a few for you to have it memorized."

"Let's just say more than once. Besides, I've become friendly with the head of security at the NRD facility, Kat Gentry, and she told me basically the same thing—they've updated their procedures to ensure that Crutchfield has no communication with the outside world."

"And yet you don't sound convinced," Dr. Lemmon noted.

"Would you be?" Jessie countered. "If your dad was a serial killer known to the world as the Ozarks Executioner *and* you'd personally seen him eviscerate his victims and he was never caught, would your mind be set at ease by a few platitudes?"

"I admit I'd probably be a bit skeptical. But I'm not sure how productive it is to dwell on something you can't control."

"I was meaning to broach that with you, Dr. Lemmon," Jessie said, dropping the sarcasm now that she had a genuine request. "Are we sure I don't have any control over the situation? It seems that Bolton Crutchfield knows a fair bit about what my father has been up to in recent years. And Bolton…enjoys my company. I was thinking another visit to chat with him might be in order. Who knows what he might reveal?"

Dr. Lemmon took a deep breath as she considered the proposal.

"I'm not sure playing mind games with a notorious serial killer is the best next step for your emotional well-being, Jessie."

"You know what would be great for my emotional well-being, Doctor?" Jessie said, feeling her frustration rise despite her best efforts. "Not fearing that my psycho dad is going to jump out from around a corner and get all stabby on me."

"Jessie, if just talking to me about this gets you so riled up, what's going to happen when Crutchfield starts pushing your buttons?"

"It's not the same. I don't have to censor myself around you. With him I'm a different person. I'm professional," Jessie said, making sure her tone was more measured now. "I'm tired of being a victim and this is something tangible I can do to change the dynamic. Will you just consider it? I know that your recommendation is pretty much a golden ticket in this town."

Dr. Lemmon stared at her for a few seconds from behind her thick glasses, her eyes boring into her.

"I'll see what I can do," she finally said. "Speaking of golden tickets, have you formally accepted the FBI's National Academy invitation yet?"

"Not yet. I'm still weighing my options."

"I think you could learn a lot there, Jessie. And it wouldn't hurt to have it on your résumé when you're trying to get work out here. I worry that passing on it might be a form of self-sabotage."

"It's not that," Jessie assured her. "I know it's a great opportunity. I'm just not sure this is the ideal time for me to up and move across the country for almost three months. My whole world is in flux right now."

She tried to keep the agitation out of her voice but could hear it creeping in. Clearly Dr. Lemmon did too because she shifted gears.

"Okay. Now that we've gotten a big picture view of how things are going, I'd like to dig a little deeper on a few subjects. If I recall, your adoptive father came out here recently to help get you squared away. I want to get into how that went momentarily. But first, let's discuss how you're recovering physically. I understand you just had your last physical therapy session. How was that?"

The next forty-five minutes made Jessie feel like a tree having its bark peeled back. When it was over, she was happy to leave, even if it meant her next stop was getting checked to reconfirm she could have kids in the future. After nearly an hour of Dr. Lemmon poking and prodding her psyche, she figured getting her body poked and prodded would be a breeze. She was wrong.

*

It wasn't so much the poking that set her off. It was the aftermath. The appointment itself was pretty uneventful. Jessie's doctor confirmed that she hadn't suffered any permanent damage and assured her that she should be able to conceive in the future. She also gave the all-clear to resume sexual activity, a notion that had genuinely not crossed Jessie's mind since Kyle attacked her. The doctor said that barring something unexpected, she should return for a follow-up in six months.

It was only when she was in the elevator on the way down to the parking garage that she lost it. She wasn't completely sure why but she felt like she was falling into a dark hole in the ground. She ran to the car and sat in the driver's seat, letting the heaving sobs wrack her body.

And then, in the middle of the tears, she got it. Something about the finality of the appointment had hit her hard. She didn't have to come back for six months. It would be a normal visit. The pregnancy stage of her life was, for the foreseeable future, over.

She could almost feel the emotional door slam shut and it was jarring. On top of her marriage ending in the most shocking way possible and learning that the murderous father she thought she'd put in the past was back in her present, the realization that she'd had a living being inside her and now she didn't was too much to bear.

She peeled out of the parking garage, her vision blurred by tear-stained eyes. She didn't care. She found herself pressing down hard on the accelerator as she roared south on Robertson. It was early afternoon and there wasn't much traffic. Still, she weaved wildly in and out of lanes.

Ahead of her, at a stoplight, she saw a large moving truck. She hit the gas hard and felt her neck snap back as she accelerated. The speed limit was thirty-five, but she was at forty-five, fifty-five, passing sixty. She was sure that if she hit that truck hard enough, all her pain would vanish in an instant.

She glanced to her left and as she whizzed by, she saw a mother walking along the sidewalk with her toddler son. The thought of that little boy being witness to a mass of crumpled metal, blistering fire, and charred remains snapped her out of it.

14

Jessie hit the brakes hard, squealing to a stop only feet from the back of the truck. She pulled into the gas station parking lot to her right, parked, and turned off the car. She was breathing heavily and adrenaline coursed through her body, making her fingers and toes tingle to the point of discomfort.

After about five minutes sitting there motionless with her eyes closed, her chest stopped heaving and her breathing returned to normal. She heard a buzzing and opened her eyes. It was her phone. The caller ID said it was Detective Ryan Hernandez of the LAPD. He'd spoken to her criminology class last semester, where she'd impressed him with how she'd solved a sample case he presented to the class. He'd also visited her in the hospital after Kyle tried to kill her.

"Hello, hello," Jessie said out loud to herself, making sure her voice sounded normal. Close enough. She answered the call.

"This is Jessie."

"Hi, Ms. Hunt. This is Detective Ryan Hernandez calling. Do you remember me?"

"Of course," she said, pleased that she sounded like her usual self. "What's up?"

"I know you graduated recently," he said, his voice sounding more hesitant than she remembered. "Have you secured a position yet?"

"Not yet," she answered. "I'm weighing my options right now."

"In that case, I'd like to talk to you about a job."

CHAPTER FOUR

An hour later, Jessie was sitting in the reception area of the Central Community Police Station of the Los Angeles Police Department, or as it was more commonly called, Downtown Division, where she was waiting for Detective Hernandez to come out to meet her. She expressly refused to think about what happened with the near crash. It was too much to process at the moment. Instead, she focused on what was about to happen.

Hernandez had been cagey on the call, telling her he couldn't go into detail—just that a junior position was opening up and he'd thought of her. He asked her to come in to discuss it in person as he wanted to gauge her interest before mentioning her to the higher-ups.

While Jessie waited, she tried to recall what she knew about Hernandez. She had met him earlier that fall when he'd visited her master's program forensic psychology class to discuss the practical applications of profiling. It turned out that when he was a beat cop, he'd been instrumental in catching Bolton Crutchfield.

In the class, he'd presented an elaborate murder case to the students and asked if anyone could determine the perpetrator and the motive. Only Jessie had figured it out. In fact, Hernandez had said she was only the second student ever to solve the case.

The next time she saw him was in the hospital when she was recovering from Kyle's attack. She was still a bit drugged up at the time, so her memory was a little hazy.

He had only been there in the first place because she'd called him, suspicious about Kyle's background before she'd met him at age eighteen, hoping to get any leads he could offer. She'd left a voicemail with the detective and when he couldn't reach her after multiple calls back—primarily because her husband had tied her up in their house—he'd tracked her cell and found she was in the hospital.

When he visited, he'd been helpful, walking her through the state of the pending case against Kyle. But he'd also quite clearly been suspicious (with good reason) that Jessie hadn't done all she could to come clean after Kyle killed Natalia Urgova.

It was true. After Kyle had persuaded Jessie that she had killed Natalia herself in a drunken rage that she couldn't remember, he'd offered to cover up the crime by dumping the woman's body at sea. Despite her misgivings at the time, Jessie hadn't been forceful about going to the police to confess. It was something she regretted to this day.

Hernandez had sussed that out but as far as she knew, never said anything about it to anyone after that. Some small part of her feared that was the real reason he'd called her here today and that the job was just a pretense to get her in the station. She figured that if he took her to an interrogation room, she'd know which way things were headed.

After a few minutes, he came out to greet her. He was much as she remembered him, about thirty, well-built but not overly imposing. At about six feet tall and a little under 200 pounds, he was clearly in good shape. It was only as he got closer that she remembered how ripped he was.

He had short black hair, brown eyes, and a wide, warm smile that probably even made suspects feel at ease. She wondered if he cultivated it for that very reason. She saw the wedding band on his left hand and remembered that he was married but had no kids.

"Thanks for coming in, Ms. Hunt," he said, extending his hand.

"Please call me Jessie," she said.

"Okay, Jessie. Let's go to my desk and I'll fill you in on what I had in mind."

Jessie felt a stronger than expected surge of relief when he didn't suggest the interrogation room but managed to avoid making it obvious. As she followed him back to the bullpen, he talked softly.

"I've been keeping up with your case," he admitted. "Or more accurately, your husband's case."

"Soon to be ex," she noted.

"Right. I heard that too. No plans to stick it out with the guy who tried to frame you for murder and then kill you, huh? No loyalty these days."

He grinned to let her know he was kidding. Jessie couldn't help but be impressed by a guy willing to make a crack about a murder to the person who was almost murdered.

"The guilt is overwhelming," she said, playing along.

"I'll bet. I've got to say, it's not looking good for your soon-to-be former hubby. Even if prosecutors don't seek the death penalty, I doubt he's ever getting out."

"From your lips..." Jessie muttered, not needing to finish the sentence.

"Let's move to a happier subject, shall we?" Hernandez suggested. "As you may or may not recall from my visit to your classroom, I work for a special unit in Robbery-Homicide. It's called Homicide Special Section, or HSS for short. We specialize in high-profile cases—the kinds that generate lots of media interest or public scrutiny. That might include arsons, murders with multiple victims, murders of notable individuals, and of course, serial killers."

"Like Bolton Crutchfield, the guy you helped capture."

"Exactly," he said. "Our unit also employs profilers. They're not exclusive to us. The whole department has access to them but we have priority. You may have heard of our senior profiler, Garland Moses."

Jessie nodded. Moses was a legend in the profiling community. A former FBI agent, he'd relocated to the West Coast to retire in the late 1990s after spending decades bouncing around the country hunting serial killers. But the LAPD had made him an offer and he agreed to work as a consultant. He was paid by the department but wasn't an official employee, so he could come and go as he chose.

He was over seventy years old now but still showed up to work just about every day. And at least three or four times a year, Jessie read a story of him cracking a case no one else could nail down. He supposedly had an office on the second floor of this building in what was said to be a converted broom closet.

"Am I going to meet him?" Jessie asked, trying to keep her enthusiasm in check.

"Not today," Hernandez said. "Maybe if you take the job and have settled in for a while, I'll introduce you. He's a little on the crusty side."

Jessie knew Hernandez was being diplomatic. Garland Moses had a reputation for being a taciturn, short-tempered asshole. If he wasn't great at catching murderers, he'd probably be unemployable.

"So Moses is kind of the department's profiler emeritus," Hernandez continued. "He only shows his face for really big cases. The department has a number of other staff and freelance profilers it uses for less celebrated cases. Unfortunately, our junior profiler, Josh Caster, tendered his resignation yesterday."

"Why?"

"Officially?" Hernandez said. "He wanted to relocate to a more family-friendly area. He has a wife and two kids he never got to see. So he accepted a position up in Santa Barbara."

"And unofficially?"

"He couldn't hack it anymore. He worked robbery-homicide a half dozen years, went to the FBI's training program, came back all gung ho and really pushed hard as a profiler for two years after that. Then he just hit a wall."

"What do you mean?" Jessie asked.

"This is an ugly business, Jessie. I feel like I don't need to tell you that, with what happened with your husband. But it's one thing to have a brush with violence or death. It's another to face it every day, to see the foul things human beings can do to each other. It's hard to keep your humanity under the onslaught of that stuff. It grinds you down. If you don't have somewhere to put it at the end of the day, it can really mess you up. That's something to think about as you consider my proposal."

Jessie decided now wasn't the time to tell Detective Hernandez that her experience with Kyle wasn't the first time she'd seen death close up. She wasn't sure if watching her father murder multiple people as a child, including her own mother, might hurt her job prospects.

"What exactly is your proposal?" she asked, steering clear of the topic entirely.

They had reached Hernandez's desk. He motioned for her to sit down across from him as he continued.

"Replacing Caster, at least on an interim basis. The department isn't ready to hire a new full-time profiler just yet. They put a lot of resources into Caster and they feel burned. They want to do a big candidate search before hiring his permanent replacement. In the meantime, they're looking for someone junior, who won't mind not being a full-time hire and won't mind being underpaid."

"That's sure to reel in top applicants," Jessie said.

"Agreed. That's my fear—that in the interest of keeping costs low, they'll go with someone who doesn't have the chops. Me? I'd rather try someone who might be green but has talent rather than a hack who can't profile worth a damn."

"You think I have talent?" Jessie asked, hoping she didn't sound like she was fishing for a compliment.

"I think you have potential. You showed that in the classroom scenario. I respect your professor in the class, Warren Hosta. And he tells me you have real talent. He wouldn't get specific but he indicated that you'd been granted permission to interview a high-value inmate and that you'd established a rapport that might prove fruitful in the future. The fact that he couldn't read me in on something a fresh-scrubbed master's graduate is doing suggests you're not as untested as you seem. Plus, you managed to uncover your husband's elaborate murder plot and not get killed in the process. That's nothing to sneeze at. I also know you were accepted into the FBI's National Academy without any law enforcement experience. That almost never happens. So I'm willing to take a flyer on you and throw your name into the mix. Assuming you're interested. Are you interested?"

CHAPTER FIVE

"So you're not doing the FBI thing?" Lacy asked incredulously as she took another sip of wine.

They were sitting on the couch, halfway through a bottle of red and devouring the Chinese food that had just been delivered. It was after 8 p.m. and Jessie was exhausted from the longest day she could remember in months.

"I'm still going to do it, just not now. They gave me a one-time deferment. I can join with another Academy class, as long as I attend at some time in the next six months. Otherwise I have to reapply. Since I was lucky to get in this time, that pretty much guarantees I'll be going soon."

"And you're bailing to do grunt work for the LAPD?" Lacy asked, disbelieving.

"Once again, not bailing," Jessie pointed out, taking a big glug from her own glass, "just delaying. I was already on the fence with everything going on with the house sale and my physical recovery. This was just the clincher. Besides, it sounds cool!"

"No it doesn't," Lacy said. "It sounds totally boring. Even your detective buddy said you'd be doing routine tasks and handling the low-profile cases no one else wanted to take on."

"At first. But once I've got a bit of experience I'm sure they'll throw me on something more interesting. This is Los Angeles, Lace. They're not going to be able to keep the crazy away from me."

*

Two weeks later, as the patrol car dropped Jessie off a block from the crime scene, she thanked the officers and headed for the alley where she saw police tape already up. As she crossed the street, avoiding the drivers who seemed more intent on hitting than avoiding her, it occurred to her that this would be her first murder case.

Looking back on her brief time at Central Station, she realized that she'd been wrong to think they couldn't keep the crazy away from her. Somehow, at least so far, they had. In fact, most of her time these days was spent in the station, going through open cases to make sure the paperwork Josh Caster had filed before he left was up to date. It was drudgery.

It didn't help that Central Station felt like a busy bus station. The main bullpen area was massive. People swarmed around her all the time and she was never quite sure if they were staff, civilians, or suspects. She had to repeatedly move desks as profilers without the "interim" tag used their seniority to lay claim to work stations they preferred. No matter where she ended up, Jessie always seemed to be situated right below a flickering fluorescent light.

But not today. Stepping into the alley just off East 4th Street, she saw Detective Hernandez at the far end and hoped this case would be different from the others she'd been assigned so far. For each of those, she'd shadowed detectives but wasn't asked for her opinion. There wasn't much need for it anyway.

Of the three field cases she'd shadowed, two were robberies and one was arson. In each instance, the suspect confessed within minutes of arrest, once without even being questioned. The detective had to Mirandize the guy and get him to re-confess.

But today might finally be different. It was the Monday just before Christmas, and Jessie hoped the spirit of the season might make Hernandez more generous than some of his colleagues. She joined him and his partner for that day, a bespectacled forty-something guy named Callum Reid, as they investigated the death of a junkie found at the end of the alley.

He still had a needle sticking out of his left arm and the uniformed officer had only called in the detectives as a formality. As Hernandez and Reid talked to the officer, Jessie ducked under the police tape and approached the body, making sure not to step anywhere sensitive.

She looked down at the young man, who didn't look any older than her. He was African-American, with a high fade haircut. Even lying down and shoeless, she could tell he was tall. Something about him felt familiar.

"Should I know who this guy is?" she called out to Hernandez. "I feel like I've seen him somewhere before."

"Probably," Hernandez shouted back. "You went to USC, right?"

"Yeah," she said.

"He likely overlapped with you for a year or two. His name was Lionel Little. He played basketball there for a couple of years before going pro."

"Okay, I think I remember him," Jessie said.

"He had a gorgeous left-handed finger roll shot," Detective Reid recalled. "Reminded me a little of George Gervin. He was a highly touted rookie but he ended up washing out after a few years. He couldn't play defense and he didn't know how to handle all the money or the NBA lifestyle. He only lasted three seasons before he was out of the league entirely. The drugs pretty much took over at that point. Somewhere along the line, he ended up on the streets."

"I'd see him around from time to time," Hernandez added. "He was a sweet kid—never cited him for more than loitering or public urination."

Jessie leaned over and looked more closely at Lionel. She tried to imagine herself in his position, a lost kid, addicted but not much trouble, wandering the back alleys of downtown L.A. for the last few years. Somehow he'd managed to maintain his habit without overdosing or ending up in jail. And yet here he was, lying in an alley, needle in his arm, shoeless. Something didn't feel right.

She knelt down to get a closer look at where the needle jutted out from his skin. It was jammed in deep on his otherwise smooth skin.

His smooth skin...

"Detective Reid, you said Lionel had a nice left-handed finger roll, right?"

"Thing of beauty," he replied appreciatively.

"So can I assume he was left-handed?"

"Oh yeah, he was totally left-hand dominant. He had real trouble going to his right. Defenders would overplay him to that side and completely shut him down. It was another reason he never made it in the pros."

"That's weird," she muttered.

"What is it?" Hernandez asked.

"It's just...can you guys come over here? There's something that doesn't make sense about this crime scene to me."

The detectives walked over and stopped right behind where she was kneeling. She pointed at Lionel's left arm.

"That needle looks like it's halfway through his arm and it's not anywhere near a vein."

"Maybe he had bad aim?" Reid suggested.

"Maybe," Jessie conceded. "But look at his right arm. There's a precise line of tracks that all follow along his veins. It's pretty meticulous for a drug addict. And it makes sense, because he was a lefty. Of course he'd inject his right arm with his dominant hand."

"That does make sense," Hernandez agreed.

"So then I thought maybe he was just sloppier when he used his right," Jessie continued. "Like you said, Detective Reid, maybe he just had bad aim."

"Exactly," Reid said.

"But look," Jessie said pointing at the arm. "Other than the spot with the needle in it right now, his left arm is smooth—no track marks at all."

"What does that tell you?" Hernandez asked, starting to see where she was going.

"It tells me that he didn't shoot up in his left arm, pretty much ever. From what I can tell, this isn't the kind of guy who would let someone else shoot him up in that arm either. He had a system. He was very methodical. Look at the back of his right hand. He's got marks there too. He'd rather shoot up his hand than trust someone else. I bet if we took off his socks, we'd find track marks between the toes on his right foot too."

"So you're suggesting he didn't overdose?" Reid asked skeptically.

"I'm suggesting that someone wants to make it look like he OD'd but did a sloppy job and just jammed the needle somewhere in his left arm, the one right-handed people would typically use."

"Why?" Reid asked.

"Well," Jessie said cautiously, "I started thinking about the fact that his shoes are missing. None of his other clothes are. I'm wondering if, him having been a former pro player, his shoes were expensive. Don't some of them go for hundreds of dollars?"

"They do," Hernandez answered, sounding excited. "Actually, when he first joined the league and everyone thought he was going to be a big deal, he signed a shoe contract with an upstart company called Hardwood. Most guys signed with one of the big sneaker companies—Nike, Adidas, Reebok. But Lionel went with these guys. They were viewed as edgy. Maybe too edgy because they went out of business a few years ago."

"So then the sneakers wouldn't be that valuable," Reid said.

"Actually the opposite is true," Hernandez corrected. "Because they went bankrupt, the shoes became a hot commodity. There are only so many in circulation, so each one is quite valuable with collectors. As a spokesman for the company, Lionel probably got a truckload of them when he first signed on. And I'd be willing to bet that's what he had on tonight."

"So," Jessie picked up, "someone saw him wearing the shoes. Maybe they were desperate for cash. Lionel's not viewed as a tough guy. He's an easy mark. So this person takes Lionel down, steals the shoes, and shoves a needle in his arm, hoping we'd just mark it down as another overdose."

"It's not a crazy theory," Hernandez said. "Let's see if we can get a search going for someone in the area wearing a pair of Hardwoods."

"If Lionel didn't overdose, then how did the perp kill him?" Reid mused. "I don't see any blood."

"I think that's a great question…for the medical examiner," Hernandez said, grinning as he stepped back to the other side of the police tape. "Why don't we call one in and get some lunch?"

"I've got to run to the bank," Reid said. "Maybe I'll just meet you back at the station."

"Okay. It looks like it's just you and me, Jessie," Hernandez said. "How do you feel about a street vendor hot dog? I saw a guy across the street earlier."

"I feel like I'm going to regret it but I'll do it anyway because I don't want to look like a wuss."

"You know," he pointed out, "if you say you're doing it so you won't look like a wuss, everyone knows you're just eating it for the credit. That's kind of wussy. Just a pro tip."

"Thanks, Hernandez," Jessie replied. "I'm learning all kinds of new stuff today."

"It's called on-the-job training," he said, continuing to rib her as they walked down the alley to the street. "Now if you put both onions *and* peppers on the dog, you might earn some street cred."

"Wow," Jessie said, grimacing. "How does your wife like lying next to you at night when you stink of that stuff?"

"Not much of a problem," Hernandez said, then turned to the vendor to place his order.

Something in Hernandez's response struck her as odd. Maybe his wife was simply unfazed by the smell of onions and peppers in bed. But his tone suggested that perhaps it wasn't much of a problem because he and his wife weren't sharing a bed these days.

Despite her curiosity, Jessie let it lie. She barely knew this man. She wasn't about to interrogate him about the state of his marriage. But she did wish she could somehow find out if her gut was way off or if her suspicions were correct.

Speaking of guts, the vendor was looking at her expectantly, waiting for her to place her order. She looked at Hernandez's dog, overflowing with onions, peppers, and what looked to be salsa. The detective was eyeing her, clearly ready to mock her.

"I'll have what he's having," she said. "Exactly what he's having."

*

Back at the station a few hours later, she was emerging from the ladies' room for the third time when Hernandez approached her with a broad smile on his face. She forced herself to seem casual and ignored the uncomfortable gurgling in her lower abdomen.

"Good news," he said, thankfully oblivious to her discomfort. "We got word that someone was picked up a few minutes ago wearing Hardwoods that match Lionel's foot size, which was a sixteen. The person wearing the sneakers has size nine feet. So that's—you know—a little suspicious. Good job."

"Thanks," Jessie said, trying to play it off as no big deal. "Any word from the M.E. on possible cause of death?"

"Nothing official yet. But when they turned Lionel over, they found a massive welt on the back side of his head. So a subdural hematoma isn't a crazy hypothesis. That would explain the lack of blood."

"Great," Jessie said, happy that her theory seemed to have panned out.

"Yeah, except not so great for his family. His mother was down there to identify the body and apparently she's a total mess. She's a single mom. I remember reading in some article about him that she worked three jobs when Lionel was a kid. She had to think she'd be able to scale it back once he hit it big. But I guess not."

Jessie didn't know what to say in response so she simply nodded and stayed silent.

"I'm cutting out for the day," Hernandez said abruptly. "Some of us are going out for a drink, if you want to join us. You've definitely earned one on me."

"I would but I'm supposed to go to a club tonight with my roommate. She thinks it's time I get back in the dating scene."

"Do *you* think it's time?" Hernandez asked, his eyebrows raised.

"I think that she is relentless and won't let this drop unless I go out at least once, even if it's on a Monday night. That should give me a few weeks' grace before she starts in again."

"Well, have a good time," he said, trying to sound optimistic.

"Thanks. I'm positive I won't."

CHAPTER SIX

The club was loud and dark and Jessie could feel a headache coming on.

An hour ago, when she and Lacy had been getting ready, things seemed much more promising. Her roommate's enthusiasm was infectious and she found herself almost looking forward to the evening as they put on their dresses and did their hair.

When they left the apartment, she couldn't say she disagreed with Lacy's contention that she looking "smokin' hot." She was wearing her red skirt with the slit up the thigh, the one she never got to bust out in her brief but tumultuous Orange County suburban existence. She wore a black sleeveless top that accentuated the muscle tone she'd developed during physical therapy.

She even deigned to put on a pair of three-inch black pumps that officially put her over six feet and in the Amazon woman club alongside Lacy. Originally she wore her brown hair up but her fashion impresario roommate convinced her to let it down, so that it cascaded past her shoulders to her upper back. Looking in the mirror, she didn't think it was totally ridiculous when Lacy said they looked like a couple of models slumming for the evening.

But an hour later her mood had soured. Lacy was having a great time, playfully flirting with guys she wasn't interested in and seriously flirting with girls that she was. Jessie found herself at the bar talking to the bartender, who was obviously well practiced in entertaining girls not used to the scene.

She wasn't sure when she'd gotten so lame. It was true that she hadn't really been single in nearly a decade. But she and Kyle had gone out to exactly these kinds of clubs back when they lived here, before the move to Westport Beach. She had never felt out of place.

In fact, she used to love to check out new downtown L.A.— DTLA to locals—clubs, bars, and restaurants, a few of which seemed to open every week. The two of them would swoop in and take over the place, trying the most unconventional menu item or drink, dancing goofily in the center of the club,

28

oblivious to the dubious glances they got. She didn't miss Kyle but she had to admit she longed for the life they'd shared together before everything went sideways.

A young guy, likely not older than twenty-five, sidled up next to her and eased onto the empty bar stool to her left. She gave him the once-over in the bar mirror, quietly sizing him up.

It was part of a private game she liked to play with herself. She informally called it "People Prediction." In it, she would try to guess as much about a person's life as possible, based only on how they looked, acted, and spoke. As she surreptitiously gave the guy a sideways glance, she was delighted to realize that the game now had professional benefits. After all, she was a junior, interim criminal profiler. This was fieldwork.

The guy was moderately attractive, with shaggy, dirty-blond hair that swept down over the right side of his forehead. He was tan, but not in a beachy kind of way. It was too even and perfect. She suspected he visited a tanning salon periodically. He was in good shape but looked almost unnaturally lean, like a wolf that hadn't eaten in a while.

He'd clearly come from work, as he was still in "the uniform"—suit, shiny shoes, slightly loosened tie to show he was in relaxed mode. It was approaching 10 p.m. and if he was only just getting off work, it suggested he worked a job that required long office hours. Maybe finance, though that usually meant early starts more than late nights.

He was more likely a lawyer. Not for the government though; maybe an associate in his first year at some fancy firm in a nearby high rise where they were working him to death. He was well-paid, as the tailored suit proved. But he didn't have much time to enjoy the fruits of his labor.

He seemed to be deciding what line to use on her. He couldn't offer her a drink as she already had one that was still half full. Jessie decided to give him a hand.

"What firm?" she asked, turning to face him.

"What?"

"What legal firm are you with?" she repeated, nearly shouting to be heard over the pulsating music.

"Benson & Aguirre," he answered in an East Coast accent she couldn't quite identify. "How did you know I was a lawyer?"

"Lucky guess; looks like they're really working you to the bone. You just get off?"

"About a half hour ago," he said, his voice betraying a tone more Mid-Atlantic than New York. "I've been looking forward to a drink for about three hours now. I could really go for a water ice but this'll have to do."

He took a swig from his bottle of beer.

"How does L.A. compare to Philadelphia?" Jessie asked. "I know it's been less than six months but do you feel like you're adjusting okay?"

"Jeez, what the hell? Are you some kind of private detective? How do you know I'm from Philly and that I only moved here in August?"

"It's kind of a talent I have. I'm Jessie, by the way," she said, extending her hand.

"Doyle," he said, shaking it. "Are you gonna tell me how you do that parlor trick? Because I'm kind of freaking out over here."

"I wouldn't want to spoil the mystery. Mystery's very important. Let me ask one more question, just to complete the picture. Did you go to Temple or Villanova for law school?"

He stared at her with his mouth agape. After blinking a few times, he regrouped.

"How do you know I didn't go to Penn?" he asked, feigning insult.

"Nah, you didn't order any water ices at Penn. Which is it?"

"'Nova all the way, baby!" he shouted. "Go Wildcats!"

Jessie nodded appreciatively.

"I'm a Trojan girl myself," she said.

"Oh, jeez. You went to USC? Did you hear about that Lionel Little guy—former ball player there? He got killed today."

"I heard," Jessie said. "Sad story."

"I heard he was killed for his shoes," Doyle said, shaking his head. "Can you believe that?"

"You should take care of yours, Doyle. They don't look cheap either."

Doyle glanced down, then leaned over and whispered in her ear, "Eight hundred bucks."

Jessie whistled in fake awe. She was fast losing interest in Doyle, whose youthful exuberance was starting to be overwhelmed by his youthful self-satisfaction.

"So what's your story?" he asked.

"You don't want to try to guess?"

"Oh man, I'm not so good at that."

"Give it a try, Doyle," she coaxed. "You might surprise yourself. Besides, a lawyer needs to be perceptive, right?"

"That's true. Okay, I'll give it a shot. I'd say you're an actress. You're pretty enough to be one. But DTLA isn't really actress territory. That's more like Hollywood and points west. Model maybe? You could be. But you seem too smart to have that be your main thing as like, a career. Maybe you did some modeling as a teenager but now you're into something more professional. Oh, I've got it, you're in public relations. That's why you're so good at reading people. Am I right? I know I am."

"Really close, Doyle. But not quite."

"So what do you do then?" he demanded.

"I'm a criminal profiler with the LAPD."

It felt good to say it out loud, especially as she watched his eyes widen in shock.

"Like that show *Mindhunter*?"

"Yeah, kind of. I help the police get inside the heads of criminals so they have a better chance of catching them."

"Whoa. So do you hunt serial killers and stuff?"

"For a while now," she said, neglecting to mention that her search was for one particular serial killer and that it had nothing to do with work.

"That's awesome. What a cool job."

"Thanks," Jessie said, sensing that he'd finally built up the courage to ask what had been on his mind for a while now.

"So what's your deal? Are you single?'

"Divorced actually."

"Really?" he said. "You seem too young to be divorced."

"I know, right? Unusual circumstances. It didn't pan out."

"I don't want to be rude but can I ask—what was so unusual? I mean, you seem like a catch. Are you a psycho or something?"

Jessie knew he didn't mean any harm with the question. He was genuinely interested in both the answer and in her and he'd just fumbled it horribly. Still, she could feel all her remaining interest in Doyle drain from her at that moment. In the same instant, the weight of the day and the discomfort of her high heels reared their heads. She decided to close out the evening with a bang.

"I wouldn't call myself a psycho, Doyle. I'm definitely damaged, to the point of waking up screaming most nights. But psycho? I wouldn't say that. Mostly we got divorced because my husband was a sociopath who murdered a woman he was sleeping with, attempted to frame me for it, and ultimately tried to kill me and two of our neighbors. He really embraced the 'death do us part' thing."

Doyle stared at her, his mouth so wide it could have caught flies. She waited for him to recover, curious to see how smoothly he'd extricate himself. Not very, as it turned out.

"Oh, that really sucks. I would ask more about it but I just remembered I have an early deposition tomorrow. I should probably get home. Hope to see you around some time."

He was off the stool and halfway to the door before she could get out a "Bye, Doyle."

*

Jessica Thurman pulled the blanket up to cover her half-freezing little body. She'd been alone in the cabin with her dead mother for three days now. She was so delirious from lack of water, warmth, and human interaction that sometimes she thought her mother was talking to her, even as her corpse slumped, unmoving, her arms held in the air by manacles attached to the wooden roof beams.

Suddenly there was banging on the door. Someone was just outside the cabin. It couldn't be her father. He had no reason to knock. He entered whatever place he wanted whenever he wanted.

The banging came again, only this time it sounded different. There was a ringing sound mixed in. But that made no sense. The cabin didn't have a doorbell. The ringing came again, this time without any knocking at all.

Suddenly Jessie's eyes popped open. She lay there in bed, allowing her brain a second to process that the ringing she'd heard had come from her cell phone. She leaned over to grab it, noting that while her heart was pumping fast and her breathing was shallow, she wasn't as sweaty as usual in the aftermath of a nightmare.

It was Detective Ryan Hernandez. As she answered the call, she glanced at the time: 2:13 a.m.

"Hello," she said, with almost no grogginess in her voice.

"Jessie. It's Ryan Hernandez. Sorry to call at this hour but I got a call to investigate a suspicious death in Hancock Park. Garland Moses doesn't do middle of the night calls anymore and everyone else is already spoken for. You up for it?"

"Sure," Jessie replied.

"If I text you the address, can you be here in thirty minutes?" he asked.

"I can be there in fifteen."

CHAPTER SEVEN

When Jessie pulled up in front of the mansion on Lucerne Blvd. at 2:29 a.m., there were already multiple police cars, an ambulance, and a medical examiner's vehicle out front. She got out and walked toward the front door, trying to look as professional as possible under the circumstances.

Neighbors stood on the sidewalk, many wrapped up in robes to protect against the chill of the night. This sort of thing wasn't typical for a wealthy neighborhood like Hancock Park. Nestled between Hollywood to the north and the Mid-Wilshire district to the south, it was an enclave of old money Los Angeles; or at least as "old money" as anything in a city so unconcerned with historical tradition could be.

The people who lived here weren't so much the movie stars or Hollywood moguls one might find in Beverly Hills or Malibu. These were the homes of the generationally wealthy, who might or might not actually work. If they did, it was often merely to avoid boredom. But they didn't have to worry about being bored tonight. After all, one of their own was dead and everyone was curious as to who.

Jessie felt a bit of thrill as she walked up the stairs to the front door, which was marked off with yellow police tape. This was the first time she'd arrived at a crime scene unaccompanied by a detective. And that meant it was the first time she'd have to show her credentials to access a restricted area.

She remembered being so excited when she'd first gotten them. She even practiced flashing them to Lacy a few times back at the apartment. But now, as she fumbled through her coat pocket, trying to find them, she felt surprisingly nervous.

She needn't have been. The officer at the top of the stairs barely glanced at them as he pulled back the police tape and let her pass.

Jessie found Hernandez and another detective standing just inside the foyer of the house. The younger man looked like he'd drawn the short straw. Detective Reid's seniority must have allowed him to beg off this call. Jessie wondered why Hernandez hadn't pulled rank too. He saw her and waved her in.

"Jessie Hunt, I don't know if you've met Detective Alan Trembley. He was the detective on call tonight and he'll be working the case with me."

As Jessie shook his hand, she couldn't help but notice that, with his unkempt curly blond hair and glasses halfway down the bridge of his nose, he looked as scattered as she felt.

"Our victim is in the pool house," Hernandez said as he started walking, leading the way. "Her name is Victoria Missinger. Thirty-four years old. Married. No children. She's in a small, hidden nook off the main room, which may help explain why it took so long to find her. Her husband called in this afternoon, saying he hadn't been able to reach her for hours. There was some concern that it might have been a ransom situation so a full house search wasn't done until a few hours ago. Her body was found by a cadaver dog."

"Jesus," Trembley muttered under his breath, making Jessie wonder just how experienced he was to be set off by the notion of a cadaver dog.

"How did she die?" she asked.

"The M.E. is still on sight and no blood work has been done yet. But the initial theory is an insulin overdose. A needle was found near the body. She was a diabetic."

"You can die from an insulin overdose?" Trembley asked.

"Sure, if left untreated," Hernandez said as they walked down a long hallway of the main house toward the back door. "And it looks like she was alone in the room for hours."

"We seem to be dealing with a lot of needle-related incidents lately, Detective Hernandez," Jessie noted. "You know, I am willing to handle a shooting now and then."

"Purely coincidence, I assure you," he replied, smiling.

They stepped outside and Jessie realized that the massive house in front hid an even larger backyard. An enormous pool took up half the space. Beyond that sat the pool house. Hernandez headed that way and the other two followed.

"What makes you suspect it wasn't just an accident?" Jessie asked him.

"I haven't drawn any conclusions yet," he answered. "The M.E. will be able to tell us more in the morning. But Mrs. Missinger has had diabetes all her life and, according to her husband, she's never had an accident like this before. It sounds like she knew how to take care of herself."

"Have you spoken to him yet?" Jessie asked.

"No," Hernandez replied. "A uniformed officer took his initial statement. He's currently being babysat in the breakfast room. We'll talk to him after I show you the scene."

"What do we know about him?" Jessie asked.

"Michael Missinger, thirty-seven years old. Scion of the Missinger oil fortune. He sold his interest seven years ago and started a hedge fund that invests exclusively in environmentally friendly technologies. He works downtown in the penthouse of one of those buildings you have to crane your neck to see the top of."

"Any priors?" Trembley asked.

"Are you kidding?" Hernandez scoffed. "On paper, this guy is as straight as arrows come. No personal scandals. No financial issues. Not even a traffic ticket. If he's got secrets, they're well hidden."

They had arrived at the pool house. A uniformed officer pulled back the police tape so they could enter. Jessie followed Hernandez, who took the lead. Trembley brought up the rear.

As she stepped inside, Jessie tried to clear her head of all extraneous thought. This was her first high-profile potential murder case and she didn't want any distractions pulling her from the job at hand. She wanted to focus exclusively on her surroundings.

The pool house was all understated, old-world glamour. It reminded her of the cabanas she imagined movie stars from the 1920s would use when they visited the beach. The long couch at the back of the main room had a wood frame but luxurious cushions that looked extremely nap-friendly.

The coffee table appeared to have been hand-crafted from reclaimed wood, some of which looked to be old sections of boat hulls. The art on the walls looked to be Polynesian in origin. In the far corner of the room was a bumper pool table. The flat-screen TV was hidden behind a thick, silky-looking beige curtain that Jessie suspected might have cost more than her Mini Cooper out front. There was no sign that anything untoward had happened in here.

"Where's the hidden nook?" she asked.

Hernandez led them past the bar that ran along the near wall. Jessie saw more police tape in front of what looked like a linen closet. Hernandez peeled it back and opened the closet door with a gloved hand. Then he stepped inside and seemed to disappear.

Jessie followed and saw that the closet did indeed have shelves with towels and some cleaning products. But as she got closer, she saw a narrow opening to the right between the door and the shelves. There appeared to be a sliding wooden door that receded into the wall.

Jessie put on a pair of gloves of her own and pulled the door closed. To an undiscerning eye, it looked like just another panel in the wall. She slid it open again and stepped inside the small room where Hernandez stood waiting.

There wasn't much to it—just a little loveseat and a small wooden table beside it. On the floor was a lamp that had apparently been knocked over. Some shards had broken off and settled onto the plush white carpeting.

Slumped on the loveseat in a relaxed pose that could easily be mistaken for sleeping was Victoria Missinger. A needle rested on the cushion beside her.

Even in death, Victoria Missinger was a beautiful woman. It was hard to gauge her height but she was trim, with the look of a woman who met regularly with her trainer. Jessie made a mental note to follow up on that.

Her skin was creamy and vibrant, even as rigor mortis was setting in. Jessie could only imagine what it was like when she was alive. She had long blonde hair that covered part of her face, but not enough to obscure her perfect bone structure.

"She was pretty," Trembley said, understating it.

"Do you think there was a struggle?" Jessie asked Hernandez, nodding at the broken lamp on the carpet.

"Hard to be sure. She could have just bumped it trying to get up. Or it could mean there was a tussle of some kind."

"I feel like you have an opinion but are holding back," Jessie pressed.

"Well, as I said, I hate to draw conclusions too early. But I found this a little odd," he said, pointing at the carpet.

"What?" she asked, unable to discern anything notable other than how thick the carpeting was.

"You see how deep the indentations in the carpet are from our footsteps?"

Jessie and Detective Trembley nodded.

"When we first came in after the dog found her, there were no footprints at all."

"Not even hers?" Jessie asked, starting to figure it out.

"Nope," Hernandez answered.

"What does that mean?" Trembley asked, not getting it yet.

Hernandez filled him in.

"It means that either the luxurious carpeting in here has unprecedented bounce-back capabilities or someone vacuumed it after the fact to hide the existence of footprints other than Victoria's."

"That's interesting," Jessie said, impressed by Detective Hernandez's attention to detail. She prided herself on reading people but would never have picked up on a physical clue like this. It reminded her that this was the man who'd been instrumental in catching Bolton Crutchfield and that she shouldn't underestimate his skills. She could learn a lot from him.

"Did you find a vacuum?" Trembley asked.

"Not out here," Hernandez said. "But folks are checking the main house."

"Hard to imagine either of the Missingers did a ton of housework," Jessie surmised. "I wonder if they'd even know where the vacuum was kept. I assume they have a housekeeper?"

"They do indeed," Hernandez said. "Her name is Marisol Mendez. Unfortunately, she's out of town all week, on vacation in Palm Springs apparently."

"So the maid is out," Trembley said. "Anyone else work around here? They've got to have a ton of employees."

"Not as many as you might think," Hernandez said. "Their landscaping is largely drought-resistant, so they only have a groundskeeper come in twice a month for maintenance. They have a pool management company and Missinger says someone comes around once a week, on Thursdays."

"So who does that leave us with?" Trembley asked, afraid to voice the clear answer for fear of being too obvious.

"It leaves us with the same person we started with," Hernandez said, unafraid to go there. "The husband."

"Does he have an alibi?" Jessie asked.

"That is exactly what we're going to find out," Hernandez replied as he pulled out his radio and spoke into it. "Nettles, have Missinger transported to the station for questioning. I don't want anyone else asking him a thing until we get him in an interrogation room."

"Sorry, Detective," came a crackly, apprehensive voice over the radio. "But someone already did that. He's en route now."

"Dammit," Hernandez swore as he turned off the radio. "We have to go now."

"What's the problem?" Jessie asked.

"I wanted to be there waiting when Missinger got to the station—to be the good cop, his lifeline, his sounding board. But if he gets there first and sees all those blue uniforms, guns, and fluorescent lights, he's going to spook and demand to see his lawyer before I can ask anything. Once that happens, we'll never get anything useful out of him."

"Then we better get moving," Jessie said, brushing past him and out the door.

CHAPTER EIGHT

By the time they arrived at the station, Missinger had already been there for ten minutes. Hernandez had called ahead and ordered the desk sergeant to have him taken to the family room, which was intended for crime victims and families of the deceased. It was a little less sterile than the rest of the station, with a couple of old couches, some curtains on the windows, and a few months-old magazines on the coffee table.

Jessie, Hernandez, and Trembley rushed to the family room door, where a tall officer stood guard outside.

"How's he doing in there?" Hernandez asked.

"He's fine. Unfortunately, he demanded his lawyer the second he walked through the front door."

"Great," Hernandez spat. "How long has he been waiting to make the call?"

"He already did, sir," the officer said, shifting uncomfortably.

"What! Who let him do that?"

"I did, sir. Was I not supposed to?"

"How long have you been on the force, Officer...Beatty?" Hernandez asked, looking at the name tag on the guy's shirt.

"Almost a month, sir."

"Okay, Beatty," Hernandez said, clearly trying to keep his frustration in check. "There's nothing that can be done about it now. But in the future, you don't have to immediately hand a potential suspect a phone the second he requests it. You can put him in a room and tell him you'll get right on that. 'Right on that' might take a few minutes, maybe even an hour or two. It's a tactic to give us time to develop a strategy and keep the suspect off-balance. Will you please try to remember that in the future?"

"Yes, sir," Beatty said sheepishly.

"Okay. For now, take him to an open interrogation room. We probably don't have much time before his lawyer gets here. But I'd like to use what we do have to at least get a sense of the guy. And Beatty, when you're moving him, don't answer any of his questions. Just put him in a room and leave, got it?"

"Yes, sir."

40

As Beatty went into the family room to collect Missinger, Hernandez led Jessie and Trembley to the break room.

"Let's give him a minute to settle in," Hernandez said. "Trembley and I will go in. Jessie, you should watch from behind the mirror. It's too late to ask substantive questions but we can try to establish some kind of rapport with the guy. He doesn't have to tell us anything. But *we* can say a lot. And that can have an effect on him. We need him feeling as uncertain as possible before his attorney gets here and starts setting him at ease. We need to get those lingering doubts in his head, so that he wonders if maybe we're better allies to him than his high-paid lawyer. We don't have much time to do it, so let's get in there."

Jessie went to the observation room and took a seat. It was her first chance to get a look at Michael Missinger, who was standing awkwardly in a corner. If anything, he was more beautiful than his wife had been. Even at 3 a.m., wearing jeans and a sweatshirt that he must have thrown on at the last minute, he looked like he had just stepped out of a photo shoot.

His short, sun-bleached blond hair was just mussed enough to look unpretentious but not so much as to seem disheveled. His skin was tan in parts, but white in others, the sign of a regular surfer.

He was tall and lanky, with the look of a guy who didn't have to work out much to get that way. The redness and puffiness of his blue eyes—likely from crying—didn't make them any less gorgeous. Jessie had to admit, despite herself, that if this guy had approached her at the bar last night, she would not have been so cavalier toward him. Even his nervous shifting from foot to foot was frustratingly endearing.

After a few seconds, Hernandez and Trembley walked in. They looked less impressed.

"Have a seat, Mr. Missinger," Hernandez said, making the instruction sound almost warm. "We know you've asked for your lawyer, which is fine. My understanding is that he's on his way. In the interim, we wanted to fill you in on where things stand with our investigation. Let me first start by offering my condolences on your loss."

"Thank you," Missinger said in a slightly raspy voice that Jessie wasn't sure was permanent or a result of the night's stresses.

"So we don't yet know if this was foul play," Hernandez continued, sitting down across from him. "But my

41

understanding is that you told one of our officers that Victoria was extremely proficient in regulating her condition and that you can't recall an incident anything like this in the past."

"I..." Missinger started.

"No need to answer, Mr. Missinger," Hernandez interrupted. "I don't want to be accused of violating your Miranda rights, which I understand have been read to you, correct?"

"Yes."

"Of course, that's all standard. And though we don't really view you as a suspect, you're well within your rights to request your attorney. But from our perspective, we're trying to move as quickly as we can to get to the bottom of this. Time is of the essence. So the more details we can confirm, like the one you shared about Victoria's proficiency with self-medicating, the less likely we are to go down dead ends. Does that make sense?"

Missinger nodded. Trembley stood silently to the side, as though not sure if or when he should jump in.

"So," Hernandez continued, "also just confirming, you said your housekeeper, Marisol, is on vacation this week in Palm Springs. You gave her cell number to an officer and I believe we're reaching out to her. By the way, without formally replying, if you find that I'm stating something inaccurate, perhaps you could make me aware. No need to answer any questions, of course. Just steer me in the right direction if I get off course. Fair?"

"Fair," Missinger agreed.

"Great. We're making progress here. We know you tried to reach out to Victoria several times over the course of the afternoon and she never responded. My understanding is that it was late yesterday afternoon, when you came home to meet up for a dinner reservation and found her car but not her, that you became concerned enough to call the police. If I'm getting any of this wrong, just tap your finger on the table or something to let me know."

Hernandez continued to walk through the rest of the timeline but Jessie found herself only half-listening. She had noticed something during the last exchange and was wondering if what she'd seen was real or imagined. Right around the time that Hernandez said "over the course of the afternoon," Michael Missinger had flinched slightly, almost reflexively. Not when Hernandez said "you tried to reach out." Not when he said "she never responded." Only at the words "over the course of the afternoon."

What had he been thinking about when the afternoon was mentioned? It was so imperceptible that Missinger himself might not have noticed it. That seemed unlikely if he was recalling murdering his wife in the afternoon. She would have expected either a bigger reaction or a concerted effort to have no response at all. At yet, something about the mention of the "afternoon" had thrown him, if only slightly.

Jessie's thoughts were interrupted by a new person entering the interrogation room.

"Hello, Detectives," a short, balding, forty-something man said buoyantly. "I'm Brett Kolson, Mr. Missinger's attorney. I hope we're all having a good time here. And I'm confident that you haven't been questioning my client after he called me."

He breezed in and pulled out the metal chair beside Missinger. Jessie typed Kolson's name into the attorney database to see what she could glean about him.

"Nice to meet you, counselor," Hernandez replied with a tone that suggested he wasn't being entirely sincere. "I'm sure your client will tell you that we've been nothing but gentlemen prior to your arrival."

Missinger nodded.

"They've just been reconfirming stuff," he said quietly.

"That's right," Hernandez agreed. "But now that you're here, Mr. Kolson, we'd love to get a little clarity on some timeline-related matters."

"You're welcome to try. But I reserve the right to advise Mr. Missinger to refuse to answer anything I think is out of bounds. And I will pull him if I deem it appropriate. Mr. Missinger wants to help get to the bottom of this horrible event. I trust it won't be a witch hunt."

"Of course, not," Hernandez said, pretending not to be troubled by the very developments he was concerned would happen.

"Give us a moment to confer, privately, would you?" Kolson said.

"Sure," Hernandez said. "We'll be back momentarily."

A few seconds later he and Trembley stepped into the observation room and looked at Missinger huddling quietly with his lawyer.

"We're not going to get anything out of this guy," Hernandez said, dispirited. "His lawyer is going to advise him not to answer anything of consequence. When we go back in there, he's going to shut down every path we take."

"Maybe not," Jessie said, still studying the screen.

"What do you mean?" Hernandez asked.

"This Kolson guy isn't a criminal lawyer. He may be putting on a good show but he's the corporate attorney for Ecofund Investment Partners, Missinger's hedge fund."

"Does it really matter?" Trembley asked. "He's still not going to let us start peppering his client with probing questions."

"No," Jessie agreed. "But Kolson's legal obligation is ultimately to the fund, not to Missinger personally. If we can get Missinger to believe that his interests and his attorneys aren't aligned, maybe he'll say something useful."

"Any suggestions?" Hernandez asked. "Because I can't think of any way to go at him that doesn't get shut down immediately."

"There's definitely something up with what he was doing yesterday afternoon. He flinched when you mentioned that timeframe. Maybe go back to that. See if he can walk you through his calendar for Tuesday afternoon at work. Maybe Kolson won't balk if he thinks the answer won't incriminate his client. I want to see how he reacts when you bring up that stretch of time."

"What are you looking for?" Hernandez asked.

"I have no idea," Jessie admitted.

The detectives returned to the room. Missinger and Kolson stopped whispering. Jessie tried to read their faces. But other than generalized anxiety on the client's part, nothing jumped out at her.

"Let's talk about yesterday afternoon, Mr. Missinger," Hernandez started. "I know you told our officer you came home to meet your wife for a planned dinner out. What were you doing prior to that?"

Missinger looked at his lawyer, who nodded.

"We had a conference call all afternoon," he said.

"You led it?"

"No. I made a few introductory remarks. But it was mostly run by our CFO, Sven Knullsen. It was a reevaluation of the EIP portfolio heading into Q one, sort of a last review before we lock everything in for the holidays. He had a big presentation planned so I deferred to him."

"This consumed your entire afternoon?" Hernandez asked.

Jessie saw Missinger tense up involuntarily, almost imperceptibly, before responding.

"It did. I had to prep for it and then I was on the call for well over an hour."

"The meeting was in your downtown office?" Hernandez asked.

"Technically, yes. That's where it originated. But our team is dispersed throughout the world. It's not like we were in the conference room. Everyone called in remotely, even within our offices."

"Is there a recording of the call?" Trembley asked.

"There usually is," Missinger said. "We maintain them so that folks who couldn't make it can listen later."

Kolson piped up at that point.

"Anything from that meeting is work product and I would object to it being used for anything other than to verify my client was on the call."

"Were you on the call the whole time, Mr. Missinger?" Hernandez asked.

"Yes," he answered.

Again, his jaw muscles flexed ever so slightly. Jessie had seen enough. She decided it was time to be more than just an observer.

CHAPTER NINE

Jessie left the observation room and knocked on the next door, ignoring the army of butterflies in her stomach. Trembley opened it.

"Mind if I join for a moment?" she asked.

Hernandez raised his eyebrows in surprise but quickly recovered.

"Mr. Missinger, this is one of our police consultants, Jessie Hunt."

Missinger nodded.

"I'm so sorry for your loss, sir," Jessie said, sitting down across from the man in the chair next to Hernandez.

"Thank you," he said quietly.

"I know this is a really raw time for you so I hope you'll forgive me for being so direct. But you have to realize that the thing you're hiding is going to come out."

"What is this?" Kolson demanded, his voice rising.

"And unless you killed your wife," Jessie continued, barreling past the lawyer's protestations, "whatever you're hiding isn't worth protecting."

"Don't respond to that, Michael," Kolson insisted.

Hernandez gave Jessie a look that was half fury and half befuddlement. She plowed on, aware that unless she got something now, her career with the LAPD might be over before it really got started.

"Remember, Michael," she said softly, "Mr. Kolson's obligation is to your company, not to you personally. I suspect that if you had called a lawyer with no connection to your firm, rather than the only one you had on speed-dial, you'd already have told us the secret you're clearly holding back right now."

"This conversation is over," Kolson said huffily, standing up. "Either arrest my client or we're leaving right now."

"Is this conversation over, Michael?" Jessie asked, staring into his still-red eyes. "Or do you have something to share?"

"Come on, Michael, let's go," Kolson said, grabbing Missinger's arm and tugging.

"Wait," his client said in a near-whisper.

Jessie sat in front of him, waiting, not breathing for fear it might influence his decision.

"Can you promise me some kind of confidentiality?" Missinger asked.

"What do you mean?" Jessie asked.

"If I reveal something that isn't illegal but could affect my company in a negative way, are you able to look into it quietly, and *keep* it quiet if it doesn't impact the investigation?"

Jessie began to suspect the universe of "somethings" that Missinger might be hiding and tried to ease his concerns as best she could.

"I can't make any promises, Mr. Missinger. But I can tell you this. Whatever you're hiding, we will uncover it. If you're forthcoming now, we can investigate with a scalpel rather than an axe. We can be diplomatic. We can keep a low profile. We can do those things if we know what we're dealing with. But if we don't, we have to cast a wide net. We might have to be more forceful—warrants, subpoenas, that sort of thing. You can limit those kinds of actions by giving us the information we need up front."

Missinger looked at Jessie helplessly. She could feel the other three men in the room staring at them both.

"How do I know I can trust you?" he asked with pleading eyes.

"You don't," Brett Kolson insisted, "which is why you shouldn't say another word."

"He's right," Jessie said quickly. "If you're responsible for Victoria's death, you shouldn't say another word. But if you aren't and you want us to find out who is, you'll bite the bullet and take the hit for whatever you've done that has you feeling guilty. We'll do our best to be discreet in following up, but only if you are forthcoming here and now. So what's her name, Michael?"

Missinger's eyes widened. But then something unexpected happened. His whole body seemed to relax, like a balloon once the air is let out.

"Mina," he said.

Out of the corner of her eye, Jessie noticed Brett Kolson tense up.

"Who's Mina?" she asked.

"She's Sven's wife."

"Who's Sven again?" Trembley asked. Jessie wanted to punch him.

"He's the chief financial officer for Ecofund," Missinger reminded him. "He's the one who was giving the presentation that day."

"So you were with Mina...during the conference call?" Jessie asked.

"Yes. I made my introductory remarks from the office but I was on my cell phone. Once Sven took over, I stayed on the line but left the building. He was in his own office and never saw me go. I walked three blocks to the Bonaventure Hotel, where I had a room held using a corporate credit card. I went straight upstairs to the room. Mina was waiting there."

"You had sex with your CFO's wife while listening to him make a presentation?" Trembley asked, sounding equal parts horrified and impressed.

"My phone was on mute," Missinger told him. "He couldn't hear anything. But I could hear the meeting, so that if I needed to speak, I could. I actually did make occasional points."

"Why did you meet her then?" Hernandez asked.

"Because I knew we couldn't get caught, at least not by Sven. He was obviously busy. But I have to admit the risk element was exciting. It was very illicit."

"Do you think your wife knew about the affair?" Jessie asked.

"No. I always used the EIP corporate card for our...visits. Mina and I met during the day, near work. Victoria would have no reason to be suspicious."

"How long had this been going on?" Jessie pressed.

"A couple of months. It wasn't anything serious. We started flirting at a dinner party one night and things just developed. But I love my wife and Mina has great affection for Sven. We both just wanted a little excitement."

"That little excitement could have billions of dollars' worth of consequences," Kolson muttered, despite himself.

"That's exactly why this has to stay quiet," Missinger replied.

"That's the least of your concerns right now, Michael," Hernandez said. "We have to verify your alibi."

"I'm sure cameras can show me leaving my office, entering the hotel, maybe even going into my room," Missinger insisted. "Can't you check the geo-location on my phone? There have to be ways to confirm where I was without going around asking a bunch of questions. If this got out, it would send the company into a tailspin. I've already lost my wife. I can't lose my business too."

"We'll check it all out," Hernandez told him. "If you provide all the details, fully and completely, we'll do our best to investigate tactfully. I can't promise it won't eventually get out in some future legal proceeding. But if you're straight with us and you aren't involved in your wife's death, we'll try to be sensitive. Fair?"

Missinger nodded. Hernandez pointed to the legal pad and pen lying on the table.

"Write it all down. Start with the dinner party you mentioned. List every date you can recall where you met Mina Knullsen. Then go through all of yesterday, listing everything you did, everywhere you went and everyone you met. Include times as best you can. Leave nothing out. Got it?"

"Yes," Missinger said.

"After that, we'll have more questions for you. We'll want to know about Victoria's doctors, everyone who knew about her diabetes, everyone who had access to your home, etc. You're going to be here for a while, Mr. Missinger, so get comfortable."

They left him in the interrogation room to write up his statement and returned to the observation room.

"Good catch on the affair, Jessie," Hernandez said, "even though you took a massive risk pushing him on it. You're lucky it worked out."

"What you call luck, I call talent," Trembley said.

"Don't encourage her, Alan," Hernandez said before turning back to Jessie. "How *did* you know to go there?"

"I didn't know," she admitted. "He seemed tense and guilty about the afternoon but wasn't even aware that he was projecting that. If he'd killed her, I would have expected either a bigger reaction or none at all. And when he conceded that he'd done something wrong but not illegal, something that could hurt his company, I was able to narrow it down. It wasn't drugs or financial impropriety. Either of those would be admitting law-breaking. But an affair wouldn't rise to that level. So I guessed."

"It may not be illegal, but it's the sort of thing that could get him killed if Sven found out and got pissed," Trembley said.

"I suspect Sven's not the 'get pissed' type," Jessie noted, "which may be why Mina was looking for some excitement in the first place."

"All that is very interesting," Hernandez said brusquely, "but we've got a problem."

"What's that?" Trembley asked.

"If Missinger's alibi checks out, we've just lost our primary suspect. We're back to square one."

CHAPTER TEN

Jessie felt like a churning cocktail of frustration and exhaustion. She hadn't expected to watch the sunrise from a desk in that Central Community Police Station, but that's exactly where she was as dawn began to settle over Los Angeles. And they still didn't have any promising leads.

Trembley was running down the list of people Missinger said accessed their home regularly. Hernandez had a message in to Victoria Missinger's doctor and expected a return call momentarily. He'd gotten an emergency warrant to access her phone and was now trying to track her movements over the course of the previous day. A few more detectives who had just arrived were helping him run down leads.

Jessie left the traditional investigation to them and instead studied the online calendar that Hernandez had downloaded from Victoria's phone. There were multiple events listed during the last few days—including a fundraising meeting for a children's charity called the Downtown Children's Outreach Center and a Hancock Park homelessness reduction seminar.

Jessie noted that both events and several others over the last few weeks took place at the same location—the Beverly Country Club. It occurred to her that the club might not be a bad place to check out. Since she wasn't technically a cop, she might be able to show up, ask around and glean some information that a more official law enforcement visit wouldn't allow.

She glanced at the clock. It was 7:37 a.m. The club would likely be open at this hour to accommodate the early morning golf crowd. But she doubted those were the folks she needed to talk to. Even on a Wednesday, the wealthy wives gang was more likely to amble in around brunch time.

"I'm going home for a bit," she announced to Hernandez and Trembley. "I figured I'd take a quick nap and clean up. Then I plan to go to her country club. I'm hoping that if I keep a low profile, I might overhear some scuttlebutt from the ladies who lunch. I'm sure by then, they'll all have heard about Victoria and be anxious to talk about it."

"That actually sounds like a really good idea," Hernandez agreed. "In my experience, once the cops show up, people are

51

either really forthcoming or completely clam up. You going in as a civilian might allow you to hit the sweet spot of getting info without dealing with agendas."

"Okay. I'll let you know if I learn anything worthwhile. In the meantime, happy detectiving, gentlemen."

She left the bullpen and headed for her car, excited to do a little probing on her own but even more excited to get a little shut-eye.

*

Jessie, wearing her best smart casual outfit, walked into the main entrance of the Beverly Country Club at 10 a.m. sharp. She'd called ahead and learned that brunch started at 10:30, but she wanted to be there well in advance in case anyone arrived early to trade rumors.

She had made a point of driving past the Missinger home on her way over. There was still one police car out front and tape surrounding the entire house. But other than that, it was quiet. Jessie had continued on, driving through the small neighborhood known as Larchmont Village.

The homes were an eclectic mix of ostentatious mansions and more modest cottages that had been here since before property costs in the area had skyrocketed. The business stretch of Larchmont Boulevard, just east of the country club, was a cornucopia of artisanal cheese shops, vegan-friendly cafes, organic markets, and fair trade coffee shops.

Jessie turned left on Beverly and right on Rossmore, where the guest parking lot for the club was situated. Once inside, she approached the reception desk and expressed her interest in joining the club. Could she get a quick tour, she wondered, and perhaps mill about to get a sense of the place?

A hostess happily showed her around before giving her a ticket for a complimentary brunch, which, she noted, conveniently started in a few minutes. She told Jessie to make herself comfortable and returned to help greet the ladies who were just starting to arrive.

Jessie sat down in the den-style main room, settling into a comfy easy chair near the fireplace with a view of the front door. She grabbed an old copy of *Vanity Fair* and pretended to read it as she peeked up occasionally to look at people as they walked through the doors.

A server came by and offered her a mimosa. She declined but asked if she could get a seltzer and orange juice. That way, she could mix with the crowd without drawing suspicion because she wasn't holding a beverage. Once it arrived, she got up and walked over near a particularly chatty group of three women. She pretended to study a painting on the wall nearby.

After a few minutes of discussion about the dip in the quality of the club's seafood over the last few months, the women seemed to feel they had waited a respectful period of time and, as Jessie expected, dived into discussing Victoria Missinger's death. It was challenging to distinguish individuals among the cacophony of voices with her head turned the other way.

"I heard they dragged Michael down to the police station in the middle of the night."

"Poor, sweet man."

"The medical examiner truck was there all night. That makes me think it must have been a bloody crime scene."

"I assume they'll check security camera footage. It has to show something."

"But Andi, don't you remember? There was that power outage yesterday. I wonder if there's even anything to see."

"I wouldn't be surprised if it turns out the pool boy came by hoping to get some action and got violent when she said no."

"Um, Marlene, how can you be sure she would have said no?"

"You know how those guys are. A 'no' wouldn't matter."

"Nice, Marlene. Any other stereotypes you'd like to toss out before brunch?"

"Sure, Andi. Now that you mention it, maybe the maid got jealous and decided to take out the lady of the house. I know I've thought about it just so I could get my hands on that man's body."

"Marlene, she's not even cold yet."

"Yeah, how can you be so bad?"

"Oh, don't be so prudish, Cady. You all know you'd take that ride if you could."

"What do *you* think?"

The conversation stopped and Jessie glanced up. All eyes were pointed in her direction and she realized she had been the focus of the question.

"Are you talking to me?" she asked innocently.

"Yes," said the woman who'd taken issue with the stereotyping, a blonde mid-thirty-something apparently named Andi. "I couldn't help but notice you listening in and thought you might have an opinion on the matter."

"Were you eavesdropping on us?" a pale, dark-haired woman wearing too much makeup demanded. Jessie recognized her voice as belonging to Marlene, the pool boy–suspecting one who wanted to get her hands on Michael's body.

"I was," she admitted. "Can you blame me? Talk of bloody crime scenes and violent pool boys. You ladies are like catnip."

"Who are you?" Marlene asked, her face a mix of suspicion and borderline disgust.

"My name's Jessie," she answered.

For the first time, perhaps ever, she was glad for the months she'd spent living in the ritzy Orange County enclave of Westport Beach. While there, she'd been reluctantly initiated into a secret club comprised of women much like the ones in front of her now. Back then, she'd been vulnerable and uncertain. Now she was working with the LAPD to solve a murder. She was not intimidated by Marlene.

"No, I mean who *are* you?" Marlene repeated. "Are you a member here or did you just wander in off the street for some free mid-morning food?"

"Marlene, you are an unbelievable bitch," Andi said before turning to Jessie. "I'm so sorry. Please ignore her. It's just that you seemed interested in our conversation and we didn't recognize you and…never mind, it's not my business."

"No, it's okay," Jessie said. "I don't want Marlene over here to stroke out. I'm happy to share. I work with the Los Angeles Police Department and I thought you ladies might be able to answer a few questions for me."

"Are you a detective?" the one who'd suspected a bloody crime scene asked, full of awe and trepidation. She was small, about five-foot-two, with long brown hair and a delicate frame that reminded Jessie of a baby bird that didn't yet know how to fly.

"No, I'm a consultant. I'm just trying to fill in some blanks. I saw in her calendar that Victoria spent a lot of time here and hoped that her friends here could be of assistance."

"So you came in here under false pretenses?" Marlene asked, only slightly tempering her vitriol.

"False pretenses?" Jessie asked, plastering a pleasant a smile on her face. "I was just appreciating the art here at the club while I waited for the right moment to interrupt. Why so much animosity, Marlene?"

The woman opened her mouth to respond when Andi jumped in.

"Of course, we'll help in any way we can," she said, extending her hand. "My name is Andrea Robinson but everyone calls me Andi. You've met Marlene Port. That's Cady Jessup. What would you like to know?"

"You were all friends of Victoria's?" Jessie asked, shaking her hand.

"Acquaintances at the very least," Andi replied. "I knew her and Michael casually. Marlene and Cady were closer, weren't you ladies?"

Marlene stared stone-faced but Cady answered.

"I'd say we were friendly, if not friends," she said. "Victoria wasn't the most outgoing person in the world. But she was nice and genuinely committed to the causes the club supports. But we didn't go for drinks together, if that's what you mean."

"Okay," Jessie pressed, "then what makes you think she was involved with the pool boy?"

"Oh, that's just talk," Cady said dismissively.

"Not really," Marlene said, finally engaging in the conversation. "There really is a pool cleaning service that has some boys who offer extra services. And I know the Missingers use that company. Whether she partook of what they were willing to provide, I have no idea."

"And you think that even if Victoria wasn't interested, the technician might be aggressive?" Jessie asked.

"Look, police consultant," Marlene said derisively, lowering her voice. "I know it's not proper to say this. But most of the 'technicians,' as you call them, are of Latin American derivation. And we all know that those kinds of men can be very forceful when they want something."

"*Do* we know that, Marlene?" Andi asked disdainfully. "Because it seems like you're painting with a pretty broad brush there."

"Here we go again," Marlene replied, rolling her eyes, "always standing up for the little guy, this one. Guardian of morality. Sometimes I wonder if you're Andi Robinson or Andy Griffith."

"I'm just not a fan of assuming everyone with skin darker than ours is prone to criminal activity," Andi whispered back.

Jessie noted to herself that just about everybody on the planet had darker skin than the ivory-toned Marlene.

"Look, the police consultant woman asked what the pool guy thing was about. I'm telling her. She can do what she wants with the information. Right, Jessie?"

"Sure," Jessie said, not taking the bait. "Better to have too much info than not enough. Any other service providers in the area that might not make the official list?"

"You mean the list of men that rich women pay to satisfy them while their husbands are off playing Masters of the Universe or golf?" Marlene nearly spat.

"That's exactly what I mean."

"There's a personal trainer some girls use," Cady offered. "His name's Dan Romano. But I think Victoria only used him once. So either she wasn't interested or she wasn't satisfied."

"I can assure you it wouldn't have been the latter," Marlene piped in.

"Listen, Jessie," Andi said quietly. "I didn't know Victoria that well. But I never got that kind of vibe from her. She never really expressed an interest in that sort of thing, at least to my recollection. I never saw her give a hot guy a second glance. I think her passions were of the more philanthropic variety. The only times I ever truly saw her get... zealous was when she talked about helping sick or homeless kids."

"She didn't have any of her own though?" Jessie asked, though she knew the answer.

"Barren as the Sahara," Marlene cracked.

"Jesus!" Cady muttered

"What?" Marlene retorted. "It's not like it was a secret. She said it had something to do with her form of diabetes; too risky or something."

"She wasn't interested in adoption?" Jessie asked, pretending not to notice that none of the women seemed surprised to hear of Victoria's diabetes. Apparently it was common knowledge, which increased the number of potential suspects substantially.

"I think she was. But Michael wasn't," Cady said. "So until she could change his mind on that, she considered the kids she worked with her children."

"Frickin' Mother Teresa," Marlene muttered under her breath.

Andi glanced over at Jessie, clearly mortified.

"And the comment about the maid, Marlene?" Jessie asked. "Were you serious about that?"

"What? That she might have murdered her boss so that she could have Michael all to herself? Obviously I was kidding. But if I was around that man every day, the thought would occur to me. He's yummy."

"She's just being catty," Andi said apologetically.

"Last question," Jessie said, wondering if that really was all there was to it. "What was this about a power outage yesterday?"

"Oh yeah," Cady said. "A transformer blew out some time in the early afternoon. It affected all of Larchmont Village. They didn't get things up and running again until after four p.m."

"Good thing it wasn't summer," Marlene said. "Or we'd have all boiled."

"And you think it might have affected the security cameras?" Jessie asked, trying to keep them all on task.

"I know when I got home the backup battery for our system was beeping," Cady said. "We had to reset the whole thing to get it operational again. I don't know what that does to video footage and that sort of thing."

"I wouldn't be surprised if it fried everything," Andi said. "That happened to my computer once."

"Listen," Marlene said, "I'd like to help you some more. But I need to find one of those hardworking, law-abiding Hispanic workers and get a mimosa refresh. Do you mind?"

"Not at all," Jessie said, stepping back. "Thanks for your time, Marlene. And don't forget to pick up your white robe and hood from the cleaners later."

Marlene stared at her for a second before breaking into a smile.

"I kind of like you, police consultant. You've got some fire in your belly."

Then she turned and headed off in the direction of the kitchen.

"It was nice to meet you," Cady said before scurrying off after her.

That left only Andi.

"I'd apologize again," she said, shrugging. "But I feel like it's getting old."

Jessie nodded. She noted that Andi seemed conflicted, as if she wanted to say more but wasn't sure that she should. Jessie decided to give her the opportunity.

"I have to head back to the office now," she said. "Care to walk me out?"

"Sure," Andi said, obviously glad not to have to share what she wanted to say in the confines of the club.

"Lead the way," Jessie said. "You're the member."

Andi did just that. As they headed out the front door, Jessie studied her more closely.

Now that her attention wasn't split among three women, she was able to take in more detail and she realize that Andi was younger than she'd thought at first, closer to thirty than thirty-five. Her blonde hair was shoulder-length and far less fussy than either of her club mates'. She was attractive in a nondescript sort of way and clearly tried to stay in shape. About five-foot-five and 125 pounds, she was unremarkable in almost every way. That is, except for her eyes.

They were a deep blue and twinkled with a playful sharpness that was at odds with the rest of her conventional bearing. Jessie got the distinct sense that the woman was appalled, or at least unenthusiastic, about her social circle. She couldn't help but like her.

"So what was it you couldn't tell me in there?" she asked when they were outside.

"I just wanted to make sure that you had a little context on the neighborhood before you went back to your colleagues and started suggesting lines of inquiry," Andi said.

"I'm listening."

"All right," Andi said. "Well, Marlene gave the impression that this community is teeming with blue collar workers just itching to commit crimes on residents. But that's not been my experience."

"Wait, did you come out here with me to tell me that your friend is kind of racist? Because I figured that one out on my own."

"No," Andi said. "Clearly you don't need to be a police consultant to pick up on that. I wanted to make clear that in addition to her overt racism, Marlene is also wrong. I don't have statistics at my fingertips. But I can't remember the last time someone from Hancock Park, especially the Larchmont Village area, was murdered by a worker of some kind. And I've lived here my whole life."

"So you don't think it was some pool boy slash gigolo?"

"I don't have any idea. I just don't want someone getting railroaded because they fit some preconception of what a criminal might look like."

"Well, Ms. Robinson, I can assure that we won't be railroading anybody. We'll go where the evidence takes us. But as long as we're on the subject, exactly how many murders do you remember in your neighborhood?"

"First of all, please call me Andi. That is, if you're allowed. To answer your question, I don't know. I'd be guessing but... less than a half dozen. And they were almost always crimes of passion or drug-related. Jealous spouse or a local kid high on something."

"So do you think Michael Missinger was the jealous spouse type?" Jessie asked.

"I don't know about that," Andi said. "I wasn't super tight with them. But he seemed pretty happy with his life to me. He didn't strike me as the sort of guy to get riled enough about anything to kill someone, much less Victoria. She didn't engender a lot of venom. The harshest thing I could say about her was that she was really intense about helping underprivileged children. Is that something that's going to make someone want to kill them? Seems hard to fathom."

"It's true," Jessie said, failing in her attempt to stay totally professional. "Enthusiastic philanthropy isn't often a motive for murder. But we can't rule anything out just yet."

"Well, here's my number," Andi said, handing over a card. "Don't hesitate to call if you have other questions. I may not be especially useful when it comes to the details of the Missingers' lives but I can probably give you some solid background on the neighborhood more generally if you need it."

"I appreciate that," Jessie said, handing over her card in return. "I may actually take you up on that."

Andi smiled warmly and returned to the club. Jessie watched her go before getting in her car. It occurred to her that she didn't really have many good female friends. There was Lacy, but she'd known her since college. Most of her other friends from those days had faded away as she and Kyle focused on couple-dom.

She'd gotten friendly with one of the wives down in Orange County, who was married to Kyle's high school buddy, Teddy. Unfortunately, things had gotten awkward with Mel once Kyle tried to kill all three of them in the same night.

She had confided the truth about her dad to Kat Gentry, the head of security at NRD, where the serial killer Bolton Crutchfield was being held. Other than Dr. Lemmon and Crutchfield himself, Kat was the only person in Los Angeles who knew the truth. Did that make them friends? If so, it was the weirdest friendship ever.

Once this Missinger case was resolved, Jessie resolved to see if Andi Robinson might like to get a drink. In her current circumstances, it was rare to find someone worth hanging out with. And if that meant having to find friends during a murder investigation, then so be it.

My life is weird.

CHAPTER ELEVEN

"So just to be clear," Hernandez said, the sarcasm in his voice unmistakable, "the ladies who lunch think we should be looking exclusively at pool boys, trainers, and maids as our primary suspects."

"Well, the other two were less definitive," Jessie clarified. "But the racist one definitely thought that was a good start."

"Sadly, she's far from the only one. As a dark-skinned guy, I was just waiting for someone to call *me* out."

"You are a little sketchy," Jessie poked.

"Not the first time I've heard that," conceded Hernandez, grinning. "As to those other folks, we've already run some of them down. Her trainer was from Florida and moved back there a month ago, so he's out. You'll recall the maid had a vacation in Palm Springs. We're locking that alibi down. In the meantime, she's returning to town right now so we should be able to interview her this afternoon. The pool boy, whose name is Raul Reyes, has gone missing. So maybe your friend from the club was on to something there. Let's not rule him out just yet. Any other leads?"

"Not really," Jessie admitted. "I can go back but I'm not sure how much I'll glean from another visit."

"Hold off until we have a reason," Hernandez advised. "If we upset them, then we inevitably upset their sugar daddies. And we don't want to make any enemies before we have to."

"Fair enough."

"I'm going to go find Trembley and see if he's had any luck hunting down Reyes. What are your plans?" he asked.

"I was thinking of going through the records on Victoria's phone some more to see if I can find anything out of the ordinary. Do you mind if I use your work station? I still don't have my own computer."

"That's fine. If you need to access any databases, all my log-ins are taped to the inside of my top drawer."

"Thanks," Jessie said, pretending but failing to sound casual as he walked off.

"Everything okay?" he asked, noticing the hitch in her voice.

"Yeah, fine," she assured him.

But everything was not fine. And it was Hernandez's fault. For reasons she'd have to address with Dr. Lemmon, his use of the phrase "sugar daddies" had made Jessie think of her own father. And it was while she had that thought in her head that he'd mentioned that she could access all the police databases using his log-ins.

That series of events had caused an idea—likely a very bad idea—to pop into her head. She sat there for a long moment, deciding whether to pursue it or just continue following up leads on the Missinger investigation.

Before she had officially made a decision, she found herself typing in the website for the FBI's unsolved crimes database. She entered Hernandez's log-in information and waited while the page loaded.

I can still exit the program and no harm will be done.

But then the search screen popped up and she found her fingers on the keyboard typing in a name: Xander Thurman— the proper name of the Ozarks Executioner, her father.

Almost immediately, a litany of criminal incidents began to populate the screen. The first crimes on the list were from years before she was even born, back when her father was a teenager. They included everything from cruelty to animals to petty theft.

She scrolled down the screen, scanning quickly through her father's criminal history. She was just getting to the details of his first murder victim when she sensed that she was being watched. She swiveled in Hernandez's seat to find Captain Roy Decker standing directly behind her.

Decker was tall and rail-thin, with only a few wisps of gray hair preventing him from being totally bald. He was in his late fifties but the deep creases in his face made him look a decade older. His sharp nose and beady, penetrating eyes reminded Jessie of an eagle hunting its prey. In this case, she appeared to be that prey.

Decker was one of the Central Station commanders and supervised both her and Hernandez, among many others. He hadn't hired her—that was done by a special department that liaised with profilers. But he could fire her. And right now, he looked like he wanted to.

"Ms. Hunt, do you want to explain why you're searching a federal database for information on a serial killer when you're supposed to be investigating the death of a local socialite?" he asked derisively. "Has the Ozarks Executioner come out of hiding to start injecting rich Hancock Park women with insulin overdoses?"

"I'm sorry, sir," Jessie muttered quietly as she exited the site. Out of the corner of her eye, she saw Hernandez returning to the desk. She felt her face flush with embarrassment.

"I know you profilers all want to make that big catch that will jump-start your career," Decker said. "But you can't use department time and resources to pursue an unrelated cold case when we have an unsolved murder on our hands. Is that too much to ask, Hunt?"

"No sir."

"Not a great start to your time here," Decker added.

"That's my fault, sir," Hernandez said as he arrived. "I asked Hunt to search the database for recent crimes with similar M.O.s but I didn't walk her through department restrictions and regulations. It's my bad."

Decker looked at him skeptically, clearly not convinced, but unable to prove otherwise.

"Don't let it happen again," he said. "I'm too busy to have to deal with this crap."

"No sir," Hernandez said, aggressively changing the subject. "By the way, we found out where Raul Reyes is."

"Where?" Decker asked, taking the bait.

"In the hospital. He's been there since Sunday night with pneumonia. It's an airtight alibi. He's not our guy."

So where does that leave us?" Decker asked.

"Back to the drawing board, sir," Hernandez admitted.

"Great," their supervisor said as he turned and started back to his office, before shouting back over his shoulder, "Keep me posted."

When he was gone, Hernandez turned to Jessie, his expression grim.

"Let's go get a bite," he ordered more than suggested. "We need to talk."

*

Hernandez had picked Nickel Diner, which was a five-minute walk from the station. It was packed, but when the greeter saw him, he created a table up front near the cashier counter and dropped two mugs of coffee on it. Jessie hadn't even looked at the menu before Hernandez came out with it.

"You can't pull that kind of thing again, Jessie," he said severely. "Even if we weren't in the middle of a case, you can't go hunting through an FBI database just to find out what's going on with your ex's case."

"That's not what I was doing," she said, realizing he hadn't been around when Decker first called her out. He had no idea that she'd been looking for information on her father.

"What then?" he demanded. "What was worth risking your brand new very interim job profiling for the department? A job I helped get you, by the way."

Jessie looked at Hernandez closely, trying to gauge how much she could trust him. If she stayed at Central Station, as she hoped, they would likely work together a lot. They needed to be able to count on each other. They needed to know what made the other one tick. Maybe she should tell him the truth about what was driving her. If she was going to be around him that much, this seemed like too big a secret to keep.

Besides, it was possible that he could help. He had access to resources like the database. Perhaps he'd let her use them. Beyond that, he was a detective; his job was to catch criminals. And he wasn't just any detective, but one who had been instrumental in capturing Bolton Crutchfield, the very man who had told her that her dad was looking for her. It seemed like an almost criminal waste *not* to pick his brain. But that meant coming clean about her past.

"You want to know what made me check that database?" she asked.

"I do."

"All right, I'll tell you," she said, diving in before her internal warning system went off. "But I need to know I can count on your discretion. Besides me, only four people in the world know what I'm about to tell you. One of them is my therapist, two are serial killers, and the last one makes a living ensuring one of those two serial killers doesn't get out of prison."

"Um, what?" Hernandez said, looking mildly stunned.

"Do you remember how Professor Hosta mentioned that I'd been granted permission to interview a high-value inmate and that I'd established a rapport with him?"

"Yeah, I think about it a lot, actually," he admitted.

"Well, that inmate is Bolton Crutchfield."

"Bolton Crutchfield, who butchered at least nineteen people over six years just for kicks? The guy who gave me this scar when I apprehended him?"

Hernandez pulled up the left side of his shirt to reveal a long, thick angry red line that ran vertically along his side from the hip bone up to the middle of his rib cage.

"The very same," she said, forcing down a gasp. She hadn't realized he'd been injured when bringing down Crutchfield.

"I'm still incredibly confused," Hernandez said, pulling his shirt back down and tucking it in.

"I haven't even gotten to the crazy part yet," Jessie warned him. "So you're going to need to buckle up and just let me say this, okay? No interruptions. Just let me get it out."

"Okay," Hernandez said, though he sounded like he was wishing he could bail on the whole conversation.

"Okay then, here goes. My father is Xander Thurman, better known as the Ozarks Executioner. My mother—her name was Carrie—and I had no idea. We lived in southeast Missouri. Money was short and jobs were hard to come by. So for many years, he worked in construction, doing jobs in various towns throughout the area. He'd be gone for days or even weeks at a time. Then he'd return and we'd be a family again.

"He was a decent dad—loving, sometimes tender. He used to call me Junebug. But he also had a volcanic temper. If he got angry he'd get very still and quiet and you knew the explosion was coming soon. He was never violent with me but I think he hit my mother a few times out of my sight. She didn't speak of it.

"What we didn't know was that, while he was off on these construction trips, he was also abducting, torturing, and murdering people. The cops aren't sure when it started. Because of the itinerant nature of his work, it was hard to track his movements. But they think it escalated once he bought a cabin in the Ozarks, in part paid for with money he took from his victims. He used the cabin to hide and eventually murder his victims.

"He took us out to the cabin a few times but my mom didn't love the place. It was sparsely furnished and she said it smelled strongly of antiseptic, like a hospital room. After a while, he just went there by himself for 'hunting weekends.' But all that changed one day when I was six."

The server walked over but Hernandez waved him off and the woman walked away without a word.

"My mother got jealous," Jessie continued. "She accused him of using the cabin as some sort of love nest. Looking back on it, I think she must have been following him one day when I was at school and seen him drive in that direction with a woman. She couldn't know the woman was actually a future victim.

"I guess something in my dad snapped at the accusation. He was offended at the notion that he'd been unfaithful. So he took us out there to show us the truth. Apparently he had no problem revealing that he was a killer. But being called an adulterer offended him.

"He drove us to that cabin on a dreary, snowy day in the middle of winter. I remember getting out of the car and walking to the cabin, my worn-out sneakers squishing into the slushy snow and the cold, wet stuff seeping through to my socks. I hadn't dressed properly for the visit.

"Once inside, he pulled open a trap door to reveal a basement and told us to go down there. I remember thinking how odd it was that an isolated backwoods cabin had a basement. When we got down, it was pitch-black. He turned on a kerosene lamp. That was when we saw them, a man and a woman, I assume the one my mother had been jealous of, completely naked and manacled to a supporting beam of the basement roof."

CHAPTER TWELVE

Hernandez had been about to sip his coffee. But at those words he put it down and rested his hands, palms down, on the table.

"The man looked like he'd been there for days," Jessie continued. "He was emaciated and had cuts—more like precise incisions—all over his body. He barely lifted his head when we came in. The woman didn't look like she'd been there as long. She had fewer cuts and seemed less beaten down somehow. She still had enough energy to be terrified. I heard a muffled scream come from her direction and saw that something had been stuffed in both their mouths."

Hernandez gulped hard, trying not to look overwhelmed.

"My mom began screaming," Jessie said. "That's when my dad covered her mouth with an ether-soaked rag. She got quiet and slumped into his arms. Then he carried her back upstairs, instructing me to follow them. I could barely move my muscles but I did what he told me. He had me sit in a wooden chair in the living room while he stripped my mom of her clothes and tied her up the same way he'd done the others. I was so shocked and terrified that I never even thought of running. He manacled her arms to a wooden support beam and let her hang there with her arms limply holding her up."

Hernandez put his head in his hands. Jessie wondered if he was going to make it.

"You okay?" she asked him.

"No," he admitted. "But keep going anyway."

So she did.

"My father explained to me that there was a lot of evil in the world and that it was his job to root it out and destroy it. I remember asking him if what he was doing wasn't evil too. He told me that sometimes it took a sinner to save the world. I said that Mommy wasn't evil and that he didn't need to destroy her. He said that she did have evil in her but promised that he would try to get it out of her as best he could and would only destroy her as a last resort.

"And that's what he did. Between tormenting and killing the people in the basement, he would 'test' my mom by cutting

67

her or burning her. I don't remember him ever doing anything special to get the evil out. I don't remember him asking her any specific questions. And anyway, she had the rag in her mouth so she couldn't answer."

An older woman sitting at nearby table got up, dropped a ten-dollar bill on the table, and left, her plate still half full. She cast Jessie a dirty glance on her way out.

I guess I should lower my voice.

"While we were there, he went away a few times," she went on, speaking just above a whisper now. "I remember finally loosening the ropes on my arms and legs enough that I could have escaped. But that would have meant leaving my mom and I couldn't do that. Besides, I never knew when he might come back.

"He always returned with new victims, whom he dragged down to the basement. He brought in three more people, in addition to the two that were already downstairs. Over the course of what I now believe to be about ten days, he brutalized and murdered them all. Then he turned to my mom."

The server approached us again.

"Give us a couple more minutes," Hernandez said quietly without taking his eyes off Jessie.

"He began whispering to her in this frenzied voice," she said. "He took his hunting knife and told her he was going to gut her with it. That's when I decided to make a run for it. I figured it was the only way to stop him from killing my mother right then and there.

"So while his head was turned, I snuck out of the cabin. I don't think he even noticed at first, he was so focused on my mom. But eventually I heard him coming after me. I was barefoot and freezing and lost and eventually came to a cliff overlook a raging, ice-filled river. I thought about jumping. But in the end I couldn't. He caught up to me and brought me back. He tied me up again and taped my eyes open so I couldn't look away. He said, 'You have to see, little Junebug. You have to know the truth.' He called me Junebug. Then he plunged the knife into my mother repeatedly. After that, he used the same knife to cut this into me."

Jessie pulled down the left side of her top to reveal a scar that ran horizontally just below her collarbone from her shoulder to her neck. She saw the server approaching again and pulled the shirt back up.

"I'll have toast and fruit," Jessie said.

"French fries with a side of bacon," Hernandez added.

The server nodded and left as quickly as she'd come.

"Interesting order," Jessie noted, trying to lighten the mood a bit.

"What happened then?" he asked quietly, refusing to change the subject.

"My father left me there, bleeding, staring at my mother's dead body. He never came back. A couple of hunters found me three days later and got help. When I recovered enough to speak, I told the authorities everything that had happened. Except for my mother, my father had burned all the bodies. They had some physical evidence to back everything up— videos he'd made and human remains, mostly pieces of bone. But some of the cops still couldn't believe it.

"They decided to move me out of town to protect me. Back then they were still hoping they might catch him and I was the only witness. They had both my written statement and my video testimony. There was no reason I had to stay there. So I was put in Witness Protection, relocated to live with a couple in Las Cruces, New Mexico, Bruce and Janine Hunt. They had recently lost their toddler son to cancer. The husband was an FBI agent there. The wife was a teacher."

"So that's where you spent the rest of your childhood?" Hernandez asked.

"Yeah. I started going by Jessie because I couldn't stand to hear the name my mom had called me after everything that happened. I was given a back story to use. No one but my adoptive parents and a couple of U.S. marshals based in New Mexico knew the truth. I stayed there through high school, and then came out here when I got accepted to USC."

"Are you still close with them?"

"I used to be very close to both of them. And I'm still close with Janine, my adoptive mother."

"But...?" Hernandez said, obviously picking up on her hesitation.

"Unfortunately, she got cancer in my junior year of college, just as her son had all those years earlier," Jessie said matter-of-factly. "She's been in and out of remission for almost a decade now. It's taken a real toll on her both physically and mentally and she's mostly bedridden now. She was always the bridge between me and my adoptive father, Bruce. We're both pretty stubborn. But in recent years, with her so weak, Bruce and I kind of drifted apart. Still, he comes out here occasionally. He was even here a few weeks ago to check on me after the whole 'your husband is a sociopathic killer' thing. But we don't talk a ton."

"Does he still work for the bureau?" Hernandez asked.

"He's semi-retired. He still consults for them and for Las Cruces PD. But he's not formally an employee."

"Kind of like you," Hernandez noted with a wry smile.

"I guess I never thought of it that way, but yeah."

"Forgive me for asking this," Hernandez said, "but what does any of this have to do with Crutchfield?"

Jessie appreciated that he didn't try to pursue any questions about the cabin and answered before he could change his mind.

"I heard about the Crutchfield case while I was in college and something about it sounded familiar to me. So I did some research and realized that he'd used many of the same techniques as my father. He kept his victims alive in the basement of his place. As you know, basements are rare out here. I learned that he'd had one built special after he bought the place. He also manacled them to the beams of the ceiling. He used the same brand of hunting knife to kill them."

"Jesus, that's right," Hernandez exclaimed. "He did use a hunting knife."

"There's no reason anyone out here would make the connection," Jessie noted. "The case was over a decade old at the time. It was halfway across the country. The perpetrator was never caught. But it obviously jumped out to me."

"You never mentioned it to anyone?"

"Not to the authorities. I couldn't risk having my identity revealed. And I wasn't sure how some random guy in Los Angeles even knew about the Ozarks Executioner. So I did my own poking around. But there was only so much I could learn from the public record. So I set about trying to get access to Crutchfield directly."

"What made some college student think she could get in to see a serial killer being held in a secure lockdown facility for deranged killers?" he asked incredulously.

"I have access to …resources I'm not at liberty to discuss."

"Okay," he replied slowly. "I'll let that one go for now even though every part of me is screaming to pursue it. Let's try this. You obviously got in to see him. Did he confirm your suspicions?"

"He did," Jessie said. "Crutchfield told me he'd been an admirer of the Ozarks Executioner. He said he'd committed his crimes the same way, almost in homage. I'm still not sure how he learned of him, although I know he's from Louisiana. Maybe it made the news down there. Regardless, he was eventually forthcoming, in his own circuitous way. He even helped me realize that Kyle was manipulating me. It was something he said that helped me start to unravel my husband's plot."

"Good guy then," Hernandez replied drily.

"Anyway, he wasn't surprised to see me," Jessie said, pressing on despite the detective's quip. "My father had told him that there might be a day when a woman would come to visit him asking about the connection between the two sets of murders. He wanted Crutchfield to give me a message."

"What was the message?"

"It was: *BE SEEING YOU, JUNEBUG.*" No one else—at least no one else alive—knew he called me that. That's how I was sure it was legitimate."

"He's looking for you," Hernandez said quietly.

"He is," Jessie confirmed. "That's why I was in the FBI database; because I have to find him first."

CHAPTER THIRTEEN

They sat there silently for the next few minutes. The server brought their food but neither ate. Jessie sipped at her coffee. Hernandez stared into space, lost in thought. Finally he spoke.

"Crutchfield knows your new identity," he said urgently. "What if he tries to contact your father to tell him?"

"Thanks, Hernandez," she replied sarcastically, trying to inject a little lightness into the atmosphere. "I hadn't thought of that."

"Sorry," he said, chastened. "Of course you've considered all of this. But it's new to me."

"That's okay. It's a lot to take in. The truth is I've gotten friendly with the head of security at the hospital where he's being held. Do you know Katherine Gentry?"

"I've met her," Hernandez said, finally deciding to take a bite of his fries. "By the way, try these. They're the best in the city."

"Well, she's one of the four—now five—people I've told the truth," Jessie said, trying one. "And she's working to ensure there's no way for Crutchfield to reach out. They've been reevaluating their security protocol to plug any leaks. Beyond that, she says she doubts Crutchfield would even say anything."

"Why not?" he asked.

"She thinks Crutchfield is fond of me, that he passed along the message as a warning."

"Do you agree with her?"

"I think he likes playing with me, like a pet mouse. But I worry he'd happily feed me to a snake to see me get chomped if he thought it would be entertaining enough."

Jessie snagged a few more fries and popped them in her mouth, despite the imagery she'd just evoked.

"These are good. So what's your story, Hernandez?" she asked, attempting to move on to any other subject.

"I'm afraid I don't have anything to share that could come close to that," he admitted. "Somehow 'nearly dying while helping catch a serial killer' just doesn't sound all that compelling after listening to you."

"You're right. That sounds totally boring. Still, I'm happy to hear from someone with even a smidge less life drama. Give me the mini-bio."

"Okay, I grew up in East L.A. Started gang-banging in my early teens; met a teacher in high school who used to be a cop and convinced me to try a different path. I graduated, went to a couple of years of community college before applying to the police academy. Spent three years in uniform before the Crutchfield thing jump-started my career and I got on the detective track. I've been doing that for five years, the last two with HSS."

"And when you're not working?"

"Married for six years now. We live in the Mid-Wilshire district. I like to go hiking in the Santa Monica Mountains when time allows. I'm a decent cook."

"Any kids?" Jessie asked, taking a sip of water to clear the catch in her throat.

"Not yet," he answered, his voice getting suddenly tight. "That topic remains under discussion."

Jessie sensed he didn't want to elaborate and moved on quickly.

"So what do you do when all your leads on a case dry up, Hernandez?" she asked in a perky tone.

"I think we've worked together enough for you to call me Ryan," he replied.

"Okay, Ryan, what do we do now?"

"We regroup and review what we have while we wait to see if the M.E. has anything interesting to share. We interview the maid when she gets back into town later today. We check the Missingers' financials to see if there's anyone they owe who might have decided to teach the husband a lesson. Basically, we circle the wagons until something pops."

"It sounds like we've hit a dead end," Jessie said skeptically. She took another glug of water to try to loosen the uncomfortable feeling in her throat.

"I prefer to call it a lull in the action," Ryan replied.

"Well, do you think that I could take few hours off during the lull?" she asked, wheezing slightly. She was having a bit of trouble getting the words out. "I have something I need to take care of."

"I think you're good, as long as you don't try to improperly access any more classified databases," he said, smiling slightly.

"Speaking of, do you think you could maybe help me access them properly, now that you know what I'm looking for?"

She grabbed a napkin to dab at her suddenly watering eyes and found herself hacking into it.

"Let's deal with the case at hand right now. Maybe we can work something out down the road," he answered, a concerned look on his face. "Hey, are you okay?"

"I feel like I'm having an allergic reaction to something," she croaked. "My throat is closing up."

"Oh jeez," Ryan said, looking stricken. "Are you allergic to peanuts?"

Jessie nodded between coughs. Her skin felt like it had been doused in poison ivy and every breath was now a challenge.

"The fries are cooked in peanut oil," he said urgently, standing up and moving to her side of the table. "I didn't even think about it."

Jessie reached into her purse, unzipped the side pocket, and pulled out an inhaler. She took a huge puff, waited briefly, and then inhaled another one. Within about thirty seconds, she felt her constricted windpipe start to relax. She took a long, slow, deep breath. Ryan reluctantly sat back down.

"Is it working?" he asked. "Are you feeling better?"

Jessie nodded, still not quite ready to speak again.

"I'm so sorry," he said. "I should have asked."

"It's okay," she rasped. "That's what the inhaler is for. I even have an emergency inhaler in my jacket in case I don't have my purse with me. It's my backup plan."

"That came on quick," he said, still looking slightly unsettled. "What would have happened if you didn't have your inhaler?"

"Nothing good," Jessie said, taking another swig of water. She felt like she was finally returning to normal. She stood up and tossed her napkin on the table. "I assume you've got this?"

"Why do you assume that?" he asked.

"Because you almost killed me," she teased. "Also I'm leaving now. And if you don't pay, that means no one does. And I think that's a crime or something."

She turned and headed for the door, pleased at her snark. But leaving now also served two other purposes. First, she could hide just how scared she'd been only moments earlier. And second, she could conceal her certainty that she was getting back into that database at some point, whether she had permission or not.

*

Jessie was almost to her destination—the Non-Rehabilitative Division of the Department of State Hospitals in Norwalk, about a half-hour drive southeast of DTLA—when she finally stopped dithering and made the call. Her adoptive father, former agent Bruce Hunt, picked up on the second ring.

"Jessie? Is everything okay?" he asked, concerned.

"I'm fine, Pa," she assured him, using the same name she'd chosen for him all those years ago when she first moved in. She couldn't go with "Dad," and "Father" seemed too formal. She'd considered "Bruce" briefly, but somehow that felt disrespectful.

"I just hadn't heard from you since I was last out there visiting and I worried that you were calling because…something had gone wrong."

"Something *else* you mean?" Jessie asked, regretting it immediately.

"I didn't say that."

"No, of course not," she said quickly, trying to barrel through. "Everything's fine. I'm still living with Lacy but I'm looking for my own place. How are you settling into yours?"

Just last month, Pa had finally consented to move out of the house he and his wife had shared for twenty-seven years. He'd recently gotten a hip replacement and having the bedroom on the second floor had become impractical, especially since the dining room had been converted into Ma's bedroom years ago. Now they lived in a condo complex for seniors, many of whom were also retired law enforcement. It had an affiliated assisted living unit that Ma transferred to temporarily when she was really struggling.

"Not too bad," he replied. "It's nice having everything on one level. And everyone treks to the Coco's down the block together for the early bird special."

"I can't tell if you're serious or not," Jessie said.

"I wish I was joking," he said wryly. "That place gets pretty crowded around four thirty in the afternoon. So what's up?"

"Does something have to be up for me to call you, Pa?"

"Usually," he said.

"I just wanted to check in, make sure you were okay and thank you for helping me square everything away after what happened."

"How's your gut?" he asked, referring to her injury. For as long as Jessie had known the man, Bruce Hunt had never willingly taken a compliment or a thank-you.

"Pretty good," she said, unable to hide the pride in her voice. "I'm actually working, doing some consultant work, profiling for the LAPD. I'm in the middle of a murder case right now."

"What happened with the FBI Academy?" he asked gruffly, almost as if he hadn't heard her. "Is that still happening?"

"I put it on hold for now" she replied, trying not to take offense. "I can still go for the next cycle if I want. I just couldn't pass up this opportunity, you know?"

"You have to do what you think is best," he said, his tone indicating that he doubted she was doing so.

"Right, thanks, Pa," she said as she pulled into the hospital parking lot. "I actually need to run. I have to conduct an interview now. But I'll check back again in a few days, all right?"

"Whatever you like."

"Okay," Jessie said, doing her best not to let his brusqueness get to her. "Talk to you later, then."

The phone went dead and she realized he'd hung up.

CHAPTER FOURTEEN

Jessie parked the car and sat quietly for a minute, trying to push the interaction from her mind so she could focus on what lay in front of her. Somehow her talk with Ryan Hernandez had spurred her to take the reins on multiple troubled relationships in her life.

First, she had initiated a conversation with her adoptive father, a rarity in its own right. Now, she was about to confront the serial killer who'd alerted her to the fact that her serial killer birth dad was seeking her out. At this rate, she'd be heading to Orange County tonight to chat up her murdering soon-to-be-ex-husband.

Jessie couldn't help but chuckle as she got out of the car and made her way to the facility's perimeter security gate entrance. She pushed the button on the gate and waited for whoever was manning the security camera above to buzz her in. They were familiar with her here now and the head of security, Katherine Gentry, had authorized her visit.

She entered the small courtyard and walked to the dual doors that served as the entry point to the unit. As the metal gate clanged shut behind her, she felt her mood change. Remembering the kind of people who were held here and what they'd done to fellow human beings, she felt any sense of lightness drain from her.

The NRD unit was a stand-alone annex to Norwalk's Department State Hospital-Metropolitan. The main facility housed other mentally disordered offenders deemed unfit to serve their time in a traditional prison. But none of the felons kept there—all men—had been convicted of sex crimes or murder. That's what NRD was for.

The Non-Rehabilitative Division was a special unit. A closely guarded secret, the facility was unknown to the general public and most of the Southern California mental health and law enforcement community. That was because it held the most extreme offenders—also only men so far—who were each serial murderers or rapists.

The facility had been built on the Norwalk hospital campus exclusively to house the worst of the worst in a maximum security environment that met state requirements for housing disordered offenders. There was enough space to hold ten inmates but there were currently only five residents, including Bolton Crutchfield.

Once admitted, Jessie passed through the outer door of the facility into a small vestibule. When that door closed, the inner door opened, allowing her entry into NRD's small main lobby, where she handed over her belongings to a guard and passed through an airport-style millimeter wave scanner. Once she cleared that, she found Officer Gentry waiting for her.

"Hi, Jessie," she said warmly. It was a far different reaction from how the NRD head of security had greeted Jessie the first time she'd visited the facility. Back then, it was all skepticism, bordering on suspicion.

At the time, Kat couldn't understand how or why a graduate student had gotten into her facility to interview a notorious killer. She still wasn't privy to the "how" but now that she knew the "why," she was much more sympathetic. Even though that first meeting had only been four months back, it felt like a lifetime ago.

"Hey, Kat," Jessie said. "Thanks for letting me come on such short notice."

"No problem. Let's get you changed."

They entered a room formally titled "Transitional Prep" with Kat in the lead. Jessie once again noted how imposing her new friend was. It wasn't so much her size. Kat was of average height, about five-foot-seven. But her body was powerfully built, 140 pounds of chiseled muscle. Even without flexing, the muscles in her arms bulged.

She was attractive in a casual "I don't give a crap" way. That was reinforced by her lack of makeup and the hurried bun she'd tied her hair in. It was slightly undercut by multiple facial burn marks and the long scar that ran vertically down her left cheek from just below her eye. Jessie knew these were the remnants of her time as an Army Ranger but how exactly Kat had gotten them hadn't ever come up.

Even if she hadn't been wearing a uniform, Katherine Gentry had the bearing of an authority figure, one not to be messed with. She walked quickly and purposefully. She spoke directly. And her haunted gray eyes were seemingly always on alert. Apparently two tours in Afghanistan left more than just physical marks.

Once inside, Jessie, who knew the drill well after multiple visits, changed into gray hospital-style scrubs. Having already removed all her jewelry and left it in the car, she quickly wiped what little makeup she was wearing off her face. Anything that might excessively stimulate the patients was prohibited.

"Let's go to my office," Kat said after Jessie had finished prepping. "You can fill me in on what's going on before we go visit your not-so-secret admirer."

"Has he actually mentioned me?" Jessie asked as they started down the hall. "I would have thought he'd consider it a sign of weakness."

"Not to me," Kat said, as they passed into the darkened hallway with several small offices and seemingly countless security cameras. "You know he never speaks to me. But Cortez says he's mentioned you a few times during supervised shower time."

"He mentioned me while he was naked? I'm not sure how I feel about that."

"Beggars can't be choosers," Kat said, chuckling to herself as they entered her cramped office. Jessie realized that was the first time she'd ever seen NRD Chief of Security Katherine Gentry laugh.

"Are you developing a sense of humor all of a sudden?" she asked, smirking.

"I've always had one," Kat replied, as she sat down and motioned for Jessie to sit in the chair across the desk from her. "I just like to hide it from civilians—keeps them on edge."

"Whoa, does this mean I've entered the vaunted Gentry circle of trust?" Jessie asked in her best Bambi voice, crossing her legs elaborately as she sat down.

"When you've had my back during a firefight in Helmand Province, you're in the circle of trust. For now, I'm putting you in the oval of 'not totally irredeemable.'"

"I'll take it," Jessie announced with faux pride.

She saw Kat force back the smile that was starting to play at her lips.

"All right, enough idle chitchat, Professor. Do you want to know where we stand with your gentleman caller, security-wise, or not?"

"First, I am not a professor. Having a master's is not the same thing, just in case it comes up down at the local hard-ass bar or something. And second, yes, I would very much like to know where we stand in terms of preventing one serial killer from passing information about me to another serial killer."

"Well, we're pretty sure that's not happening," Kat assured her. "He knows where all our old recording equipment is. But we've added extra hidden cameras and mics to his cell when he's showering so he doesn't know when we're watching or listening."

"You mean you did it when he was off chatting about me with Cortez?"

"Exactly. As you know, that thirty-minute period is the only time he's not in his cell each week. So while they're having Big Boy Jessie Talk Time, we also do a full search of the cell to make sure there's no contraband, that he hasn't found a way to slip messages through some tiny hole in the floor or that he hasn't somehow gotten Wi-Fi access in there; that sort of thing. Even the newspapers he's allowed to read are burned when we remove them from his cell."

"And?"

"Nothing," Kat said. "The place is clean as a whistle. As best we can tell, there is no way for him to communicate with anyone on the outside, which means your secrets are safe from dear old dad."

"Why, despite all that, do I not feel reassured?"

"Because," Kat answered, her voice now straightforward and serious, "you're a normal person. And any normal person who found out her serial killer father was looking for her would be freaked out, no matter how confident she was that he couldn't find her. It would be strange if you *weren't* unsettled."

"Any suggestions for how to remedy that?" Jessie asked.

"I do have one," Kat said reluctantly. "But it's a little unusual."

"I'm intrigued," Jessie said, raising her eyebrows. "Please continue."

"Okay, but if this idea is just too weird, feel free to tell me," she began. "I've eaten boiled rats and pulled shrapnel from a fellow soldier's butt crack so I'm not overly sensitive."

"Noted."

"I know that the last time we talked you mentioned you were thinking of moving out of your friend's apartment and getting a place of your own. It just so happens that my lease in picturesque City of Industry is up at the end of the month and I was thinking of moving to a community that didn't have a skyline of factory smokestacks and billboards for strip clubs.

80

You have any interest in having a roommate, specifically one who is expert rated with a service weapon, knows multiple forms of martial arts, and can rig an effective booby trap in under sixty seconds?"

Jessie was quiet for a second, pondering the possibility. Kat apparently misinterpreted the silence and jumped back in.

"Never mind, it's a stupid idea. I just—"

"No, sorry," Jessie interrupted. "It's not stupid. I was just thinking about the logistics."

"What logistics?" Kat asked, looking relieved.

"Well, I've only been looking at one-bedroom apartments so this reboots my whole mind-set, you know? I'm just playing with the options in my head."

"So you don't think it's a crazy idea?"

"I'm not saying it's *not* crazy," Jessie admitted. "I am saying I can't think of any reasons at this exact moment that it definitely *is* crazy. Can I sit with it for a bit?"

"Of course. I should have waited until after to bring it up anyway. You should be focusing on meeting with Crutchfield. We can discuss it later... or never."

"Let's go with later," Jessie suggested. "But for now, I think I should set my attention on what's about to happen. Is he in his cell now?"

"He is. You want to head over?"

Jessie nodded. Kat got up and they walked down the hallway to the security door that led to the resident cells area. As they did, she went over the rules again.

"I know you've probably committed all this to memory. But as it's been a while since you were here, let me just refresh you a little. Remember, don't approach the inmate. Definitely don't touch the glass barrier. Normally, I would say don't share any personal information. I realize we're kind of past that in your case, but still, try to show some discretion. The less he knows about you, the less he can mess with you. Lastly, do you remember the red button?"

"Of course," Jessie said. "My security blanket of sorts."

"That's right. Keep the key fob remote I'll give you in your hand, hidden from his sight. If things get too intense, push the button and it will alert me that you want out without him realizing he'd gotten to you."

"I'll take it," Jessie said. "But you do know he's likely aware of the button and that if you suddenly jump in, he'll know that I've probably pushed it."

81

"I know. But it's the best option we've got right now."

The security door buzzed as they reached it and Kat pulled it open. Someone inside must have seen them approaching. They stepped in and Jessie looked around. The security station looked the same as it had the last time she was here six weeks earlier. It was configured like a hospital nurses' station, with a long, central desk covered in a bank of computer monitors. Surrounding the station were multiple doors leading to resident cells.

There were four officers situated at the security station. Two were doing paperwork of some kind. A third was restocking a cabinet. And then there was Cortez, Bolton Crutchfield's shower chaperone. He looked up from the monitor he'd been studying and gave Jessie a big smile.

Officer Ernie Cortez was a massive human. A Hispanic man in his mid-thirties, Cortez was easily six-foot-six and well over 250 pounds. His genial expression couldn't hide the fact that if he wanted to do some physical damage, it wouldn't take much.

"Look who it is," he said happily, "my favorite Vogue Chick. How's it going, Jessie?"

Vogue Chick was the pet name Cortez had given her the first time he'd met her. Apparently he considered her model material.

"Good, Cortez. I hear you've been spending a lot of quality time with Crutchfield lately."

"What?" he asked, looking taken aback.

"The shower," Kat prompted.

"Oh yeah," Cortez said. "I pulled the short straw on that one. That guy's a real chatterbox when he's naked."

"Say anything especially interesting?" Jessie asked. "Maybe about me?"

"He's mentioned you on occasion. He read about that thing with your husband in the paper and wanted to know if you were okay. Sounded almost genuine."

"You guys don't cut out the articles about me before you gave him the papers?" Jessie asked, surprised.

"It's not like we go through them before handing them over," Cortez said slightly defensively. "How could we have known you'd be plastered all over them?"

"Fair point," Jessie said, relenting. "So that was it, just asking about my well-being?"

"Mostly," Cortez. "It's not like he's describing having dreams about you or something. Get over yourself, Vogue Chick."

"No, that's you, Cortez," Kat teased.

"Well," Cortez said, unperturbed, "now that you mention it, since Mr. Vogue Chick is out of the picture these days, maybe you're looking for a little companionship?"

Jessie just stared at him.

"Too soon?" he asked before cackling at his own cleverness.

"All right, enough flirting, you too," Kat said. "Let's get serious. Jessie, are you prepared to enter the cell?"

Jessie nodded.

"I need a verbal 'yes' for the record."

"Yes," Jessie said, the lightness she'd felt a moment earlier completely evaporating.

"Okay, last bit of business. Sign this form releasing the Department State Hospital-Metropolitan, Non-Rehabilitative Division from any liability should an incident with the inmate occur."

Jessie signed it.

"Here's your key fob," Kat said, handing over the small piece of plastic. "Are you ready to get reacquainted with one of the most dangerous people on the face of planet Earth?"

Before Jessie could answer the door buzzed. Kat held it open for her to enter. She took one last big gulp and stepped inside.

CHAPTER FIFTEEN

Despite having been in the cell multiple times, Jessie still felt a surge of adrenaline course through her body, making her fingertips tingle. She breathed out slowly, reminding herself that everything in the world was essentially the same as it had been ten seconds prior.

You can handle this.

She forced herself not to dwell on the fact that she was entering the same confined space as a man who had butchered nineteen people, and those were just the ones the authorities could verify. Some law enforcement officials thought the true number might be more than double that.

Don't fixate on the past. That gives him the advantage. Stay in the moment.

She forced herself to concentrate on the details of the room. It was divided into two sections, separated by a thick glass wall. On Jessie's side were a small desk and chair with a pad of paper and a pencil. On the other side of the glass was the secure portion of the cell, which was dimly lit.

It was sparsely furnished, consisting of a narrow metal bed attached to the wall, hovering three feet above the ground. A thin mattress was connected to the bed frame and a small rubber pillow rested at the head. There were no sheets.

In the back right corner of the cell was a toilet, with a curved sliding plastic door to provide some minimal privacy. Next to it, also attached to the wall, was a tiny metal sink. Beside that was a combination chair and desk, with the far end of the desk actually melded into the wall so the thing couldn't be moved. This was where Crutchfield sat.

He was facing away from her and had given no indication that he was aware that Jessie had entered the room. He was dressed in his own set of scrubs, only his were a bright, aqua blue shade. His blond hair was shorn tight against his skull, which was bony and almost alien-looking from the back.

Jessie sat down at the desk and waited a moment to see if he'd speak. After a good thirty seconds of silence, she took the initiative.

"Hello, Mr. Crutchfield. It's been a while."

He still didn't respond so she tried again.

"Mr. Crutchfield?"

Still no reaction. Crutchfield sat at his desk, facing away from Jessie, unresponsive. She glanced over at Kat, who had stationed herself in the corner of the room.

"He's pouting," she explained, "since you haven't been here in a while."

"Is that true?" Jessie asked.

"Can you blame me?" Crutchfield finally said, in the languorous, gentlemanly southern drawl she'd never quite been able to associate with the man who'd committed all those crimes.

"What do you mean?" she asked innocently, though she suspected she knew what he was getting at.

Crutchfield stood up and turned to face her. As she was on every other visit, Jessie found herself stunned that such an unimposing-looking man was capable of such horrific violence. Bolton Crutchfield was about five-foot-eight and barely 150 pounds.

He was soft-looking despite his smallish-frame, with a doughy appearance. His face was appealing in a boring, unmemorable sort of way. He was pale, with a soft chin and crooked teeth. She knew he was thirty-five, but he looked boyish, almost half a decade younger. Only his wolfish brown eyes suggested something more menacing underneath the mild façade.

"I thought I was useful to you, Miss Jessie," Crutchfield said mournfully. "I let you know your suspicions about your husband were not without merit. I warned you that your dear old daddy was interested in your whereabouts; all that in return for little more than a bit of chitchat. And yet you toss me aside like so much rubbish. No visits, no calls, not even a postcard. It's hurtful."

Jessie wasn't sure if he was serious or faux offended and decided to proceed without making any assumptions.

"My understanding is that you aren't permitted to receive calls or mail, Mr. Crutchfield."

"True, but visits are permitted," he noted. "And you had made several in the past, if you'll recall. I guess once I served my purpose I was no longer of any value to you."

Jessie weighed her next words carefully. Crutchfield liked to play games and she was increasingly confident that he was merely acting the role of the jilted man. But his teasing manner could turn vicious on a dime. And it usually happened when he thought someone was trying to work him. In the past, she'd always had the most success with him when she was at least partially honest. She decided to try a bit of that now.

"Truthfully, Mr. Crutchfield, I've been a little reticent to come back. Since we last saw each other, my husband tried to kill me and did in fact injure me pretty seriously. I've been recovering ever since. In fact, I was only recently cleared to walk without a cane. So the idea of traipsing all the way here wasn't especially appealing."

She noticed him sigh almost imperceptibly and knew she hadn't gone far enough. He wanted more and if he was going to give her any information, she'd have to spill it.

"And there's something else," she continued, noticing his previously glazed eyes suddenly come into focus.

"Pray tell," he said, feigning disinterest but well aware that he wasn't pulling it off.

"Well, I just wasn't sure I could manage it. Coming back here, looking in the face of the man who pulled the blinders off my eyes—it's a painful thing. I spent a long time with my husband and couldn't see what he really was. You saw the truth without ever actually meeting him. I knew seeing you again would remind me of my failure. It's not exactly something I was looking forward to."

"Is that all?" he asked, knowing it wasn't.

"Of course not," she admitted. "I got your message. I know my father is looking for me. I know you spoke to him about me. It's very…unsettling. I wasn't sure I was up for coming back. So I stayed away. I hope you can understand that."

"I can, Miss Jessie," he said, his voice warm for the first time since she'd entered the room. "And I know this is a lot for you to process. I believe that you needed some time to make sense of it. But can I be frank with you, my dear?"

"I wouldn't have it any other way," she said, sounding convincing even if she wasn't sure he believed it.

"Good. We both know that you're only here because you need something from me. Otherwise you'd never step foot in this place again."

"What is it you think I need?" Jessie challenged.

"You want information on your father, something that can help you find him before he finds you."

"How could he possibly find me?" she asked.

"Through me, of course. I know your new name. I know the city you live in. I could probably find your current address if I was interested."

"You don't have access to the outside world, Mr. Crutchfield," she reminded him. "There's no way for you to communicate with him."

He smiled ever so slightly before responding.

"You're not that naïve, Miss Jessie," he said, sounding almost pitying. "Deep down you know that I could snap my fingers and he'd show up at your door. It's only my amusement with your antics and my intermittent affection for your coltish curiosity that have prevented that from happening so far. So it would behoove you to keep on my good side, don't you think?"

Jessie stared at him. He stared back, unblinking. He was most likely bluffing, another tactic to mess with her head. But she couldn't take that chance and he knew it.

"How would I go about that, keeping on your good side?" she finally said.

"How lovely of you to ask," he exclaimed, clapping his hands. "I have a small favor to request of you."

"Mr. Crutchfield, even if I believed you, I'm not going to be held hostage and do you a favor just so you won't say something. That's a form of blackmail and it's not how I plan to live my life. For me to even consider doing you a favor, I'd need something in return."

"This is getting delicious," Crutchfield said, rubbing his hands together excitedly. "What are you looking for?"

"How about my father's current location? City? State? Region of the country?" she asked.

"Oh, don't be silly, Miss Jessie," he said dismissively. "That would spoil all the fun. But maybe I can offer you something else."

"What's that?"

"A clue to help you with the case you're currently working on, perhaps?"

How does he know I'm working on a case? How does he even know I have a job? Have Kat's security measures already failed?

Jessie forced a plastic smile on her face to hide her shock.

"You seem to think you know a lot about what's happening in my life, Mr. Crutchfield," she said as casually as she could under the circumstances. "How is that?"

"I'm not clairvoyant, Miss Jessie. I just read the papers, even the classifieds. I saw the LAPD interim junior profiler position listed for several weeks running, but not the last few. The job has obviously been taken. It was at Central Station, which handles an area you know well from your time studying at USC. It would be hard to imagine that you didn't somehow become aware of a position that seems so perfectly suited for you."

"Those aren't outlandish guesses, I'll admit," Jessie said. "But they don't explain your assumption that I am working on a case and need help."

"No. But I did read about a case that seemed right in your wheelhouse. A wealthy socialite in Hancock Park found dead. Foul play is suspected. I could easily see it being assigned to the new gal. The crime is not so grisly as to be off-putting to a newbie. The higher-ups, after all, have no idea the magnitude of grisliness you've see in your life. And bonus—you have recent experience dealing with crime among the rich and obnoxious. It's a perfect fit. Am I close?"

"Let's say you are. What help could you offer me?"

"First, let's discuss that favor, shall we?" he reminded her.

"What are you looking for?"

"I just need you to go to an address for me and tell me if a building is still standing there or if it is now an empty lot."

"Why?" Jessie asked.

"That is not your concern. And it shouldn't put you out in any way to do this. I doubt that even your silent, judgy friend in the corner would balk at so simple a request."

Jessie looked over at Kat, who simply shrugged. Jessie turned back to Crutchfield.

"I feel like there's a catch," she said.

"I wouldn't call it a catch. There's just one extra feature to my request. What time is it right now?"

She looked at her watch.

"Almost two p.m," she told him.

"Ah, good. Then my request shouldn't be an issue. I need you to do it by four o'clock this afternoon. You need not get back to me today. But you must check on the status of the lot by four. The sun sets very soon after that today. Understand?"

"What's the address?" Jessie asked.

"1024 Visitation Avenue, unit 2016."

Jessie wrote it down, then looked back up.

"Clue time," she said expectantly.

"Oh yes, of course. The clue is that you should be looking for someone who is unhappy with their lot in life."

"That's your clue?" she demanded, disbelieving. "That's just about the vaguest thing I've ever heard in my life. It sounds like some kind of fortune cookie. Are you serious?"

"Your testiness is off-putting, Miss Jessie. Did you really think I was just going to say it was Colonel Mustard in the Conservatory? How boring would that be?"

"So you give me a riddle?"

"It's so much more fun this way," he said, bouncing on the balls of his slippered feet.

Jessie looked at him closely and couldn't help asking the question that had been in her head from the moment he mentioned a clue.

"Do you actually know who killed the socialite, Mr. Crutchfield?'

He smiled—not a grin or a smirk but a genuine, open-mouthed, crooked-teeth-visible smile. He was delighted by the question.

"Of course I don't," he said. "I've never met or even heard of the people in that news story. But I read the article closely and it was clear to me the *type* of person who would have committed this kind of crime. And if you're any good at your job, it should be clear to you too."

CHAPTER SIXTEEN

Jessie pulled up to the address Crutchfield had given her, trying to ignore the shiver of nervous anticipation that ran down her back.

She was late. It was 4:15 and the sky had already begun to darken as the sun was beginning to fade in the west. She could have been here by 4 p.m., as he had requested. But she had intentionally chosen not to make it in time.

Am I just that stubborn? Did I do it merely out of spite? Probably some combination of both.

She'd been driving to the address when she suddenly pulled over at a coffee shop a few blocks away around 3:45 and spent the next half hour in the place, sipping a hot tea and checking her phone. She told herself it was to keep up with developments in the Missinger case. But that was a lie. She just didn't want to feel like she was doing Crutchfield's bidding.

There was an email from Ryan saying the Missingers' maid was back in town but claiming to be suffering from grief and emotional exhaustion and had postponed her interview by a day. It was good information to know but nothing that couldn't wait. Jessie considered calling the detective back and asking him to meet her at the address, but then thought better of it.

I already caused trouble once today by using department resources to investigate my father. Pulling a homicide detective off his case to further pursue it definitely crosses the line.

At 4:10, long enough after Crutchfield's deadline that she could tell herself she wasn't his lackey, Jessie got in her car and drove the last quarter mile to 1024 Visitation Avenue, where she now sat, waiting for the nerves to subside.

The lot was in an industrial area at the southern edge of downtown, surrounded by multiple warehouses, many of which looked abandoned. Jessie could see that there was indeed a building with the number 1024 on the front. Theoretically, she could call Kat right now to answer Crutchfield's question: There was a standing building on the property—it was not an empty lot. Technically, she could drive away now.

But of course she couldn't. The notion that Bolton Crutchfield sent her to this random, out-of-the-way location to simply verify the existence of a building seemed unlikely. There had to be more to it. So, despite the voice in her head loudly recommending she not do it, Jessie got out of the car.

She zipped up her jacket in a futile attempt to mitigate the growing chill she felt. It was getting dark fast and the temperature had dropped into the mid-40s, but she suspected she'd still be shivering even if it was a summer day.

She moved across the patchy, brownish grass to the front step of the building and looked up. Unlike most of the other structures in the area, this one appeared to have once been a residential building. She walked up the steps to the front door and noted the faded directory of last names in a now-shattered box to the right of the entrance. This had indeed once been an apartment complex.

But that must have been a while ago. The place looked like it hadn't been inhabited in some time. Most of the street-facing windows were gone, and only some had been boarded up. Graffiti covered the outside walls. A chain loosely wrapped around the main double doors indicated that visitors were not welcome. The sign taped to the front saying "condemned" reinforced the idea.

Jessie glanced at the directory again. Most of the names were too faded or muddy to read but some unit numbers were legible. And that's when she noticed something that should have been obvious the second she pulled up. Crutchfield had mentioned unit 2016. But the building was only three stories high. There was no twentieth floor and no unit 2016.

There was apparently a unit 206, where, according to the barely visible, smeared red ink, someone named Johnson, Jones, or maybe even Johannsen had once lived.

Could Crutchfield have made a mistake? Maybe misremembered the address?

It seemed doubtful. And yet, that was the only unit that came close to what he'd described.

Jessie looked again at the chain wrapped between the metal door handles. Even before she'd calculated with certainty that she could slip through into the building, she knew she was going to do it.

She glanced quickly around the area. Seeing no one, she quickly removed her bulky jacket, dropped it on the ground, and sidled through the narrow crack between the building's doors. The whole process had taken less than ten seconds. Once inside, she pulled out her phone and turned on the flashlight feature, shining it into the dark lobby.

It was empty, save for a couple of overturned chairs strewn about. A thick layer of dust was visible even in this dim light, which made it easier to see the multiple sets of shoe prints leading from the main doors off into various directions. Apparently she wasn't the first person to have determined the chain lock need not be an impediment to getting inside.

She saw movement to her left and gave a little jump before she realized it was just a rat scurrying away from the light. Other than the rodent, the place looked abandoned. The smell of urine and feces was strong, so much so that her eyes watered.

She moved forward quickly, looking for the stairwell to the second floor, taking care to avoid stepping on the bits of glass or the small, unidentifiable mounds of debris that littered the ground. As she passed from the lobby into the main hall with the bank of elevators, she thought things would warm up a bit. But with the broken windows, the hall formed a kind of wind tunnel, making everything colder. Without her jacket, Jessie couldn't stop herself from shaking involuntarily.

Eventually her flashlight passed over a sign at the back of the hall that read "stairwell." She followed it around the corner where she finally got a break from the currents of air whipping at her skin.

She turned the handle to the stairwell door and it gave. She pushed and the door opened easily, providing access to a set of steps that, despite being concrete, looked dangerously crumbly.

You've come this far. No point in chickening out now.

She allowed herself one deep breath before scaling the stairs, noting with relief that despite how they looked, they were still pretty stable underfoot. She reached the second floor quickly and found the door to that hallway unlocked as well.

Once it closed behind her, Jessie found herself in a different world. The ratty, carpeted floor muffled the sounds from outside, including the occasional passing truck and even the howling wind. Shafts of light from several open apartment doors created sad little spotlights dotting the length of the hallway.

She moved quickly down the hall, shining her light on the apartment numbers on each door. Most doors were closed. Some were slightly ajar. Still others were wide open. A few units were missing doors completely. She hurried past them all, unsure what she'd find inside, vaguely fearful that someone or something might reach out to grab her.

92

When she got to unit 206, near the far end of the hallway, she saw that the door was closed. As gingerly as possible, she turned the handle. It opened without complaint. Jessie pushed the door open and stepped back so she could shine the flashlight on as much of the room as possible before entering.

From her vantage point, it was unremarkable. The living room was small and still furnished, though it looked like the rats had gotten to the couch and easy chair. Stuffing poked out at various spots and a thick layer of dust coated them.

She stepped inside and passed the beam over the rest of the place. As she did, she noticed a strong putrid smell. It was different from the excrement downstairs, foul in a distantly familiar way. Unable to identify it, she focused on the details of the apartment. There was a small breakfast room that had a table but no chairs. The kitchen was tiny with several cupboards hanging loose from their hinges.

Jessie moved to the bedrooms. One had a futon-style bed that had been stripped bare. The other was empty except for a dresser that was devoid of drawers. She made her way to the bathroom. The second she stepped inside, she knew something was wrong.

The smell she'd noticed upon first entering the apartment was much stronger in here. It hung thick in the air, like a layer of rank fog. She glanced at both the sink and the toilet and saw nothing. The bowl was dry, completely devoid of water. A wooden-handled plunger sat beside the toilet seat, ready for duty but clearly not called on in some time. That left only the shower.

The curtain, once white but now various shades of mold-covered gray, was pulled across the length of the tub. Jessie grabbed the plunger and placed it at the edge of the curtain, waiting for the right time to pull it back. Deciding there was no right time, she decided to just do it.

She swung the plunger to the left, sliding back the curtain. Several of the rings snapped as she did that, making the whole contraption sag heavily. Still, she was able to get a fairly clear view of the tub. Inside, on its back, was skeleton, a sunken mass of dusty bones and hair that had clearly once been a human body.

It had obviously been there for a while. Most of the skeleton had decomposed. With the clothes, now faded and dusty, still on the body, it looked more like a scarecrow lying face-up than an actual person. The skull was still mostly intact and tufts of longish hair rested in patches nearby. She guessed this had been a woman.

Now Jessie realized why the smell had been so familiar. It was the same one that had come from the decomposing bodies in her father's cabin all those years ago.

Despite the stench, Jessie leaned in closer, hoping to glean any more identifiable details. A sound from behind made her stumble. She reached out for the curtain to steady herself but only managed to bring the whole thing down as she landed awkwardly on the edge of the tub.

Turning quickly, she flashed her light in the direction of the sound. In the bathroom doorway stood a man of indeterminate ethnicity. His long, shaggy hair covered the top half of his face. A thick beard hung off his chin. His baggy clothes draped off him, making it difficult to tell just how big he was.

"What do you want?" she demanded as she tried to scramble to her feet but only got more tangled in the curtain.

He took a step toward her. His hair moved slightly and she saw his eyes. They were shining bright with a faraway intensity that suggested he was both hyperalert and yet not totally there. His hands were twitching involuntarily.

He's on something.

"Step back," Jessie ordered forcefully. "I'm LAPD and you are interfering in an official investigation."

But the man seemed either not to hear her or not to care. He took another step forward, grunting unintelligibly. She saw one of his shaking hands dig into a pocket and pull out something that flashed in her phone's light. It looked like a cheap serrated-edged steak knife. The blade was either rusty or bloody. He gripped it by the handle and stood there, growling half-words as he rocked back and forth.

Jessie sensed that he was going to pounce at any second and decided additional warnings would be fruitless. While he still seemed uncertain about his next move, she decided she had to make hers.

She took her phone and slid it across the bathroom floor. The man's eyes followed the bright light. Jessie took advantage of the distraction to turn the plunger around so that she was gripping it near the bottom, just above the actual rubber plunger. The wooden handle was now pointed at the man.

When her phone bumped against the wall, the light stopped moving and the man turned his attention back to her. He stopped growling and for a long beat there was total silence in the bathroom. Then he leapt toward her.

CHAPTER SEVENTEEN

Jessie gripped the wooden shaft of the plunger and jabbed it at the man as she dived forward, keeping low as she aimed for his midsection. She felt the tip drive into something soft and knew she'd poked him in the stomach, even as the plunger tore from her hands.

The pained grunt from above confirmed it as her right shoulder collided with his legs, sending him sprawling over her toward the tub. She heard a loud thump as she rolled over and looked back to see that he'd slammed into the edge of the tub, almost exactly where she'd been seconds earlier.

He was groaning loudly and the knife had skittered away from him into the corner of the bathtub. Jessie scrambled to her feet as the man tried to do the same. She saw the plunger lying at her feet and grabbed it again, this time by the handle. As the man attempted to stand, she shoved him hard with the rubber end, sending him tumbling backward into the tub on top of the skeleton.

As he flailed about, Jessie grabbed her phone off the floor and rushed from the bathroom, still holding the plunger. Behind her, she could hear flailing as the man tried to extricate himself from the tub. She dashed out of the apartment and down the hall, glancing back only when she reached the stairwell door. The man was there, just exiting the apartment at the other end of the hall. He caught sight of her and began to half-run, half-limp after her.

Jessie shoved open the stairwell door and dashed down, yanking open the door at the bottom just as she heard him rip open the one a flight above her. She sprinted down the back hall, almost slipping on the dusty floor as she rounded the corner near the elevators.

As she ran through the lobby, she could see a sliver of dim daylight slashing through the chained front door. She shoved her phone back into her pocket, knowing she'd need both hands to get out.

When she got there, she dropped the plunger and yanked the doors as far apart as the chain would allow. As she started to shimmy through she heard the heavy breathing and even heavier footsteps of the man getting closer.

She had just passed through and was sliding her left arm out when she felt something grasp at her left wrist. As she pulled away, she saw the man's dirt-encased fingers clasping her tight. He dug his fingernails into her skin as he tugged her back, slamming her body against the exterior of the door.

A new wave of adrenaline surged through her system as she tried to rip herself free. It didn't work. She had managed to create some space between herself and the door but he was still holding on tight. She looked around desperately and her eyes fell on a shard of window glass lying near her right foot.

She reached down and grabbed it before he could tug at her again. Then, as he yanked her back toward him, she went with it, using the force to give her extra momentum. She kept her focus on the back of the hand that was clutching her own and jammed the glass hard into it just before her body slammed against the door.

She heard a yelp and her wrist was suddenly released as she tumbled back onto the front step of the apartment. As she got to her feet, she heard the man howling just inside the door. She was about to grab her coat, which was still lying on the ground nearby, when she saw him start to force himself through the opening.

Abandoning the coat, she turned and ran toward her car, pulling out her remote and punching the "unlock" button repeatedly. She swung open the door, got in, slammed it shut, and locked the doors just as the man got there. He threw his body at her window as if he was trying to tackle the car.

The glass seemed to ripple a bit but it held. The man stumbled backward, stunned by the collision. Jessie pushed the ignition button. The noise roused the man back into angry consciousness and he charged the car a second time. Jessie switched from "park" to "drive" and pulled out into the street just as the man dived onto her hood.

She had only gone a few yards when he started to grasp at her windshield wipers. She slammed on the brakes before he could grab anything and he went flying forward, tumbling off the hood and onto the street in front of her.

Jessie switched into reverse and screeched backward down the street, trying to avoid hitting the cars parked on either side of her. When she reached the intersection, she hit the brakes and switched back into "drive."

As she turned to go down the new street, she saw the man had just gotten to his feet. He gave himself a shake like a wet dog and started after her again. By the time she saw him reach the intersection in her rearview mirror, she was several hundred yards away and felt safe enough to breathe.

It was only then that she noticed the sharp throbbing sensation in her left shoulder.

*

Jessie had only been in the ER hospital bed for about twenty minutes when Ryan arrived.

She could hear him asking a nurse where she was and called out from behind the curtain separating her bed from the next one five feet away.

"In here."

He poked his head in and she waved him over.

"What the hell?" he asked, apparently not sure where specifically to start.

"It's a long story," Jessie said. "The short version is that a really aggressive vagrant sliced up my shoulder with an old steak knife while I was exploring an abandoned apartment building and I had to get fourteen stitches."

"I have so many questions about that one sentence that I don't even know where to begin," Ryan said, shaking his head in disbelief.

"I'm happy to give you the longer version. But before I do, why don't you update me on the Missinger investigation?"

"That's your priority right now?"

"It's just that the nice nurse gave me some pain medication a few minutes ago and I want to hear where we're at while my head is still clear. If I'm going to get fuzzy, I'd rather it be when I'm talking than when I'm listening."

Ryan looked like he was about to argue but then thought better of it.

"Where's your phone?" he asked. "I need to see it for a second."

She unlocked it and handed it to him.

"I'm adding a quick-touch dialing function," he said as he punched something into the dial pad. "From now on, if you're ever in an emergency situation like that, dial nine-nine-nine and hit 'send.' It will send a text to my phone that says "ASAP" and

I'll know you're in trouble. It's a lot quicker than calling nine-one-one or texting or calling me. Okay?"

"Okay, thank you," Jessie said, trying not to sound defensive as she took back her phone. "Now can you please update me on the case details before my brain turns to mush?"

"We still don't have anything firm to go on," he admitted, launching in without another word about the apartment incident. "As you know, the maid interview was rescheduled for tomorrow. Captain Decker was worried she was stalling so she could skip town or something. But we sent an officer to her place to check it out and she's not going anywhere. He checked on her and she was completely knocked out. Her mom said she was so messed up that she gave her a double dose of valium."

"You believe her?"

"I believe she's highly medicated right now," he clarified. "As to the reason, I'll withhold judgment until I talk to her. Besides, I'm happy to have the delay."

"Why?' Jessie asked.

"You remember Victoria's personal trainer? The one who supposedly moved to Florida?"

"I remember you mentioning that."

"Well, his name is Dan Romano and it turns out he never really left town. He only told everyone that because he'd been sleeping with a client and he wanted to throw her husband off the scent."

"How do you know that?" Jessie asked.

"Because the husband found out he was still here and came after him. Romano wants police protection."

"And you gave it to him—a suspect?" Jessie asked, surprised.

"He doesn't know he's a suspect. He doesn't even realize we're investigating Victoria Missinger's murder. He thinks we're just looking out for him. When his name popped in the system, we had Olympic Division transfer him to us. They told him they didn't have anywhere to put him and we offered him a cell for the night. He actually thanked us. We're having one of our confidential informants bunk with him to see what he might say. We're hoping to learn more by the morning."

"Sounds promising," Jessie said, noticing her tongue felt slightly heavy. "Did the M.E. have any updates?"

"Nothing official yet," Ryan answered. "But she did confirm that the levels of insulin in Victoria Missinger's bloodstream are consistent with poisoning. The chances she inadvertently gave herself that high a dose are pretty remote."

"So what does that tell us?" Jessie asked. "Nothing new, it seems."

"It tells us something weird," Ryan countered. "It suggests that whoever did this was savvy enough to know Victoria was diabetic and wanted it to look like she OD'd herself. But at the same time, the killer didn't know enough to realize a dose this high would look suspicious? That is an odd confluence of awareness and cluelessness that doesn't make sense to me."

"You're right," Jessie agreed. "It's doubtful that someone could be simultaneously that clever and that dumb. Something about it doesn't sit, er…fit."

"No, it doesn't," Ryan agreed, raising his eyebrow slightly at her slurred speech but saying nothing. "I think we're going to have more success nailing this down through motive than through method."

"Yes," Jessie mumbled, "*why* did they do it? Maybe they were unhappy with their lot in life."

"What?" Ryan asked, looking confused.

Jessie looked up at him and found it hard to focus.

"It's just something someone said to me today. Forget about it. I think these meds are starting to kick in a bit."

"I think you may be right," Ryan said, pointing at her leg. "You seem to be caressing your own thigh."

"The material is really soft," Jessie said, looking down at her slacks.

Just then Lacy poked her head in.

"Looks like I found the right place," she said.

"My ride is here!" Jessie said louder than she intended.

Lacy glanced over at Ryan, who smiled politely.

"Lacy Cartwright," Jessie announced loudly, "meet Detective Ryan Hernandez, super-sleuth. Ryan Hernandez, meet Lacy Cartwright, future famous fashion designer."

"Are you high?" Lacy asked.

"She's medicated," said the nurse, who had followed Lacy in. "Now that your friend is here, we're going to discharge you, all right, Ms. Hunt?"

"Okay," Jessie said, trying and failing not to sound loopy.

"We've given you a tetanus shot," the nurse continued. "And the pain medication has clearly started to kick in. In an hour or so, you should go from totally out of it to pleasantly numb. That should get you through the night."

"I know the drill," Jessie assured her happily. "I was stabbed in the gut with a fireplace poker in November... by my husband."

"Good to know," the nurse replied, not following up. "You'll feel pain tomorrow as well. Just follow the dosage instructions and you should be able to maintain your normal routine. You can see your primary care physician in a week to check on the stitches. Any questions?"

"Yeah, do those scrubs you're wearing feel scratchy? Whenever I wear scrubs, they're scratchy. Also, cold."

"You know," Ryan said as he moved over to help her out of bed, "I'm going to take a rain check on you telling me how this happened to you. Maybe tomorrow, when you're a little more refreshed."

"Sounds good," she said, taking his arm as she stood up. "But maybe you should talk to the officer outside who took my statement."

"I'll do that," he said, handing her off to Lacy.

"Yeah," Jessie said, too sore and sleepy to raise her head fully. "He can tell you about the skeleton in the bathtub."

CHAPTER EIGHTEEN

Jessie was pretty sure she was going to throw up. By the time they reached Lacy's apartment, she had catnapped in the car and felt no more coherent than when they'd left the hospital. She also felt nauseated.

They were just pulling into a parking space when she opened the passenger door and leaned out. But nothing happened.

"False alarm," she said, unbuckling herself and gingerly stepping out of the vehicle.

Lacy came around and offered a supportive arm as they made their way to the elevator.

"Do you still feel out of it?" she asked.

"Yes," Jessie said. "I'm still waiting for that part the nurse mentioned where I'll go from loopy to numb. Plus, I think I feel sick because I took that medication without having eaten in hours. I need to get something in my stomach."

"I have leftover salad from lunch?" Lacy offered as they stepped into the elevator.

"I'm thinking a slice of bread might be more my speed."

"We have that too," Lacy assured her as they rode up the eleven floors to her place.

When they got out, Jessie continued to use her friend for support as they made their way down the hall to the apartment. She kept her eyes on the floor, focusing on where her feet would go and trying not to lose her balance. At some point, she noticed that Lacy had stopped walking.

"What's wrong?" she asked. "Why aren't we moving?"

"Because my door is open," Lacy whispered. "I think someone broke in."

Jessie looked up. Sure enough, the door to the apartment was half open. Even in her diminished state, she could see the splintered wood on the frame where the door had been pried open.

"Call nine-one-one," she said in what she hoped was a quiet voice.

While Lacy did that, Jessie noticed a fire extinguisher on a case attached to the wall. She walked over, removed it, and, clutching it firmly like a baseball bat, headed for the door.

Stay alert.

She thought she heard Lacy say something behind her but it was too late to turn around. She was entering the apartment and needed to stay focused. Glancing around the living room, she saw that several chairs were overturned and a vase lay shattered on the floor. Other than that, the damage seemed minimal.

She thought she saw movement in the corner of the room but realized it was just a light from outside flashing through the balcony window. She stepped farther into the room, clutching the extinguisher, which felt slick and wet in her sweaty hands.

"What the hell do you think you're doing?" she heard a voice hiss from behind her.

She swiveled around, nearly toppling over before regaining her balance at the last second. It was Lacy, who was standing in the front doorway, waving for her to come back.

"They might still be in here," Jessie protested.

"Exactly," Lacy countered. "That why I called the cops. Now get out of there. Let's wait downstairs, you drugged up crazy woman!"

It was only then that Jessie remembered that she was still heavily medicated and that barreling into an apartment that could be hiding robbers while only holding a fire extinguisher might be a poor move.

"Right," she said and stumbled back to the door.

Lacy grabbed the extinguisher, wrapped her arm around her, and led her back to the elevators. As they waited for one to arrive, Jessie looked over at her friend.

"I might be a little more messed up than I realized," she said.

"You think?" Lacy asked incredulously.

When the elevator arrived, Lacy eased Jessie down to the floor, where she sat in a crouch. She watched the floors change on the digital panel until she couldn't keep her eyes open. Somewhere between the sixth and fifth floors, she passed out.

*

"Just to be clear," Detective Ryan Hernandez said the next morning in the station bullpen, "your plan was to take down potential home invaders with a fire extinguisher while you were under the influence of a mind-altering drug?"

"That is an accurate assessment of how the evening played out," Jessie said, trying to be a good sport about the whole thing. There was no point in denying it, as the officers called to the scene the night before had already spread the word.

"Well, I'm glad no one got hurt," he said, surprising her by not teasing out her shame any longer. "And I heard nothing of value was stolen?"

"That's what they told us at the hotel this morning," Jessie said.

"The hotel?"

"Yes," she said sheepishly. "I woke up this morning in a hotel bed. Apparently one of the officers had to carry me from the elevator to the squad car, after which he gave us a ride to a local hotel. Then some other officers came by this morning to say that other than some minimal damage to the door and vase, no harm had been done."

"I actually knew all that," Ryan conceded. "I just wanted to make you admit you had to be carried to a car. The shame is strong with you."

Jessie gave him her best "screw you" smirk and put her head in her hands. The loopiness and nausea of last night had faded. But because she refused to take any more pain meds, they had been replaced by a bad headache and a throbbing shoulder.

"Don't you think that's strange?" she asked without looking up.

"Not really. Cops have to carry people to their cars all the time. It's just not usually junior profilers."

"No, I mean isn't it strange that some thieves would go all the way to the eleventh floor of a secure building, bust in, and then not take anything of value?"

"It is a little odd," he admitted. "I know one of our Robbery guys is looking at the security footage from the building. There's a chance that'll give us something to go on. In the meantime, maybe today you don't charge into any potentially dangerous situations on your own, especially without any training in self-defense."

Jessie raised her head and nodded. She'd been thinking the same thing all morning.

"I was thinking it might be good for me to look into that. Do you have any suggestions?"

"Actually, I know a guy," Ryan said. "He specializes in Krav Maga; used to be in Israeli Special Forces. Now he rakes it in teaching self-defense to rich Westside wives."

"Sounds pricey."

"He is," Ryan said, smiling. "But I think I can get you the friends and family rate."

"Thanks, Ryan," she said, surprised at the lack of snark in her voice. She decided not to linger on that and pressed on. "How are we doing on the Missinger case?"

"A few developments worth mentioning," he said, also pointedly ignoring her sincerity. "Detective Trembley honchoed the interview with the maid, Marisol Mendez, a little while ago. I watched from the observation room. You can review the video later if you like. But we didn't glean a lot of new information from her. I think she was either still a bit sedated or super scared."

"Maybe both," Jessie suggested, rubbing her temples to try to make the dull ache between them subside.

"Entirely possible," Ryan agreed. "She mostly had praise for Victoria Missinger; said she wasn't bitchy like a lot of her former bosses."

"*Mostly* praise?" Jessie repeated, noting the hedge.

"Marisol essentially conveyed that she was a bit chilly, remote. Not that she was unpleasant but that sometimes she got so focused in on her causes that the niceties of human interaction became secondary. She said Mrs. Missinger was passionate about her philanthropy and it didn't leave much passion for anything outside of that."

"Did she say that was a source of tension in the marriage?" Jessie asked.

"No. Trembley asked about that. Apparently Mr. Missinger had made his peace with it. And we already know he was looking elsewhere for his passion."

That made sense, though it was hard for Jessie to imagine Michael Missinger had poured *all* his marital frustration into an extramarital affair. It had to have leaked out at home occasionally. But there was no evidence of that.

"Did her alibi hold up?" Jessie wondered, turning her attention back to Marisol and jealously imagining a resort in the California desert. "The Palm Springs trip?"

"We're still following up. But so far, yes. We tracked her cell phone and it shows her bopping around town during the time she says she was there. Her ID was copied when she paid at the hotel. We have Palm Springs PD tracking down security footage. But so far, nothing unusual has popped. And she answered all our questions with asking for a lawyer. It didn't seem to even occur to her that she might need one. It's looking like we're going to have to cross another potential suspect off our list."

"And the trainer—Dan Romano?"

"He's finishing off breakfast in the cell he used as a hotel room last night," Ryan said. "Our informant said he didn't reveal anything shocking. He also said the guy is dumber than mud. But setting that aside, apparently Romano did more than just train a lot of the local ladies. But he never mentioned Victoria Missinger and our informant worried that if he asked specifically about her, it would seem suspicious."

"Maybe it's time we asked him a few more direct questions," Jessie said.

"I was planning to go say hi now," Ryan replied. "But I still want to keep it as casual as possible. You want to observe?"

"Sure," Jessie said. "How will this work?"

"I was going to collect him and offer to get him a coffee in the break room. Maybe you're already there, sitting at a nearby table. I'll just chat him up, see what I can learn. You watch and see what jumps out at you. Sound good?"

"Sounds good," she agreed. "I'll be there."

While Ryan went to get Romano, Jessie headed to the break room. She had just prepped her coffee and sat down when the two men entered. She put her head down to avoid eye contact, focusing intently on the plastic stirrer she was using to mix in her cream. Hernandez and Romano were mid-conversation.

"…but aren't you worried about STDs?" Ryan was asking.

"Nah, man. I use protection. I've even taken a few tests, paid for in advance by the potential new lady friend. I figure if they're so worried, they're probably clean too, right?"

"That's one way to look at it," Ryan said, not quite agreeing.

"Listen, man," Romano said as if he were explaining the intricacies of a baseball triple play, "these ladies are very specific about what they want. Part of my job is to set them at ease. If it got around that I wasn't safe, my business would totally dry up."

Jessie forced herself to stifle a mocking grunt at the notion that anything about this guy's life was safe. Apart from his job, it was clear from his abnormally muscled physique and his unnaturally dark skin that Dan Romano was an enthusiastic tanner and steroid user. He looked like a young Arnold Schwarzenegger's more Mediterranean brother.

"I got ya," Ryan said, ignoring Jessie and playing along. "So how profitable was your business, Dan? Were you working every wife at the country club?"

"First of all," Romano said, getting unexpectedly serious, "let me be plain. My business is personal training—nothing illegal about that. That's what I got paid for. Any extra time I spend with the ladies is gratis. I just want to make that known. My cousin is a lawyer and he told me that I'm good. Clear?"

"I hear you, Dan," Ryan said reassuringly. "We're clear. So what's your 'second of all'?"

"Right. So the answer is no, I wasn't 'assisting' all the ladies. If you work with everyone, it stops being exclusive, you know?"

"That makes sense," Ryan said, nodding.

"And some ladies just weren't into it. Like that one who just died, Victoria something. But she never gave off even a whiff of interest. So I stayed clear."

"So you never 'worked' with her?" Ryan asked, using air quotes around "worked."

"No, man," Dan assured him. "She scheduled a few training sessions but she kept canceling. I don't know why. If you ask me, she didn't need any legit training anyway. Whatever she was doing on her own was working because her body was bangin'."

"Could she have been using another trainer?"

"I doubt it. The guys in our industry don't like to tread into another dude's territory. Bad form, you know? I would have heard if she was working with someone else for real workouts or fun workouts, if you get my drift."

"I get your drift, Dan," Ryan said, admirably managing to keep his tone mockery-free. "So what *can* you tell me about Victoria?"

"Not much. The closest I ever got to her was grabbing an orange juice for her when she fainted one time. She had diabetes—pretty bad, I think. I know what that's like. My little brother had juvenile diabetes. No fun."

Ryan couldn't help but glance over at Jessie, who raised her eyebrows. She knew they were thinking the same thing: Dan would likely be very familiar with how insulin injections worked.

107

"That sucks, man," Ryan said, returning his attention to Romano. "So if someone said you were training her, they'd be lying?"

"Or just wrong. Like I said, she booked a few appointments but she always bailed."

"Okay, thanks for the info," Ryan said. "Hey, listen, I have to get back on the clock. But I thought of a way we might be able to help you with that husband who's been bothering you."

"That would be awesome. How?"

"Take this pad and pen," Ryan said, sliding across the legal pad and ballpoint that were conveniently sitting on the table. "Write down your schedule for the last couple of days, starting on Monday morning. Don't leave anything out. Then we'll check that against records of where the hubby was at those times. If we find a lot of overlap, him showing up where you are, we might be able to get a restraining order against him."

"I don't want to make a big fuss," Romano replied. "I just don't want this guy coming after me."

"I get it," Ryan assured him. "Just write down every detail of your life for the week so far. We don't have to make anything official. But if we find that he's been tailing you, we can have a quiet chat with him that will get him to back off. Most guys, even rich, pissed off ones, will back off if the cops come knocking at his door. I promise—we'll be discreet."

"Okay," Romano said, pulling out his phone to check his calendar.

"I have to run," Ryan said, standing up and nodding at Jessie to meet him outside. "Give it to Detective Trembley and we'll follow up. It'll all work out, Dan. Don't worry."

Jessie followed Ryan back to the observation room, where they wouldn't run into Romano accidentally.

"I don't know," Ryan said once he closed the door behind them. "The diabetes connection had me wondering. But everything else about this guy makes me think he's not our man. What do you think, Junior Profiler?"

"I tend to agree, Experienced Detective," she said. "For one thing, I just don't think Romano is smart enough to pull off any element of the crime. Then there's the fact that he came to law enforcement at all. Even if there is a jealous husband after him you'd think a killer would want to stay off the radar of detectives at all costs. Plus, he's in there providing a detailed breakdown of his every movement for the last several days. If what he writes down doesn't match his phone's GPS, he'll be setting himself up to look guilty."

Ryan nodded.

"We need to find out if what he said is true about not having much interaction with Victoria Missinger. If that's a lie, the rest might be too. Let's not eliminate the possibility that this guy isn't as dumb as we think. I've been played before."

"Maybe I go back and talk to that Andrea Robinson woman from the country club," Jessie suggested. "She was pretty knowledgeable about the goings-on there. And unlike some of the other women at the club, she seemed to actually want to help. If she saw Romano and Victoria Missinger together or even just heard rumors about them, it might let us know if we're on the right path."

"Go for it," Ryan said. "Just don't be too forthcoming. If she's this chatty with you, she might be with others too. We don't need the entire Beverly Country Club knowing our business."

"I'll call her now and then we can regroup, sound okay?"

Ryan looked like he wanted to say something but seemed to think better of it and simply nodded in agreement. Something in his expression told her that whatever he was going to tell her, she wasn't going to like it.

CHAPTER NINETEEN

It didn't take long for Ryan to spill the beans.

He tried to come at it sideways by asking her a question first. He waited until they were back at his desk before diving in, after she'd finished setting up a coffee get-together for that afternoon with Andi Robinson.

"So you weren't really in any condition to give me a coherent answer yesterday, but I was hoping you could now. Care to tell me how you ended up in an abandoned apartment building, fighting off a vagrant with a steak knife in a bathroom with a years-old dead body?"

Jessie didn't see any reason not to be forthcoming. She had already told him about Crutchfield and his connection to her father. It didn't seem unreasonable to tell him about her request for information and the favor he wanted in return.

So she let him know everything about the visit yesterday, including Crutchfield's not-so-veiled threat to reveal her whereabouts to her father. She told him how she agreed to check out the address he mentioned, though she waited until past his deadline to spite him. And she walked him through the details of her trip to the apartment complex. After she'd relived the discovery of the body, the vagrant attack, and her escape, she stopped.

"I guess that's pretty much it. I drove to the hospital, got some shots and stitches, and you showed up. Now that I've told you everything, do you care to tell me whatever it is you've been holding back this whole time?"

Ryan looked momentarily surprised, before breaking into an embarrassed grin.

"I don't know if you're that good at reading people or I'm that bad at hiding things," he said.

"I think it's a little bit of both. So start talking."

Okay," he started. "First of all, the vagrant was caught near the complex. His name's Josiah Burress. He's got a long record of assaults; almost killed a man once. So it could have gone a lot worse for you."

"That's good to know," Jessie said. "But it's not what you're stalling revealing. Just tell me. You're starting to freak me out."

"It's about the body in the tub," he finally admitted. "We've identified her. She was a woman named Patrice Houston. She'd been missing for almost five years but because she was a known prostitute and drug addict, the search wasn't a top priority. The detective who originally had the case figured she OD'd in some homeless encampment and was tossed in dumpster or something."

"Sounds like the investigation was real top-notch," Jessie said derisively.

"I'll just say that the detective in charge of the case is now retired and we're all better off for it. Unfortunately, that's not the part that's going to freak you out."

"What is?" Jessie asked.

"Patrice appears to have been killed by strangulation. There are notches in her windpipe that match striations we've seen in other women who were killed by a notorious serial rapist and killer."

Jessie felt her stomach drop. Before Ryan could continue, she knew who was responsible and she knew why she had been sent to that particular apartment.

"It was Delmond Stokes, wasn't it?" she said.

Ryan nodded, not speaking.

It all made sense to Jessie now. Delmond Stokes had terrorized the Central California region for years, assaulting and sometimes murdering a series of women. He had started with prostitutes and eventually worked his way to housewives and single working women. He was known for using thick wire to choke the women he killed, wire that often left permanent grooves in the women's windpipes. By the time he was captured in Bakersfield three years ago, he was believed to have had over three dozen victims, at least four of whom he killed.

More relevant to the moment, he had spent many years in Los Angeles prior to moving north and it was assumed that he'd committed similar crimes here, though no bodies had ever been found...until now. Though it wasn't common knowledge, he was also incarcerated at NRD, the same facility as Bolton Crutchfield.

"Can't be a coincidence, right?" Ryan finally said, voicing what they were both thinking.

"No way," Jessie said. "Despite the safeguards, those two must have communicated. And Crutchfield somehow gained Stokes's trust enough to get him to reveal where he'd left a body. There's no other way he could have known that much detail."

"But you're forgetting one thing," Ryan said. "He got the unit number wrong. You told me he said unit 2016. But it was 206, correct? Maybe he heard it wrong. We could use that to figure out how they spoke to each other."

"Maybe…" Jessie murmured.

"What?" Ryan pressed. "You don't sound convinced."

"It's just that I don't think Crutchfield would make a mistake like that. He's very meticulous. He wanted me to find that body and make the connection to Stokes. He wanted to prove to me that he can reach out to anyone he chooses, whenever he wants, including my father. So he would have made certain to use the right unit number unless he had a specific reason not to."

"What reason could he possibly have?" Ryan asked.

"You're the cop who took him down," Jessie reminded him. "Don't you have any theories?"

"All I did was catch and arrest him. I've never had a substantive conversation with him. You know him way better than I do. What do you think he's up to?"

Jessie thought for a moment, then grabbed a sheet of paper and wrote down the address.

1024 Visitation Avenue, unit 2016.

She stared at it for a few moments, growing increasingly frustrated.

"He loves games," she said. "It's a riddle."

"Okay," Ryan said, prodding. "But he wouldn't give you a riddle he didn't think you could solve. He *wants* you to solve it. So it must be something important to you. What does he know you want?"

"To find out where my father is," Jessie said immediately.

"That makes sense," Ryan agreed. "But he's not going to give that up. He'd lose too much leverage."

"No," Jessie said. "But he might give me a piece of the puzzle. Like I said, he likes playing games with me. But he knows that I'll stop playing if there's nothing in it for me. So he has to give me something that will keep me coming back."

An idea flashed through her head and she gasped audibly.

"What?" Ryan asked, worried.

Jessie wrote down the address again, but this time she made a few adjustments, putting all the numbers together.

10242016, Visitation Ave. unit.

"I still don't get it," Ryan said, flummoxed.

"What if I tried this?" Jessie said, writing it again with a few small tweaks and deletions. Now it read:

10/24/2016, visitation.

"A date?" Ryan asked.

"Not just any date," she said. "Crutchfield told me that my father actually came to visit him once at NRD disguised as a doctor. I think this might be the date they met. And if we have the exact date…"

"They can check the surveillance footage," Ryan finished.

"Exactly," Jessie said. "If I can see that footage, maybe I can uncover some clue that will lead me to my dad's whereabouts."

"Do you think they'll let you look at it? Won't you have to jump through tons of bureaucratic hoops?"

"The head of security asked if I wanted to be roomies," Jessie noted. "I think I can convince her to let me take a peek."

"When are you going to go?"

"I'm not meeting with Andrea Robinson until later this afternoon," Jessie answered, standing up and grabbing her purse. "So I say no time like the present."

*

Kat had the footage cued up and waiting when Jessie arrived. If there were any hoops to jump through to get access to it, she didn't mention them. After the infuriatingly slow process of going through all the security measures, they finally walked into Kat's office twenty minutes after Jessie had arrived at the NRD.

"How do you know this is the right guy?" Jessie asked as she sat down in front of the monitor.

"Crutchfield doesn't get a lot of outside visitors," Kat said. "And they all have to be authorized. This was his only one that day, that whole month actually. He used the name Dr. Bertrand Roy. Does that name mean anything to you?"

"It's actually vaguely familiar, but I can't place where from. Do you remember him?"

"No," Kat said. "He visited Crutchfield before I took over security here. The visitation policies were less stringent back then. You ready for me to play the footage?"

Jessie nodded and Kat pushed the start button. The camera was of the cell and the image was from behind the visitor, meaning only Crutchfield's face was visible. A man walked in at 2:06 p.m. wearing a sweater vest and slacks and sat down at the very table where Jessie had been yesterday.

Even without seeing his face, Jessie knew it was him—her father. She'd recognize Xander Thurman anywhere. Even twenty-plus years later, he had the same leisurely gait, as if there was no hurry to get anywhere. His once dark hair was now sprinkled with gray but still cut short, as if he'd recently gotten out of the military.

He had the same long, angular torso she remembered. Like Jessie, he had always been tall and wiry. He had a wolfish leanness to him that even the professorial attire and the glasses he was wearing couldn't hide. He was pretending to be a nervous academic but the act was obvious to her. His lack of anxiety at being in the presence of another serial killer was evident. He seemed…comfortable.

Crutchfield said something but Jessie couldn't hear it.

"There's no audio?" she asked.

"We only had a video feed back then," Kat said.

"What the hell is the point of that?"

"My predecessor said something about a zone of privacy. It never made sense to me. I gather the administration felt like I did, which is part of why he was replaced. Now every inch of that cell is wired for sound. We can monitor his breathing patterns when he sleeps. Not that any of that helps you."

Jessie forced herself to let her frustration go and tried to zero in on the body language of both men. They had started talking almost immediately. Jessie gathered that Crutchfield recognized his visitor because his demeanor was unlike anything she'd ever seen from him. He seemed giddy, like a preteen girl meeting a member of her favorite boy band. Even at this distance on a video screen, she could see his eyes glistening with manic intensity.

It was a strange sight but it wasn't a shock. After all, Bolton Crutchfield had modeled his murders on her dad's, using the same methods. He was a fan. And now his greatest dream had come true. His hero had come to see him—was standing right in front of him—in the heart of a supposedly secure lockdown psychiatric facility. It was clearly a special moment for him.

The conversation went on for a good ten minutes before a guard came in and said something, apparently an order to wrap it up.

"There was no guard in the room for their conversation?" Jessie noted.

"Prior security regime," Kate reminded her. "Another change I instituted."

"So there's no one I can interview to see what they remember?"

"I replaced most of the staff. The only ones I kept were Berenson and Cortez. Nobody else took the job all that seriously. To be honest, this place is lucky there weren't more incidents."

Jessie had heard about the two major episodes since NRD had been established seven years prior. In one, an inmate had jumped a guard and beat his head against a wall eight times before he was subdued. The guard died after a week in a coma.

In the other one, a resident was being transferred from one cell to another when he managed to grab a pair of scissors from the security station. He had stabbed two guards to death before Cortez and another guard got him on the ground. Even then, he continued to swipe with the scissors, slicing the neck of the third guard. Cortez eventually got him in a choke hold and strangled him into unconsciousness. The inmate apparently lost too much oxygen and was declared brain dead after two days, at which point he was removed from a ventilator. As Jessie returned her attention to the monitor, she realized why Kat had kept Cortez on.

At the point in the video where the guard ended the visit, her father stood up, said one last thing to Crutchfield that seemed to make the prisoner go stiff, turned to look directly into the camera, and smiled.

Jessie was glad she was seated because she felt her knees buckle and her mouth go dry. Despite two decades, he looked much as she remembered. Yes, the wrinkle lines were deeper and the cheeks were gaunter. But the eyes—the cold, calculating eyes, the same shade of green as her own—were just as she remembered.

He seemed to be looking directly at the future her, knowing that she would one day see this footage and look at him with horror and fear. And he seemed to revel in it. Just before he walked out of the frame, he winked.

CHAPTER TWENTY

Jessie was about to enter Crutchfield's cell, to sit in the same spot, maybe even the same chair her father had occupied two years previous. She tried to ignore the dull sense of nausea she felt and focus on what she was about to do.

"You all right?" Kat asked her, handing over the red-button emergency remote as they stood outside the cell door.

"I think so," Jessie replied. "I'm trying to shut everything out so he doesn't work me too much."

"What did Detective Hernandez say?" Kat asked, referencing Jessie's call with him a few minutes ago.

"Apparently Dr. Bertrand Roy hasn't been seen in person in well over two years, since mid-October 2016. He's a professor at Cal State-Northridge who works in the field of deviant psychology. That's why his name was familiar to me. He wrote a textbook I used in an undergrad class. So it wouldn't have been that unusual for him to want to visit Crutchfield."

"But he's missing?" Kat asked.

"Kind of. Hernandez says that Dr. Roy made a written request to go on sabbatical two years ago, with no warning, in the middle of the school year. Then he just left."

"No one got suspicious about that?" Kat asked skeptically.

"He's supposedly been sending emails intermittently," Jessie said, equally doubtful. "He said he's doing work studying how isolated indigenous communities in South America handle violent behavior within their tribes. His colleagues say it was odd but not totally crazy. He'd taken sabbaticals before with little notice. He's not married and has no children. He's not really tied to the community beyond his work."

"So exactly the kind of guy a serial killer could murder, assume the identity of, and convince people he's gone on walkabout for two years?"

"It's not inconceivable," Jessie said. "His work brought a lot of money into the university. So they weren't inclined to push him too hard as long as he maintained some kind of contact."

"Are they pushing now?"

"Hernandez asked detectives up there to liaise with the university police to check around. They're on their way now. Hopefully we'll know more by the time I'm done with Crutchfield."

"Are you going to tell him what you know?" Kat asked.

"We'll see how it goes but I'm inclined to hold back. It's pretty rare that I have any cards to play when I go in there. I'm not going to show them right off the bat."

"Smart move," Kat agreed as she started to open the door. "Just remember, he's probably holding back some cards too."

*

Bolton Crutchfield seemed to have been expecting her.

When Jessie stepped into the cell, he was sitting on the edge of his metal bed, staring at her. He was not smiling.

"Why so blue, Mr. Crutchfield?" she asked as she took a seat and Kat moved to her standard spot standing in the corner.

"I'm not sad, Miss Jessie," he said, though his voice was tinged with mournfulness. "I'm just disappointed."

"Disappointed about what?"

"Disappointed that you felt the need to test me, Miss Jessie. Why you felt the need to deliberately disregard the request of a man who littered this city with broken human carcasses is beyond me."

"What are you talking about?" she asked, though she knew she wasn't fooling him.

"Shall I spell it out for you?" he asked with an edge she had only occasionally heard in his typically genteel voice. "You intentionally waited until after four p.m. to visit the address I gave you. You could easily have made it in time but you chose not to. That is something more than rude."

Jessie fought the urge to ask him how he knew that. The point was he knew and he was pissed. She'd deal with the emotional fallout that came from realizing an incarcerated serial killer seemed to know her daily movements later. Right now she had to get back on his good side.

"I'm stubborn," she said, coming as close to an apology as she could allow herself.

"Yes, I'm aware," he said, maybe slightly mollified. His voice was still firmer than usual, but the bite was gone. "Had you gone when I suggested, perhaps you would not have run into Mr. Burress, who is not usually in that area at four. Live and learn, I guess."

"I guess so," Jessie agreed noncommittally, letting him direct where the conversation went next.

"I understand you had a break-in last night," he said in a clipped tone, changing subjects without warning.

Jessie nodded, pretending not to be troubled by his awareness of it, unsure where he was going with the topic.

"Lucky you weren't home," he continued. "It could have been much worse if you were, I'd imagine. Something could have happened to your…lady's friend."

Crutchfield knows where I live. He knows about Lacy.

His odd "lady's friend" phrasing even suggested he knew Lacy was gay. More than that, Jessie got the distinct impression that Crutchfield had somehow ordered the break-in; that he was punishing her as retribution for not following his instructions.

Jessie could sense Kat tighten up in the corner of the cell, preparing to take charge of the situation if it was required. It would not be.

Jessie allowed her jaw to go slack and her eyes to grow dull. She took a slow, shallow, hopefully imperceptible breath and eased up her tight grip on the emergency remote in her hand. Crutchfield had shown his cards. He had revealed that the break-in was his doing. He was hoping to rattle her, to teach her who was boss. He wanted to see her anxious, fearful.

She would give him none of that.

"Such a control freak, Mr. Crutchfield," she said mildly as if it were merely an observation and not an insult. "Someone doesn't follow your demands to the letter and you get petty? What kind of man orders an apartment break-in just because he didn't get his way?"

Crutchfield's eyes narrowed and he seemed to be telling himself to a take a beat before responding. She could feel the self-righteous fury emanating from him.

"The same kind of man who wants to make sure his interviewer understands that she is vulnerable, that she can be reached, that there is no place she cannot be found. It would behoove a person in this situation to do what that petty control freak wishes, if only for her own self-preservation. Don't you agree, Miss Jessie?"

They stared at each for a long time, neither wanting to concede a thing. But of course, he had the advantage right now.

And Jessie, as furious as she was, didn't see much upside in poking him any further.

"What is it you wish from me, Mr. Crutchfield?" she asked, giving in without saying so.

At those words, the intensity drained from him and his southern courtliness returned.

"Nothing…for now. Just to help you in your endeavors is enough for me. Although I may make a request of you at some future date, if you'd be so accommodating."

Jessie offered a saccharine sweet smile in return.

"Normally, I would take you up on your offer of help," she said, "but how do I know I can have confidence in what you'd tell me?"

"What would possibly make you think you couldn't?" he asked.

Well, it's hard to know if you have my best interests at heart, Mr. Crutchfield," she said, preparing to drop the hammer. "I mean, it's hard to know where your loyalties lie, especially after seeing your unvarnished ardor when you met my dad. You were like a fanboy."

Jessie held her breath, waiting to see how he'd respond.

CHAPTER TWENTY ONE

Crutchfield allowed himself a small half-smile.

"And there it is," he said, with something close to pride in his voice. "You've seen the video of Daddy's visit. I wondered if you'd tease that out. I was beginning to fear my confidence in you was misplaced. I should have known better."

"You didn't answer my question," Jessie pressed, refusing to be swayed by his attempt at flattery. "Where do your loyalties lie—with me or my father?"

Crutchfield leaned back on his bed so that his back was resting against the wall behind him.

"I'm going to tell you the God's honest truth, Miss Jessie," he said quietly. "I genuinely don't know."

"You can see why that gives me pause," Jessie said, in an equally soft voice.

"I can," he admitted. "It gives me pause as well. I have such affection for you both. Your father is a hero of mine. I've modeled much of my adult life on his accomplishments. And he was as impressive in person as he'd been in my dreams."

Jessie looked down and gulped, hoping Crutchfield didn't notice her almost gag at his words. He seemed oblivious, not missing a beat.

"And yet, when I met you," he continued, "I was smitten—in a chaste, admiring sort of way, of course. You have such a fiery inquisitiveness. Your talents are still messy and unformed. You invariably let your feelings interfere with your reasoning, as you did with your former husband. Affection clouded your judgment in that case. But that's a function of your youth and inexperience, not your aptitude. I suspect that after you've learned a few more hard lessons, you'll make a fine criminal profiler. Sometimes I think it's my job to expedite those lessons in order to better prepare you for what's to come."

"What *is* to come, Mr. Crutchfield?" Jessie asked, though she wasn't sure she wanted the answer.

"Well, I assume you're planning to go after your father, to follow your lead about the doctor whose identity he borrowed. But you have to remember that Xander Thurman is not some rapacious social-climbing Orange County husband or a poison enthusiast from Hancock Park. You saw it up close so I doubt you've forgotten—he's a killer without equal. He is merciless. He is relentless. And he is after you. For what purpose I don't know. But I doubt it's to invite you to a family reunion and picnic in some local park."

He began to chuckle quietly to himself.

"What's so funny?" Jessie asked.

"I'm just imagining you and your father sitting at a picnic table in a park, balloons tied to the table. I'm picturing you eating hot dogs and potato salad and sipping sweet tea together. Oh, how I wish I could be there at the Thurman family reunion. Would you make me an honorary member, Miss Jessie? I feel so close to you both."

"I'll think about it," she replied evenly. "I have to say I'd be more inclined to invite you if you followed through on your offer."

"What offer was that?" he asked, still basking in the image of a picnic in the park with Jessie and her serial killer father.

"To help me in my endeavors," she reminded him. "Maybe Xander's current mailing address, for example."

"Oh, I don't know that. And even if I did, sharing it would spoil all the fun. I have so little to look forward to in here. Don't deny me the thrill of anticipating what happens next. But I did promise to help and it would be ungentlemanly of me not to meet that obligation. How would you like a clue that relates to both your father and your current case? A twofer, as the kids say."

"The kids don't say that. But I'm happy to hear what you've got."

"Very well. You haven't forgotten what I said about your Hancock Park perpetrator's unhappiness with their lot in life, have you?"

"No, though that could apply to pretty much every person over the age of two in L.A. County. Couldn't you just be straightforward and say the butler did it?"

She didn't mention that the Missingers didn't have a butler.

"I could say that," he answered. "But as I don't *know* who your killer is, it seems kind of silly. As I said before, I only know what *kind* of person did this. One would think that might narrow the field."

"Okay, what's your new clue?"

"Ah yes, here it is: you need to keep your focus on the never-ending battle for truth and lady justice."

"That's it?" Jessie asked incredulously. "Another vague riddle? That's supposed to help me solve this case *and* find my father?"

"You have the resources of the entire Los Angeles Police Department at your disposal, Miss Jessie. That's a lot of power. Based on what I've told you, you should be able to make serious inroads on both fronts. However..."

He trailed off. Jessie knew he was milking the moment and despised having to kowtow to him, but she was already in too deep to back out now.

"However what, Mr. Crutchfield?" she dutifully asked, doing her best to hide her annoyance.

"However, with great power comes great responsibility."

"That's what you're giving me?" Jessie exploded, unable to mask her frustration any longer. "Is that a line from a fortune cookie? You're just making this up as you go along, aren't you?"

"Perhaps I am just making it all up," he replied calmly, clearly enjoying her loss of control. "But perhaps you should look beyond that, Miss Jessie. Maybe it's not the games I play but what I do that defines me. Maybe you should ask yourself, was I making it up when I told you to go to that address?"

Jessie forced herself to stop talking before she went too far. He was right, after all. His cryptic comment about the address had led her directly to the video of her father. Crutchfield had delivered on his promise that time, in his own infuriating way.

More importantly, she reminded herself that this relationship, however messed up, was valuable. Crutchfield had given her useful information on more than one occasion. Maybe this would somehow pan out.

And as he was so fond of reminding her, he somehow had the ability to communicate with the outside world, including if he so chose, her father. All it would take was one misstep from her for him to decide to give up her identity and location. He seemed to enjoy their banter, even when it was acrimonious. But it probably wasn't wise to push him too far.

"Thanks for your assistance, Mr. Crutchfield," she said, having regained some semblance of composure. "I'll look into the leads you offered."

"I hope they serve you well, Miss Jessie," he said, standing and bowing slightly as she got out of her chair. "Please don't be a stranger."

"I'll try not to be," Jessie said as she turned for the door. She was halfway out of the cell when she turned and added, "And if you would be so kind, please refrain from having your minions engage in any more home invasions. It makes it very hard to concentrate."

She turned and left the room before he could reply.

CHAPTER TWENTY TWO

"His office was empty?" Jessie asked, repeating what Ryan Hernandez had just told her.

She was driving back from NRD to the city as he updated her on what was happening in the investigation of Dr. Bertrand Roy.

"Not empty, exactly," Ryan corrected. "They just didn't find anything suspicious. A basic search history on his computer showed that he did buy a ticket to La Paz, Bolivia, in October of 2016. A team is trying to track down if he ever got on the plane. But it's been over two years so it might take a while. They're also thinking of bringing in the FBI to compare the emails he supposedly sent from South America to his writing style in other correspondence. But so far, nothing overtly unusual has jumped out."

"That'll be a dead end," Jessie said dispiritedly. "My father would have been careful to make sure he wrote like Bertrand. And if none of his co-workers noticed anything odd initially, it's unlikely that the feds will find any smoking gun now. Do they know about my dad?"

"No," Ryan assured her. "They're treating it seriously enough as just a standard missing person investigation. As to your father, I figured the fewer people that were aware of his potential involvement, the better. We don't need to tip him off that we know he's connected. That's not good for the case, or for you."

"I appreciate that," Jessie said, only now realizing how relieved she was at that news. She felt her grip on the steering wheel relax involuntarily.

"How did it go with Crutchfield?" Ryan asked. "Did you tell him that you figured out the clue?"

"Eventually. He seemed tickled that I got it. He even promised to give me a clue that he said would help me with my dad's whereabouts and the Hancock Park murder. But all he ended up doing was spouting cliché aphorisms. He sounded like a bad psychic."

"How so?" Ryan asked. "What did he say?"

"He was blathering on about truth and lady justice and power and responsibility. It was like a Hallmark card started throwing up or something."

"Wait a second," Ryan said, his voice suddenly dead serious. "Tell me his exact words."

"I don't remember his exact words," Jessie said, surprised at the detective's reaction. "He was throwing so much at the wall, it all started to run together."

"Try, Jessie," he insisted. "I think it might be important. Tell me everything he said that sounded like a lame cliché."

"Okay, there was something about power requiring responsibility."

"With great power comes great responsibility?" Ryan suggested.

"Yeah, that was it," Jessie said.

"What else?"

Jessie played back the conversation in her head.

"He said something about him not being defined by the games he plays but by what he does," she recalled.

"It's not who I am underneath but what I do that defines me?"

"He didn't say exactly that but it was in that universe."

"Okay, tell me the truth and justice one," Ryan demanded, sounding more excited than she'd ever heard him.

"What is this about, Ryan?" Jessie asked impatiently. "What am I missing?"

"I'll explain in a moment," he promised. "But please, just tell me what he said."

"He said I needed to focus on the battle for truth and lady justice."

"Did he say 'the never-ending battle for truth, justice, and the American way'?" Ryan pressed.

"He didn't say anything about the American way. And he specifically said lady justice. But that's the gist. Can you please tell me what the hell has you so amped?"

"Jessie, have you never read a comic book?" he asked incredulously.

"I can honestly say that I never have. And I'm kind of proud of it. What does that have to do with anything?"

"All of those lines he slipped into your conversation are from superhero comic books. The one about power and responsibility is from *Spider-Man*. The one about what you do

126

defining you is from *Batman*. And the truth and justice line from *Superman*."

"Okay," Jessie said. "First of all, I had no idea you w such an incredible nerd. Second, what has that got to do v anything?"

"Because," he replied excitedly, "in addition to Dr. Rc main office on campus, he also occasionally used a lab tc psychiatric studies. A university police officer is headed there now to check it out. It was going to just be a formality. I don't think it should be anymore."

"Why not?" Jessie wanted to know.

"Because Roy's campus lab is in the Kent Clark building."

"Like Kent Clark, Superman's alter ego?" Jessie asked, recalling the character.

"His alter ego is actually Clark Kent. But it's close enough, especially considering the line from Crutchfield. And it was only after World War Two that the catchphrase added the reference to the 'American way.' According to the school's website, which I'm looking at now, the Kent Clark Building was built in 1942, when the comic book line was simply "truth and justice.' I think he's hinting that any clues about your father can be found there."

"That makes sense," Jessie said, getting excited herself. "You're brilliant."

"I thought I was just a nerd," he replied.

"If it gives us a fresh lead, I'm happy to move past nerd to genius."

"The only thing is the lady justice thing. The quote never referred to 'lady.' It seems odd that he would throw that in there."

"Maybe there's statue of a lady in the lab or something," Jessie suggested. "Is the university cop there yet?"

"I'll call him and loop you in," Ryan said.

While he did that and Jessie waited, an uncomfortable thought entered her head: had her father simply been loitering in Southern California because that's where Crutchfield was? Or did he somehow know that Jessie was here too? She felt a shiver of anxiety at the thought that he might be only a few miles from her at this exact moment.

"Officer Plumley," Ryan said, bringing her back into the present, "you're on the line with myself and our profiler on the case, Jessie Hunt. Can everyone hear?"

"I can," Jessie said.

"Me too," Plumley added. "But why does a missing person case need a profiler?"

There was silence for a second as both Jessie and Ryan realized the oddness of her involvement.

"Sometimes," Jessie said, jumping in, "it helps to create a profile of a potential victim as much as it does a perpetrator. We can often determine if someone was the victim of foul play or just took off on their own based on behavior patterns prior to his disappearance."

"Got ya," Plumley said, apparently satisfied. Jessie was pretty pleased with herself. In addition to sounding convincing, her answer had the added benefit of being true.

"So are you in Dr. Roy's lab now?" she asked.

"I was. Now I'm having a custodian unlock a small office annex connected to it. That'll just be a minute."

"Is there any chance we can video chat?" Jessie asked. "Maybe you can show us what the lab looks like?"

"I can do that," Plumley said. "Give me a sec."

As he set up the video, Jessie pulled off the freeway and parked in a nearby gas station parking lot. By the time she turned off the ignition, the video was up and running.

"Are there any images of ladies in the room?" Ryan asked. "Maybe a tchotchke or a photo or something?"

"No," Plumley replied as he panned across the lab. "The place is pretty sterile—just a bunch of desks with monitors on them. I don't see anything in the way of personality at all."

"Damn," Jessie heard Ryan mutter under his breath. "I thought that would be it for sure."

"Hold on," Plumley said. "We've got the office open now. It's tiny. I think it used to be a closet. You want me to show you what's in there?"

"Can't hurt," Jessie said.

Plumley slowly moved the camera around the room. The whole thing took about five seconds. There was a small, uncluttered desk in the corner next to a mini filing cabinet and a trash basket with a poster on the wall above it.

"I don't see anything that screams 'lady' in there either," Ryan said, disappointed. "Maybe we have him look through the filing cabinet?"

"Hold on a second," Jessie said. "Officer Plumley, can you zoom in a little on that poster?"

"Sure," he said and got tighter on the image, which appeared to be a university logo. As he got closer, she recognized it as a yellow and black tiger.

"That makes sense," Ryan said, clearly thinking along what he thought were the same lines as Jessie. "Dr. Roy went to Princeton. Their logo and team mascot is a tiger."

Jessie stared more closely at the poster, allowing a hazy memory from her childhood to bubble to the surface. After a few seconds, she spoke.

"That doesn't fit, Ryan. There's nothing personal anywhere else. But Dr. Roy puts up a poster of his alma mater?"

"Okay, good point," Ryan said. "I have a feeling you're about to make another one."

"Just that it's not actually the Princeton logo. Princeton's is orange and black. This one is yellow and black. It's for Mizzou—the Missouri Tigers."

"You a big fan?" Officer Plumley asked.

"No," Jessie said. "But my father was."

CHAPTER TWENTY THREE

Jessie couldn't hear a word.

Officer Plumley was saying something, blathering on about college football. But all Jessie could hear in her head was the thundering shout of "Go Mizzou!" as her dad jumped up from his easy chair to cheer on the team after they'd scored a touchdown.

She couldn't have been more than four. But she could clearly recall him scooping her up in his arms and spinning her around. She remembered the contact high she got off his enthusiasm even if she didn't really understand what he was so happy about. It was one of her only good memories from childhood that involved her dad.

"Officer Plumley," she said, interrupting his monologue about the primacy of the west coast offense, "can you please pull the poster off the wall and see if there's anything on the back of it? But before you do, put on your evidence gloves."

Officer Plumley did as he was asked. Both Jessie and Ryan waited silently. After several seconds, the phone, which had been resting on the desk pointed up at the ceiling, focused in on the back of the poster, which Plumley placed on the filing cabinet.

"Can you see that?" he asked them.

"Not really," Ryan admitted. "It's not very clear."

"It looks like a note written in pencil," Plumley said. "It reads: *Junebug's dad was here. He can't wait to see her again.*"

*

Jessie finally felt something close to normal again.

After a forty-five-minute drive, she was almost to the coffee shop in the Larchmont Village district of Hancock Park where she was supposed to meet Andi Robinson. It had taken her this long to fully process the situation. But there was no way around it—just as her father knew that she would eventually see the video of him talking to Crutchfield, he had anticipated that she would find the note on the poster too.

When the note was written two years ago, no other person alive, save for Bolton Crutchfield, even knew of his pet name for her. And not even Crutchfield knew about the importance of the University of Missouri in their shared memory. This was the work of her dad, intended to get her attention, to unsettle her, and just maybe to reach out to her in his own warped interpretation of paternal affection. It was all too much to process in the moment so she let it go as best she could.

She had a call to make anyway. So once she arrived on South Larchmont Blvd., she parked in a spot under the shade of a huge tree in front of an artisanal cheese shop and dialed. Lacy picked up on the first ring.

"Did they find out who did it?" her friend asked anxiously, skipping pleasantries altogether as she referred to the break-in culprit.

"Not the individual who actually did it, at least not yet. But we know who ordered it."

"Wait—someone ordered a break-in of my place?" Lacy asked, confused. "It wasn't just some random thing?"

Jessie was hesitant to get into particulars. But if she was going to set Lacy's mind at ease that it wouldn't happen again, she had to give a few details.

"No," she admitted. "It was related to a case I'm working on. Someone was trying to send me a message. That's why nothing was taken."

"A case? But the apartment's in my name. How did this person even know you're staying there?"

"That's a very good question," Jessie said, "one that I intend to look into in more detail soon. But the important thing to know is that I confronted this person and that sort of thing won't be happening again."

Instead of a sound of relief on the other end of the line, there was silence. Jessie suddenly felt uneasy. Lacy was almost never quiet. Something was wrong.

"What is it, Lace?" she asked.

"I'm sorry, Jessie," Lacy said, her voice thick with emotion. "But this isn't going to work. I can't be worrying all the time about some suspect in one of your cases deciding to teach you a lesson or send a message. I have the beginnings of an ulcer from the break-in, even before you told me that. Now I'll never get a night of sleep."

"But this was an aberration," Jessie protested. Even as the words came out, though, she wondered if it was true. There was no guarantee Crutchfield wouldn't do something else. And what if her father discovered where they lived? Lacy was right to be concerned.

"You can't know that," Lacy said, voicing the same concern. "I don't feel safe. And I don't think I ever will if we're roommates. I don't want to be a bitch but you've got to move out, sweetie. And I mean like right away."

Jessie nodded even though no one could see her. She could almost feel her friend's sense of guilt through the phone.

"I get it," she said quietly. "That makes total sense. I should have been more sensitive to your concerns. I'll pack up my stuff and be out tonight."

"You're still my girl," Lacy said, clearly fighting back tears, an amazing thing since Jessie had never known her to come close to crying. "We can still hang and get drinks and do whatever. I just need to know that the place where I rest my head at night is safe."

"I understand," Jessie said. "Don't feel bad. I'm not upset with you. We're cool, okay?"

"You sure?"

"Of course. We'll hang out this weekend," Jessie promised.

Just then, she saw Andi walk by on her way to Coffee Klatch. She was dressed casually in sporty sweatpants, a light sweater, and a windbreaker. She wore a Dodgers baseball cap with a blonde ponytail poking through the hole in back. Jessie looked at her watch. It was 3 p.m. She was right on the dot.

"What do you want to do?" Lacy asked, obviously trying to soften the blow.

"We'll figure something out," Jessie replied, hoping she didn't sound too harsh. "Listen, I actually have a witness interview starting right now so I have to run. But we'll do something. Don't feel guilty, Lace. This is on me."

She heard her friend start to reply just as she hit "end."

Damn. She's going to think I'm pissed.

She quickly texted a heart emoji before getting out of the car and hurrying to the coffee shop. Walking in, she saw that Andi had secured a table in the corner of the near-empty café and was waving her over.

"I already placed my order," she said. "I had to get over here and lay claim to this sweet table before it got pinched. You never know when there's gonna be a rush."

"Smart move," Jessie said, playing along. "Plus, you want to be there to bat away the tumbleweeds, right?"

"I like the way you think," Andi said approvingly. "You want to sit?"

Jessie nodded. She placed her order and sat down, trying to determine how best to broach the subject of Victoria Missinger's potential infidelity with a personal trainer. She decided to ease into it.

"Is that hair choice Beverly Country Club approved?" she asked, pointing at Andi's cap.

I like to live on the edge," she said as her drink arrived, "except when it comes to beverages, of course."

"Of course," Jessie agreed before fake whispering, "Why the safety precautions around beverages?"

"I'm lactose intolerant," Andi fake whispered back. "So this is a soy milk latte. My rebel streak only goes so far."

"I see. Well, you can't always be fighting the man. Take me, for example. I once drank a shot of goat's blood during spring break in Mexico, so you know I'm hardcore-ish. But the other day, I ate one of my friend's french fries. I started wheezing so badly he nearly had to call an ambulance. Turns out it was fried in peanut oil."

"Pretty allergic, huh?" Andi asked sympathetically.

"I had to bust out the emergency inhaler. If I hadn't had it, I might not be here chatting with you today."

"They really should note that sort of thing on the menu," Andi said. "I'm sure you're not the only one who's had that happen."

"You know, they might have. I should have looked before having one."

"It's funny,' Andi said as she took a sip, "my father had a theory about all that. He said that our whole generation is soft, that back in the day no one had allergies or intolerances. They just sucked it up."

"Maybe the survivors did. Too bad for the rest of them though," Jessie quipped before she could stop herself. "I'm sorry but your dad sounds like a real piece of work."

"Yeah. He's dead now."

"Oh jeez," Jessie said, her face turning crimson. "I didn't mean…"

"It's okay," Andi said, waving her off and giving a rueful smile. "A piece of work is a diplomatic way to describe Thoreau Robinson. Other people have been far more colorful. I guess when you're that brilliant, you forget some of the social niceties."

133

"Smart fella?" Jessie asked, trying to lighten the mood a bit.

"He wasn't too shabby in the brains department. He taught chemical engineering at Caltech until he hit it big. Invented some new polymer, patented it, and just like that, we were richer than the Beverly Hillbillies."

"And rather than go into the family business, you decided to go into the lucrative… country clubbing industry?" Jessie asked, her eyebrows raised.

"Yup," Andi said, taking another sip of her drink. "But don't think I was always this ambitious. I actually did follow in his footsteps for a while. I got in to the same school, although it was more of a legacy thing. How were they going to refuse the daughter of a former professor who paid for a wing named after him? I even got solid grades, though I had to work pretty hard for them."

"Sounds like it was working out okay," Jessie said neutrally, unsure where the story would end up.

"It was. I was working on my master's when he passed away. For a while after I studied even harder, sort of in honor of him. I had a four-point-oh the semester he died. But over that summer I started to question it."

"Question what exactly?" Jessie asked.

"All of it," Andi said, her eyes getting hazy as she stared off into the distance. "Why I was spending all my energy pursuing something I wasn't passionate about. Once the external pressure of his expectations was gone, I just didn't care anymore. I wanted to have a little fun. My entire youth was about trying to live up to his legacy. Once I didn't have to do it anymore, I felt free. And ever since, I've just pursued what makes me happy. I have a lot of catching up to do."

"Sounds like a nice life," Jessie said.

"I like this life better than the old one—that's for sure. I may not be saving the world. But I also don't constantly feel like I'm a failure either," Andi said, then turned her attention to Jessie, her eyes now focused again. "What about you—do you have daddy issues too? Was he rough on you?'

"You could say that," Jessie said in the understatement of the millennium. "I'm still kind of working through it actually."

"I get it," Andi said. "Don't worry. I won't push. It's funny, though, how we embrace or reject our fathers. There doesn't seem to be any middle ground."

The truth of those words hit Jessie like a punch to the gut. She tried to push mixed images of two fathers—one a serial killer, the other a lawman—out of her head. It took enormous effort to reply without revealing the churning she felt inside.

"So," she said, clunkily changing the subject, "if you aren't planning to invent any polymers in the next week or so, what do you do to keep busy?"

Andi looked like she wanted to continue the deep discussion. But apparently deciding to let Jessie off the hook, she responded in kind.

"Other than playing golf and constantly remodeling my house," she said, "I'm not sure I have any true passions. It's only recently that I've allowed myself to become open to actually falling in love. Like I said, I was always go-go-go. I never even had a real boyfriend in high school or college. How embarrassing is that? I'm trying to make up for lost time, I guess."

"So have you found Mr. Right?" Jessie asked, taking advantage of the opening. "Maybe that trainer your club lady friends were gossiping about?"

"I admit I'm a romantic, Jessie," Andi said, rolling her eyes. "But even I'm not naïve to think I can find true love with a personal trainer."

"Not even with Dan Romano?" she asked facetiously. "As we've been investigating the Missinger case, we've found him to be very…popular."

"Look, I can't say I never partook of his services. He was very… accommodating. But I'd like to think I can do better."

"What about Victoria?" Jessie asked. "The consensus seemed to be that she wasn't interested in anything extra he might be willing to offer."

"From what I could tell Victoria wasn't the infidelity type. If she was cheating with anyone, it was with those kids she raised money for. Sometimes it seemed like it was all she could talk about."

"Is that a bad thing?" Jessie wondered.

"Not for the kids, obviously," Andi said. "But in a social environment, it sometimes got to be a bit much. She was relentless and not very subtle about pouring on the guilt trips if she thought someone wasn't doing their part."

"Sounds like she was a challenging personality," Jessie said, trying to tease out more details without being too obvious about it.

"Look, I don't want to speak ill of the dead, especially someone who, unlike me, actually *was* trying to save the world.

But the general consensus around here was that she could be kind of…brittle. That's how the rumors got started."

"Rumors?"

"About Michael," Andi said, lowering her voice even though there was no one else around. "It was clear that he admired his wife's passion for her work. But folks got the sense that he would have liked her to direct a little more passion his way. Some hinted that he might be compensating with other, more willing partners."

"Anyone in particular?"

"I don't have any inside knowledge," Andi said. "Like I said yesterday, I didn't hang in their circle that much. But you remember what Marlene said about the maid when you were eavesdropping?"

"About her getting rid of Victoria so she could have Michael to herself?" Jessie recalled. "She said she was kidding."

"She did say that," Andi agreed. "And she *was* probably joking. But it's not the first time I've heard there might be something going on there."

"Do you believe that?" Jessie asked her.

"I tend not to believe ninety percent of what I hear around the club. And normally I'd keep something like that to myself. But since this is a murder investigation, I figured I should mention it. Better to err on the side of caution and say something so you can check it out rather than just stay silent for the sake of propriety, right?"

"Absolutely," Jessie agreed.

Just then her phone pinged. She looked down and saw a text from Ryan. It read: *Update on the trainer, Dan Romano. Call when able.*

"Big news?" Andi asked.

"Hard to tell," she replied. "But I need to find out. You mind if we cut this short?"

"Totally cool. Let me know if I can be of any more help."

"I may do that," Jessie said.

"And when this is all over," Andi added, "maybe we can get a drink or something. You seem like you'd be a fun hang when you're not, you know, investigating murders and stuff."

"That sounds nice," Jessie agreed as she got up. "I'll call you when we get this resolved, assuming I don't reach out to pump you for more info before then."

As she got back in her car, Jessie called Ryan.

"What's up?" she asked.

"The husband that Romano was worried about beat him up with a golf club. He's unconscious at the hospital."

CHAPTER TWENTY FOUR

"What?" Jessie demanded disbelievingly as she peeled out of her parking spot and headed back to the station.

"And if you can believe it—that may actually be useful news."

"How is that possible?" Jessie wanted to know.

"It turns out that the husband—his name is John Kasdan—has been suspicious for a while. He was tailing Romano to see if he hooked up with his wife. He found them together this afternoon and just went off."

"I'm waiting for the good news," Jessie said.

"Right," Ryan remembered. "Well, I wasn't the one who interviewed him. But apparently Kasdan has been extremely forthcoming. I guess he's in that triumphant, post-golf-club-attack mode. He said he's been following Romano for days, taking photos, keeping a log of his movements. The log is very detailed. And it doesn't show Romano going anywhere near Victoria Missinger's house. In addition, the photos Kasdan took are time-stamped and some of them are for the window in which Victoria was killed. Romano was otherwise engaged at the time."

"So basically, the man who beat up Dan Romano is also his alibi in a murder case?" Jessie concluded.

"Pretty much."

"Well, that jibes with what Andrea Robinson said," Jessie said. "There was no scuttlebutt around the club about Victoria and Romano. Is he going to be okay?"

"It's too early to say. According to witnesses, he took several hard blows to the head."

"Ugh. So we can cross him off the suspect list. But he may have brain damage? I don't know if he'd take that trade-off."

"Probably not," Ryan said. "And as long as we're talking dead ends in the case, I have another one for you."

"Great," Jessie said as she hit the brakes. There was a wall of afternoon traffic in front of her. "It just keeps coming."

"Welcome to the LAPD. Anyway, our tech team looked at the security camera footage from the Missinger house. There's nothing for the window of death. The whole grid for that area went down."

"Don't those systems have battery backups?" Jessie asked.

"They do. But this one only lasted for about forty-five minutes. The blackout started at one-oh-nine p.m. The M.E.'s rough time of death was between two and four that afternoon. So there's a long stretch of unmonitored time."

"Jeez," Jessie muttered, still staring at brake lights as far as the eye could see. "Any more bad news for me?"

"Actually yes," Ryan said apologetically. "I just saw the security footage from your apartment at the time of the break-in. Whoever did it was well aware he was on camera. I can tell the perpetrator was male based on size, but couldn't discern much else. He was wearing a hoodie and gloves and kept his head down the whole time. I couldn't determine ethnicity or age. Just that he was a male, approximately five-foot-ten to six feet tall and between a hundred seventy and a hundred ninety pounds."

"Maybe I can give Lacy the update as I'm moving out," Jessie said sarcastically.

"What?"

"She says she doesn't feel safe with me living there," Jessie told him. "And I can't blame her. She's not. Crutchfield could send someone back. My father could find the place. Any new roommate is a potential target. That's why I'm going to stay in hotels until I find someplace new. I was hoping to just grab what I need for now and leave my other stuff there until I have a more permanent residence."

"When are you leaving?" Ryan asked.

"As soon as we wrap up for the night."

"Why don't you just head over there now?" he suggested. "There's nothing essential here that you have to pursue tonight. We'll pick it up in the morning."

"Thanks, Ryan. That will be a lifesaver. With traffic right now, it might still take me another hour to travel the six miles back to my place. But there is something I want to check out first thing tomorrow."

"What's that?"

"I never looked at the footage of your interview with the maid, Marisol Mendez. I know she was out of town at the time of the killing. But Andrea Robinson hinted that folks at the club thought she might be cleaning more than just floors. If that's true, maybe we can squeeze her a little and get her to pull back the curtain on things. I keep getting the sense that there's more going on with this couple than we know. If it's true that Marisol was sleeping with her boss, we'll have some extra leverage to get her to be more forthcoming."

"I'll have the interview queued up and waiting for you tomorrow," Ryan promised. "And one more thing…"

"What's that?" Jessie asked, noticing a note of hesitation in his voice.

"If you need a couple of suggestions for short-term living arrangements, I can send you some. Over the course of my wedded bliss, I've been forced to spend a few nights elsewhere when the couch wasn't getting the job done. I know a couple of places downtown that don't cost a fortune and don't require you to bunk with roaches."

"Ew! Yes, I'll take that list, please. And some bug spray too, just in case."

"I'll text them over in a bit. The list of places, not the bug spray. Have a good night, Jessie."

"Thanks. You too," Jessie said.

She hung up and tried to force the thought of cockroaches out of her head by focusing on the task directly in front of her—exiting Lacy's apartment. She just hoped it didn't mean she was exiting their friendship too.

She wanted to believe what Lacy had said—that they could still stay close. And they mostly had even when Jessie moved to Orange County. But this time was different. Lacy was upset over something that Jessie was responsible for, even if unintentionally. There was no way it wouldn't color their relationship going forward.

Jessie couldn't help but think how odd it was that just as one longtime friend was creating some space, other women were appearing to fill the void. Jessie would have to turn down Kat's suggestion of being roommates for her own safety. But the very fact that she'd brought up the idea suggested an unexpected fondness between them. Considering how combative their initial meeting had been when Jessie first went to interview Bolton Crutchfield, it was amazing how far they'd come.

And now there was the chance that Andi Robinson might become decent friend material too. Jessie appreciated how she constantly punctured holes in her own self-importance. It was clear that she was swimming in money. But she hadn't let it go to her head. It didn't hurt that she wasn't involved in law enforcement either. It might be fun to spend time with someone local who didn't know an APB from an IED.

But if they did start hanging out more, she'd have to be careful to avoid the Dearest Daddy talk. While it was clear that they had paternal issues in common, the less Andi knew about the magnitude of Jessie's, the better off she'd be.

Thinking of just how awful a parental role model Xander Thurman was reminded Jessie that her adoptive dad, Bruce Hunt, was exactly the opposite. Somehow their estrangement since Ma's cancer came back had twisted her view of him.

When she thought of him now, she pictured his disapproving face when she said she was going to marry Kyle. But it retrospect, maybe she should have been as guarded as her guardian was.

She recalled his lukewarm reaction when she said she planned to pursue a master's in forensic psychology. But she could see now that he might only have been worried that she was re-immersing herself in the world of trauma that had so defined her childhood.

Looking back, it was apparent that all the moments she'd viewed back then as judgmental or hypercritical were more likely just concerned parenting. And while he'd clearly not been enthused by some of her choices, he never actually tried to talk her out of them.

He asked questions. He probed. But in the end, the decisions were always hers and he always stood by her. Bruce Hunt had been a father in every way she needed, even if she didn't know it at the time.

So why am I so hard on him?

Jessie grabbed her phone and called him. It went straight to voicemail, usually a sign that he had turned it off to take care of Ma or so he could concentrate on poker with the boys. After the beep, she left a message.

"Hey, Pa, I just wanted to check in with you to see how you're doing. If you're playing poker, I hope you're winning a lot of M&Ms. The job here is going okay. I'm adjusting. Still dealing with a few hiccups caused by the smoldering ruins of my marriage.

"But otherwise, I'm good. I was just thinking of that first time you took me skiing on the bunny slopes near Cloudcroft. I must have fallen thirty times in the hour we were up there. I remember yelling at you, blaming you, saying you bent my skis on purpose. But you just helped me up every time, dusted the snow off me, and picked up where we left off. You never yelled. You never rolled your eyes. You never lost your patience, at least not visibly. I just wanted you to know that I appreciate that. I didn't then but I do now. Anyway, like I said, I was just checking in. I'll be in touch. Bye."

CHAPTER TWENTY FIVE

Jessie wasn't sure how she'd never noticed it before.

She was only blocks from Lacy's apartment, waiting at another endless traffic light, when she saw the sign: Downtown Children's Outreach Center. That was the charity that Victoria Missinger was involved with.

Though it was already dark outside, all the lights in the center were blazing. It was still open. Then she chastised herself for being surprised.

Of course it's open. It's not like these kids' problems stop at six p.m.

When the light turned green, she moved to the right and parked in front of the center. She turned off the ignition and sat there for a moment, not entirely sure what she planned to do next. Then, deciding to let her instincts guide her, she got out and headed for the entrance.

The first thing she noticed was the security. It wasn't NRD level, but there were outer and inner security gates and cameras mounted at various locations. Someone had paid good money to make sure this place was secure. She was pretty certain who that had been.

She buzzed the call button and a female voice came over the intercom.

"How may I help you?"

"My name is Jessie Hunt. I'd like to speak to the program director."

She was buzzed in and met at the second gate by a security guard who apologized before thoroughly patting her down. After being admitted inside the building, she was directed through a metal detector. After that, she was met by a second security guard who said words she'd probably repeated dozens of times today.

"This facility does not permit unauthorized pictures. Please remain in designated areas. Do not interact with minors without prior authorization from a staff member. Profanity is not permitted. Failure to comply will result in immediate removal and potential arrest. Please sign this release indicating that you have been informed of these policies and will follow them."

Jessie signed the form and handed it back.

"Who are you here to see?" the guard asked.

"Whoever's in charge," Jessie said.

The guard waved for her to follow her down the hallway. Jessie noticed that the second they rounded the corner from the lobby, the entire vibe of the facility changed. The entrance area had been sterile, with white walls, fluorescent lights, and tiled floors. This wing was carpeted and painted yellow, with kids' drawing framed and posted on the walls. Vaguely holiday-themed classical music could be heard playing softly from speakers set up throughout.

The guard stopped at the door to an office with a nameplate on the side that said *Roberta Watts, Program Director*. Jessie peeked inside. The place was a mess, stacked high with manila folders and banker's boxes. One corner of the office had a kid-sized couch festooned with stuffed animals. A small table nearby was covered in books.

"Ms. Watts, you have a visitor," the guard called out.

The head of a woman who had apparently been sitting on the ground popped up from behind one of the banker's boxes.

"Thanks, Kim, I'll take it from here," she said, standing up and walking over to shake Jessie's hand.

As she did, Jessie took her in. The woman was quite a sight. Well over six feet tall and 200 pounds, she looked like she could handle security all on her own. An African-American woman in her mid-forties, she moved with a bounce in her step that Jessie envied. She had a broad smile that was even more impressive considering the time of day.

"I'm Roberta Watts," she said, extending her hand. "I run this madhouse."

"Nice to meet you," Jessie said, trying not to wince at Roberta's powerful grip. "I'm Jessie Hunt."

"Jessie, what can I do for you? I know this isn't a health department check at six twenty-one at night. We're all paid up so you're not a creditor. So that means you're here with really good or really bad news. Good Samaritan here to make a generous donation, I'm hoping?"

Jessie didn't feel she could just start discussing Victoria without any preamble, so she dodged.

"I don't know that I have the resources for that right now," she said. "But I live in the area and I was curious about the facility. Do you have a moment to tell me about it?"

"Of course. We always have time for potential contributors. I'll give you the mini-tour. Follow me."

She left her office and was halfway down the hallway before Jessie could catch up. She launched into what was clearly her standard pitch.

"We're a non-profit facility designed to help children develop life skills while providing a safe, secure environment. We offer short-term housing for homeless children and kids between foster families who don't currently have access to longer-term residential facilities. We provide low-cost and free day care for parents working below the poverty line. We offer meals, on-site education, counseling, and physical and mental health and wellness resources. We are open twenty-four hours a day, seven days a week, three hundred sixty-five days a year. We are a public-private partnership, with seventy-five of our funding coming from donors and the remaining twenty-five percent provided by the city and county. In January, we'll be celebrating our fifth anniversary."

As they curled around the corner, the corridor opened up into a large room filled with plastic play structures, beanbag chairs, and a block and Lego center. In one corner was a ping-pong table. In another there was a basketball hoop. A third corner had hopscotch and jump ropes.

Kids were everywhere, running, jumping, and rolling around. They all wore navy sweatpants and light blue T-shirts with the single word "Outreach" printed on them. She watched as one little girl with pigtails did half a dozen somersaults on a row of mats at the end of the room. When she was done, she stood up and bowed as if she'd just completed a gold-medal-winning routine.

"What's up with the sweatpants and shirts?" Jessie asked.

"Even in an environment like this, where kids are struggling, there can be teasing over clothing. Some children only have one shirt. Some only have a pair of shorts and no jeans. Some are wearing taped-up flip-flops because they can't afford real shoes. Here, everyone gets a shirt and sweats and is required to wear them. That eliminates some of the conflicts, though not all. We also provide fresh underwear, socks, and, when possible, shoes."

"You said three-quarters of your funding is private. Is that mostly corporate or individual?" Jessie asked, finally finding a way to broach the topic she had come here to pursue.

"It's a combination," Roberta Watts said, her voice faltering slightly. "Our biggest resource is a foundation established by one person. It coordinates donations from everyone. Unfortunately, the woman who spear-headed it passed away earlier this week."

"I'm so sorry," Jessie said, not sure why she didn't come clean in that moment.

"Yes, it's a real loss. Obviously, we're unsettled about what will happen to the center from a financial perspective. This woman—her name was Victoria Missinger—was relentless in getting us the resources we need. But on a personal level, it's really tough as well."

"Were you close?" Jessie asked.

"Not really. She wasn't the kind of person who was personally all that warm, at least not with adults. But it was a different story with the kids. They loved her. She'd get down on the ground and play dolls with them. She'd run around and play tag. She'd read at story time. She was as soft with them as she was hard when dealing with a reluctant donor. I haven't told them yet. I'm not sure how they'll take it. These kids have been through a lot. But to them, Miss Vicky was a rock, someone they could always count on. Now they can't."

It wasn't until then that the full magnitude of Victoria Missinger's death really hit Jessie. Until now, she'd mostly looked at the woman as a piece in a puzzle that needed to be solved. The fact that Victoria Missinger had been repeatedly described as distant, even cold, had reinforced her perception.

But looking over at Roberta, who was staring at the kids with a misty look in her eyes, she realized that this was more than just a game to be won. Dozens of lives—children's lives— could be ruined by the death of this one woman.

In that moment Jessie swore that Victoria would get whatever justice she could provide.

CHAPTER TWENTY SIX

If this was what Ryan Hernandez considered a decent hotel, Jessie wondered what he viewed as unacceptable living arrangements.

True, this was just for one night and most of his suggestions had been weekly options, but still, it was not exactly welcoming. It was clean at least. She hadn't seen one cockroach. But the room smelled musty, like the windows hadn't been opened in months.

It was more of a motel, with a door that faced the noisy, overly lit parking lot. The ice machine was outside and down the hall, which meant that it could have been in Siberia. There was no way Jessie was walking down there in her sweats at night in forty-five-degree weather. The room-temperature water in her plastic cup would have to do.

She stripped off the comforter (*who knows the last time that thing was washed?*) and lay down on one of the two twin beds in the room—no queens were available tonight. The lime-green wallpaper was starting to peel at the seams and the photo on the wall was faded, though it appeared to be of a nondescript, barren hill that didn't deserve to have its picture taken.

The pillow was lumpy, as was the mattress. The bed frame creaked. The remote control didn't work and since there were no buttons on the set itself, she had to decide whether to watch a rerun of *Mama's Family* or just turn the TV off. She turned it off.

Lying there, she reminded herself that this place was infinitely preferable to the situation of many of the children she'd just seen. They didn't have their own rooms or TVs or private bathrooms. And yet, she suspected, they were happy for what they did have.

Jessie pushed the image of those kids from her mind. It was too much for one day. She was just debating whether to crash for the night even though it was only 9:30 when a text came in. It was from her Realtor. The potential buyers on the house had rejected her counteroffer. She had to either accept their initial offer or pass. And she had to decide by 9 a.m. tomorrow or they were pulling the offer entirely.

Part of her wanted to say no just to spite them. She didn't love their hardball tactics and under other circumstances she would have told them to screw off. But there was no guarantee anything better would come along soon. This was, after all, the house where a crazy man had tied up his wife and tried to kill her and two neighbors. That sort of thing tended to reduce home value. And these people knew it.

Right then, Jessie decided it wasn't worth the fight. She just wanted to be rid of the place. She'd never really wanted to be there anyway. And even taking a loss, she'd still clear seven figures on the sale. That and her take from the divorce would leave her more than comfortable—maybe not Andrea Robinson comfortable, but with more than enough to not worry. In light of what she'd just seen a few blocks away, it seemed churlish to balk at the offer. Besides, making a clean break was worth more to her at this point than getting the best deal.

She texted back that she'd accept the offer. The reply came less than sixty seconds later. They had an agreement. She should come to Westport Beach tomorrow at 10 a.m. to sign the papers. That would mean pushing back her review of the maid's taped interview. But if it meant the house issue was resolved for good, then Marisol Mendez could wait a few hours.

Jessie turned off the light and stared up at the ceiling, illuminated by the parking lot lights despite the thick curtains. She tried to push the negative thoughts out of her head and focus on the positive. She was selling the house. She was getting a fresh start. She had made what Dr. Janice Lemmon would call a "breakthrough" when it came to her perception of her adoptive father. And yet…

She couldn't help but see the other side of things. Professionally, things were sketchy. One man—Dan Romano—was no longer a viable suspect. The home security cameras that might have revealed the killer's identity hadn't recorded anything and she was reduced to tracking down uncorroborated rumors of an adulterous maid. And now even that had to be put on hold because she had to sell the house she'd bought with the man who'd tried to kill her.

Add to that, she was sleeping in a motel with a borderline nauseating hard-to-identify smell. And that was because her oldest friend had kicked her out, putting their friendship in doubt, all because a serial killer wanted to teach her a lesson. And that wasn't even the serial killer she was most worried about. Her father earned that title.

Jessie chuckled at the gallows humor of it all. But after a moment, the grim smile on her face faded as the magnitude of all those terribles hit her. She felt her body sink into the chunky, uneven mattress as the enormity of crises in her midst started to weigh her down. A dull depression rolled over her like coastal fog. It wasn't "drive your car into the back of a truck" depression. Rather, it was more like she was lugging a fifty-pound backpack around, one she could never take off. Maybe Dr. Lemmon wouldn't be so proud of her after all.

She put in the cheap pair of earplugs she'd bought at the drugstore, rolled onto her side away from the parking lot lights, and drifted off into an unsettled, restless sleep.

*

He sat in the rocking chair across from her, whittling.

Little Jessica had stopped struggling to free her arms as the cuts were deep and it hurt to move at all. Besides, he'd just retie them anyway.

Jessica glanced up at the lifeless body of her mother. Though she'd been dead for hours, every now and then the manacles holding her arms to the ceiling beam above her head shifted imperceptibly and she swayed ever so slightly. Jessica knew movement was forthcoming when the wood creaked.

Her father, Xander Thurman, seemed oblivious to his now-dead wife's tiny movements. He just whittled away, cutting that small piece of wood into something Jessica couldn't see in his big hands. She did notice the shavings hit the ground at semi-regular intervals.

"You know, Junebug," her father said in that soft, unhurried voice, "family is the most important thing. Don't ever forget that."

Then he laid the wooden carving on the ground, put on his coat, opened the door, and walked out. She didn't know it at the time but that would be the last time little Jessica would see her father.

Once he was gone, she screwed up the courage to look at the thing he'd carved and left at her feet. It was a valentine; a heart.

With what little strength she had in her tired, hoarse child's voice, little Jessica Thurman began to scream.

And lying on that lumpy motel room bed, in her churned-up mess of sleep, so did Jessie Hunt.

CHAPTER TWENTY SEVEN

Jessie pretended she wasn't nervous. She'd met with many prisoners at many jails. She'd visited with a serial killer at a lockdown psychiatric facility well over a dozen times. She thought she'd be unfazed. But this prison was very different from Bolton Crutchfield's. This was where her husband, Kyle, was being held.

The Orange County Men's Central Jail was only three miles from the beach, but you'd never know it. Situated on flat land surrounded by several hills, it was tastefully hidden from the view of the area's well-to-do residents. At first glance it looked more like a very secure office park than a prison.

But once she entered the property, that misperception was easily corrected. Jessie had already been through two metal detectors and two pat-downs just to be sitting in the communication room where she waited for officers to bring Kyle out to see her.

She sat in a bolted down chair that faced a pane of glass with an old-style corded phone on the wall. Each "communication booth" was separated by a flimsy corkboard divider intended to give some semblance of privacy.

To Jessie's left a woman with a small child in her lap sat across from a large guy with a shaved head. Both mother and son were crying but the man was dry-eyed. To her right, the guy next to her sounded like he was conducting some kind of business with the prisoner across from him. She heard the words "package" and "lieutenant" and wondered if they knew everything they said was being recorded.

As she waited, Jessie's thoughts returned to her morning so far. She'd slept poorly and woken up around 5 a.m., so she decided to head to Westport Beach early to avoid the traffic. On her way, she texted Ryan to let him know about her change of plans. He replied, saying he'd handle things with Captain Decker until she got back.

She got to Westport just after seven. And with three hours to kill before signing the house docs, she decided to drive around the old neighborhood she'd learned to despise. She passed by the home of Melanie and Teddy Carlisle, the couple whom Kyle had tried to kill along with her. Other than a few perfunctory texts, she'd lost touch with Mel, the one person she genuinely liked down here. She regretted that but it seemed a small price to pay to put this world behind her.

After that, she passed by her own house, the McMansion she'd be signing away in a few hours. It seemed so blandly innocuous from the street. One would never guess that this was where a marriage had fallen apart, a husband's plan to frame his wife for murder had been hatched, a miscarriage had occurred, and three people had almost died.

After getting some breakfast, she went to the Realtor's office to sign the sale documents, a process that was, while time-consuming, also thankfully mind-numbing.

Next she went to the harbor, where the now-shuttered Club Deseo stood forlornly on the pier. As a result of Kyle's crimes, including the murder of a club employee, local authorities did a wider investigation and uncovered that the yacht club they belonged to was also a front for a high-end call girl business. It gave Jessie no small amount of satisfaction to know a place she'd so detested now sat empty.

She found a spot on a cliff overlooking the harbor and parked. From here, she had a broad view of the Pacific Ocean. But her eyes were drawn to a rock outcropping at the edge of the harbor, jutting out of the water and surrounded by buoys intended to warn boats away.

That's where Kyle had dumped the body of Natalia Urgova, the club waitress and sometime escort he'd been sleeping with until it became inconvenient for him. Jessie had only met Natalia once and it hadn't been a warm introduction. But she remembered every detail of the girl's face, in part because she saw it so often in her dreams.

A gate slammed and Jessie was thrust back into the present. Kyle was being led over to their booth. Even in the gray jumpsuit he was wearing, her husband still looked good. He was tall and blond, with bright blue eyes and broad shoulders, and she could still recognize the man she'd fallen in love with.

Of course, that Kyle Voss—the rakish but goofy charmer who'd wooed her in college—either never existed or long ago ceased to. The man in front of her had lied to and manipulated her for months, if not years. It was infuriating how easily he'd played her, and more than a little embarrassing, considering what she did for a living. Maybe that was why she was here now—to make some sense of that.

She picked up the phone as he sat down and he grabbed the receiver on his side of the glass.

"Hi, love," he said with a mix of humor and venom. "Miss me?"

"You'd be amazed how little," she replied.

"I doubt that. Your life was so much more exciting with me in it."

"Exciting is one way to put it," Jessie mused. "But I've managed to find other things to hold my interest. You'd be surprised."

"Oh, I don't think I would be," he said, his eyes twinkling with glee. "I've got ears in here. I know you're working with the pigs full time now."

"The pigs?" Jessie repeated, almost laughing.

'I figure now that I'm behind bars, I have to talk the part," he explained, clearly not serious. "Convincing?"

"It needs a little work. But I think it's great that you're trying to adapt to your new surroundings."

Kyle stared at her, a grin playing at his lips but not quite forming.

"Funny how quickly we slip back into the old resentful banter, huh?" he noted.

"I think it reinforces why our imminent divorce is a wise move," she pointed out. "We don't have what I'd refer to as a healthy relationship."

"There's no such thing, Jessie."

"Some might suggest that it's that kind of mind-set that sent you down the road that got you in here."

"Are you profiling me right now, baby?" he asked, smirking.

"Nope. You don't have to be a criminal profiler to make that deduction. And figuring you out isn't my job anyway. I just felt I owed it to the wreckage of our marriage to see you in person and tell you that the divorce will be finalized at the start of the new year—January second, to be exact. So enjoy the remaining two weeks of our wedded bliss, dear."

"That feels petty, Jessie," he said feigning disappointment.

"Yeah," she agreed, smiling, "it kind of does."

"Well, thanks for the heads-up. But I should tell you—I have plans, my love. I intend to beat these charges. And when I do, I'm going to woo you and win you back. We'll find our way back to each other. And once we've begun our resplendent second act together, I'm going to wait until you're sleeping, get a tire iron, and beat you until you're a pulpy mess of shattered bones, shredded skin, and oozing blood. It's gonna be special."

"So," Jessie said, standing up and making sure her expression was blank, "I think our chat is over. Thanks so much for reminding why I'll never be seeing you again. And good luck on the whole 'not getting shivved in here' thing."

She hung up the phone just as he was replying. She couldn't hear what he said and she didn't turn back to find out.

*

Dr. Lemmon picked up on the first ring.

Jessie was driving back to DTLA from Westport when the panicky feeling hit her and she dialed her therapist's number, hoping she might be on a lunch break and able to talk.

"Hi, Jessie," the doctor said, her voice soothing as always. "How are you?"

"I've been better," she admitted.

"Tell me what's going on."

Jessie proceeded to fill her in on recent developments, starting with her visit to Kyle. But she also mentioned everything from the apartment break-in to her falling out with Lacy to her professional challenges on the Missinger case and finally Bolton Crutchfield's cryptic clues about her father.

"I feel like I've got an anchor tied to me as I'm sinking in a deep lake and people keep tugging me down when I try to get to the surface."

It was only as she described the feeling that she realized just how low she felt and just how much she'd been faking getting by.

"Why did you go to see Kyle," Dr. Lemmon asked, "if you were already in such a precarious place?"

"I guess I thought maybe it would give me closure. But it mostly just reopened old wounds. It just reminded me that I wasted ten years with him, that I lost my sense of self when he got me to move down there; that I lost my baby because of him. And it reminded me that I'm still facing the fallout from all that. I've moved on physically but I'm still a mess."

"I think you're doing okay, all things considered," Dr. Lemmon said.

"Really?" Jessie asked incredulously. "Were you listening to the deluge of crap I just described?"

"I was. And it does sound challenging. But there are positives, Jessie. You're officially done with that house. You're almost done with your marriage. You have a roof over your head for the night, even if it's not your preferred one. And neither you nor your friend was hurt in the break-in. The situation with your father is difficult, to say the least. But you're meeting it head-on. And you are plowing ahead professionally, headed back to work right now to try to solve this case."

"Wow, you are really are a glass-half-full kind of lady, aren't you?"

"It's kind of my thing," Dr. Lemmon quipped.

"Well, I'm not quite there yet. I don't see how I'm going to solve this case. I'm grasping at straws of innuendo here."

"Just focus on the work, Jessie. It will allow you to set aside all the other stuff that's eating at you. And we both know that when you're zoned in on the behavioral patterns of your subjects, you pick up on things others miss. It's your gift. Now is the time to use it—to help solve this woman's murder *and* to give your mind a constructive place to go. "

When Jessie hung up she felt slightly better. Yes, her personal life was a shambles. Yes, her very life might be in danger. But she knew how to read people. And that's what she was headed to do right now. She clung to that like it was a life preserver in that imaginary lake.

CHAPTER TWENTY EIGHT

Something was eating at Jessie but she couldn't quite put her finger on it.

Sitting in the dimly lit media room where the monitor displayed the interview, she rewound the footage with the Missingers' maid, Marisol Mendez, to about the halfway point. It had been conducted by Detective Trembley, who was all over the map with his interrogation, bouncing around so much that Jessie had trouble following him. Mendez looked positively bewildered as she tried to follow his line of questioning.

It was obvious that when she wasn't stressed out and sleep-deprived, the woman was startlingly attractive. Her dark hair and eyes matched her exotic Latin features. Jessie was surprised that she hadn't tried her hand at modeling and even more surprised that Victoria Missinger would have let someone who looked like her spend so much time around her husband.

Despite the lack of continuity in Trembley's questioning, her story eventually became clear. She said she'd been sent on vacation by the Missingers last Monday and that they'd paid for her hotel as a bonus of sorts. She had returned on Tuesday after being informed about Victoria Missinger's death. But she was so overwhelmed with anguish that she'd taken too many pills and wasn't able to be interviewed until yesterday.

It was a sloppy story but not necessarily suspicious. Officers had been to her home and found her in a heavily medicated sleep. The GPS on her cell phone confirmed her trip to Palm Springs on Monday and her return on Tuesday. Hotel surveillance footage matched up as well.

Trembley hadn't asked about any potential affair so there was no way to gauge her truthfulness on the matter. And in general, she was pretty monotonous and rote when answering his questions anyway. Except for one moment.

That's what Jessie had rewound to. He was asking her about her time in Palm Springs. It was a strange topic to make Marisol uncomfortable but she clearly was. Jessie hit play and watched the maid closely as she answered Trembley's questions.

"So you arrived around four p.m. in the afternoon. Was there traffic?"

"It wasn't too bad," Marisol replied. She had a Hispanic accent, but it wasn't pronounced.

"What did you do once you checked in?"

"I went to dinner with a cousin who lives there," she said.

"Do anything else that night?"

"No. I was tired from the drive. I went to bed early."

"And the next day?" Trembley asked. "What did you do before you got the call about Mrs. Missinger?'

"I mostly lounged around the room," she said, seeming to lose herself in the memory of her time there before snapping back and adding quickly, "the pool more though. I lounged around the pool."

"In December?" Trembley asked.

"It was warmer than expected. Not bikini warm. But not so bad that I couldn't lie on a poolside chaise lounge and read."

He went on to ask about how she'd found out about Victoria Missinger's death, when she'd come back, and other mechanics of the day. But that wasn't what interested Jessie. She rewound the tape two minutes to his question about what she'd done on Tuesday.

"I mostly lounged around the room."

Jessie froze the screen on Marisol Mendez in that moment. From the dreamy, recollecting look in her eyes, it was clear that she was recalling a very specific moment. She was remembering the truth.

But only a second later, she corrected herself to say she'd lounged around the pool. In that split second, her entire demeanor changed. She seemed uncertain and jumpy, as if she'd made some kind of mistake. She was lying.

But why lie about such a small detail—whether she was in her room or by the pool? What difference could that make?

Jessie sat back in her chair in the darkened media room, closed her eyes, and gently rubbed her temples. Why would someone lie about such an unimportant detail? The only possible reason was that to Marisol, it was *not* unimportant.

Jessie opened her eyes. Pulling her chair closer to the monitor, she scrolled through the other surveillance footage from the Palm Springs hotel. She knew Trembley had gone through it and found nothing out of the ordinary. But she wanted to check again.

She did a cursory review of Marisol's check-in, which didn't reveal much. She arrived in sweats and a hoodie and the encounter seemed uneventful. Later that evening she left, apparently for dinner, in nicer, but still casual clothes, with her hair in a ponytail that stuck out of her ball cap. GPS data on her phone confirmed where she'd eaten and when she returned.

Footage from the next morning showed her going down to breakfast, wearing the same cap but a different, form-fitting workout outfit. She returned to her room for about an hour before leaving again, this time in a robe with its own hood.

Marisol went to the pool and settled into a chaise lounge, where she read on and off for the next three hours until she got a call that changed her whole demeanor. Jessie checked the phone log and saw that the call had come from a Lupita Mendez. Clearly, Lupita had informed her about Mrs. Missinger's death. She packed up quickly, returned to her room, and checked out twenty minutes later. The phone GPS showed she didn't make any unusual stops on the way back to L.A.

So she hadn't lied. She really had been by the pool most of her last day at the hotel. Then why had she acted as if she'd been caught saying something false?

Jessie rewound the tape again to the moment when Marisol got the call by the pool. She watched her walk inside and into the elevator, where she removed the robe hood and hit the button for her floor. Jessie froze the video.

The image was from above and the quality wasn't great. But it looked like Marisol had a thin blonde streak running through the left side of her hair. Jessie punched up the interrogation video—no blonde streak.

She went back to the hotel footage during checkout but Marisol was wearing the baseball cap again so Jessie couldn't be sure if she'd seen things properly.

She went back through the footage she'd already reviewed and realized something she'd missed before. In every publicly visible moment of her time at the hotel, except for that one brief stretch on the elevator, Marisol's head was covered. Sometimes it was a hoodie, other times a cap and, heading to and from the pool, a robe hood. It was almost as if she was doing it on purpose.

Why hide your hair and where did that streak go?

It seemed unlikely that Marisol had gotten a dye job in the brief window of time from when she'd left Palm Springs until she was questioned by Trembley. It wasn't exactly ideal salon time.

Jessie pulled up the file on Marisol Mendez. Age twenty-six; lived at home with her single mother, Margarita, and younger sister, Lupita, age twenty-four, who had called her by the hotel pool. She did a search and came across Lupita's Instagram, which had several family pictures. When she saw them, Jessie gasped audibly.

It was hard to tell the sisters apart. Despite the two-year age difference, they could have been twins, except for one thing—the blonde streak in Lupita's hair.

*

"She'll be here for the re-interview any minute," Detective Ryan Hernandez told Captain Decker in the observation room as Jessie sat patiently next to Trembley.

"So walk me through your theory again," Decker said, shutting the door and finally giving them his full attention after spending the last ten minutes putting out fires related to other cases.

"It's not my theory, Captain," Ryan said. "Hunt came up with it. She should explain it."

"Okay, Hunt," Decker said, projecting skepticism. "Go for it."

"Yes sir," Jessie began, ignoring the butterflies fluttering near her diaphragm. "I suspect that Marisol Mendez never actually went to Palm Springs and sent her sister instead. She even had her sister take her phone."

"And you suspect this because of her hair?" he said, scoffing.

"No sir," Jessie said, trying not to visibly react to his sarcasm. "That's just what made me suspicious. With one exception, whichever Mendez sister is in Palm Springs never leaves her head uncovered. But I still wasn't sure. After all, I saw that all the meals in Palm Springs used Marisol's credit card and it was her car parked in the hotel garage."

"Sounds like a home run so far," Decker said drily.

"Give her a chance, sir," Ryan said, clearly irked.

Decker glared at the detective before turning back to Jessie, his face softening a bit.

"Go ahead, Hunt. I'm just busting your balls."

"Yes sir," Jessie replied, not sure how to respond to that. "Anyway, I decided to check out what Lupita was supposedly doing here in L.A. while Marisol was in Palm Springs. I checked out her phone GPS and financial transactions."

"And…"

"And I found that for much of Tuesday, her phone was in the same hotel where Michael Missinger took his CFO's wife, Mina Knullsen, for their afternoon delight."

"So this hotel was his standing love nest and he was going back and forth between two mistresses all afternoon?" Decker asked, sounding both stunned and impressed.

"That's possible," Jessie admitted. "There is a record of Lupita's credit card being used in the hotel lobby coffee shop mid-morning. But there are other potential scenarios too."

"Like what?"

Ryan jumped in.

"She could have been spying on him. Maybe they were sexually involved and she suspected he was sleeping with someone else and followed him to the hotel and saw him with Mina Knullsen."

"The only problem with that theory is that her phone was at the hotel for most of the day," Jessie noted, "even before Missinger met Mina there."

"That doesn't absolve her," Ryan argued. "Maybe she didn't take the phone with her everywhere. What if he did put her up in the hotel but she left her phone in the room, went for a walk, and stumbled upon him and Mina at some point? She could have followed them and the phone GPS would show her as still in her room."

"For that matter," Trembley piped in, "she could have left her phone in the room and gone to Hancock Park to knock off Victoria Missinger."

"That's possible whether she saw Missinger with Mina or not," Jessie said. "The alternatives are endless. She could have switched phones with Lupita simply to cover for an affair with Michael. Or she could have done it to provide herself with an alibi while killing Victoria. I don't know what her game was for sure. What I *do* know is that she wasn't in Palm Springs."

Officer Beatty popped his head in the room.

"She's here," he said.

"Put her in the interrogation room," Ryan said, before turning to the others. "It looks like we're about to get some answers."

CHAPTER TWENTY NINE

Even though she was only observing the questioning through a one-way mirror, Jessie felt nervous.

It was her theory on the line after all. She could only hope that Ryan and Trembley could get Marisol Mendez to confess to whatever it was she was hiding. Sitting in that interrogation room, she didn't look like she was inclined to be forthcoming.

Her elbows were resting on the table with her head in her hands. Her face was set in a grimace, as if she were preparing to face down whatever they threw at her, as if it were her lot in life to be questioned periodically by men out to bring her down. Jessie wondered if it had even occurred to Marisol to ask for a lawyer. Then her mind did a mental skip as she went back over her previous thought.

Her lot in life.

The phrase jumped into Jessie's brain and lingered. That was part of how Bolton Crutchfield had described the perpetrator of Victoria Missinger's murder. On more than one occasion he had said that the murderer was unhappy with their lot in life.

That certainly seemed to apply to Marisol Mendez. Jessie didn't want to make assumptions but she doubted that a pretty girl like Marisol dreamed that at age twenty-six, she would still be living with her mother and working as a maid.

How much more likely was it that she longed to be living with the man she saw every day but could not have to herself; that she longed to be the lady of the house? It seemed more than reasonable to conclude that Marisol was unhappy with her lot in life.

Jessie cast her mind back to Crutchfield's other clue, the one he said was a twofer that would help with both the hunt for her dad and this case. He had said she needed to keep her focus on the never-ending battle for truth and lady justice.

She had assumed that lady justice related to the hunt for her father. But maybe only the "battle for truth and justice" was about Xander Thurman. They'd established that the Superman reference was about the Kent Clark Building at Cal State-Northridge where Dr. Bertrand Roy worked. Maybe the reference to "lady"—the one word that wasn't in the original Superman line, was Crutchfield telling her that the killer in the Hancock Park case was female. It made sense.

Ryan and Trembley had just begun the questioning and Jessie didn't want to interrupt them when they were just underway. Instead, she scribbled a message on a piece of scrap paper that read:

Crutchfield hints fit. Marisol—maid, lives with mom, sleeping with unattainable man—"unhappy with her lot in life?" Also—battle for truth and LADY justice. Lady= female killer?

She folded up the note and gave it to Officer Beatty with instructions to hand it to Detective Hernandez. When Ryan got it, he looked up at the mirror as if he'd gotten an unexpected electric shock. Almost imperceptibly, he nodded in that direction before putting the note in his pocket and turning his attention back to Marisol, who was repeating her story for Trembley.

"How long have you been sleeping with Michael Missinger?" he asked, interrupting her.

She looked startled but not surprised by the question.

"Mrs. Missinger was a wonderful boss," she answered. "I respected her. I would never—"

"Let me stop you for one second, Marisol," he interrupted again. "We know you haven't been honest about a lot of things so far. But none of them constitute crimes. It sounded like you were about to deny an affair with Mr. Missinger, which would make us very skeptical of your credibility, After all, it's one thing to lie and say you were in Palm Springs when you were in fact in a downtown hotel. It's quite another to deny you were sleeping with the husband of a woman who was murdered. At a certain point, we have to ask ourselves: why is this woman lying so much? Could it be that she's trying to cover up something far worse than an affair?"

Marisol lifted her head from her hands and looked at Ryan with such a lost, forlorn expression that Jessie almost felt bad for her.

This girl is good.

"I didn't kill her," Marisol finally said quietly. "Yes, I was involved with Mr. Missinger. And yes, he paid for my hotel in Palm Springs. I had my sister go for me because I thought Mrs. Missinger was suspicious about what was going on and if she called the hotel to check up, they'd assume Lupita was me and

161

say I was there. We switched cars, phones, everything, just to be safe. But he actually put me up at the Bonaventure Hotel. He said we could use it as our special hideaway all week. And we started to. We spent Monday evening in the room he booked for me. And then he came by again on Tuesday morning."

"What about that afternoon?" Trembley asked.

"He said he had a big meeting in the afternoon but that he'd see me on Wednesday. But he surprised me and stopped by briefly for a quickie before going home. He said he was in the area."

"So what did you do all afternoon before that?" Ryan asked.

"I walked around for a few hours," she said. "I don't usually get the time to just wander."

"Without your phone?" Trembley asked. "Or should I say your sister's phone?"

"I forgot it in the room," Marisol insisted. "By the time I remembered it, I was too far away to go back so I just left it."

"That's awfully convenient," Trembley said with an air of self-satisfaction.

"Not for me," she shot back. "I couldn't order a Lyft and I couldn't find any cabs. I had to walk all the way back."

"So for over two hours you were aimlessly wandering around downtown Los Angeles?" Ryan pressed.

She nodded.

"Did anyone see you?" he asked. "Did you interact with anyone?"

"I got a taco from a street vendor for a snack. But there was a long line of people. I doubt he'd remember me."

"Did you go into any stores?" Ryan asked. "Make any purchases using a credit card?"

"I don't make enough to shop in any of the stores I walked past," she snapped. "Didn't you hear me? I bought *a* taco, not tacos. There's a reason for that."

"Are you sure you didn't go anywhere else?" Ryan asked again.

"I'm sure."

"And when you returned to the hotel, you didn't see Michael Missinger again until he came to your room?" Trembley wanted to know. "You didn't happen to see him there with someone else?"

"Who else?"

162

"Another woman," Trembley charged confidently. Ryan gave him a subtle shake of his head as if to chastise him for giving up too much information.

"I didn't see that," Marisol said, untroubled. "But it wouldn't stun me. Mr. Missinger had a big appetite when it came to sex. Mrs. Missinger wasn't very interested. I knew I wasn't the only one he spent time with. We had fun together but it's not like I thought he was going to divorce his wife for me."

"But if he did," Trembley said in a tone that suggested he thought he was about to nail her, "you'd certainly be able to buy more than one taco from a street vendor."

Marisol gave him a look of disdain that suggested she wasn't very impressed with him.

"I've told you everything I know, even things that are embarrassing for me," she said plainly. "I think I'd like a lawyer now."

Ryan stood up and Trembley followed suit. The interrogation couldn't continue and there wasn't much purpose at this point. She wasn't going to give them anything more.

Jessie leaned back in her chair, frustrated but impressed. Marisol's alibi was almost impossible to corroborate but would be difficult to puncture. She admitted to lying and bad behavior but not to murder. In fact, acknowledging her misdeeds seemed to buoy her claims of innocence when it came to Victoria Missinger's death. There were only two real options. Either Marisol Mendez was telling the truth, or she was a far more sophisticated killer than Jessie had given her credit for.

The detectives came out and Trembley headed straight for the restroom.

No wonder he was pushing so hard. He had other things on his mind.

"That wasn't very satisfying," Jessie said to Ryan. "I kept waiting for the big Perry Mason moment and it never came."

"Nope," Ryan agreed. "Oftentimes suspects only confess when they're already busted or know they can't be. Marisol Mendez fits in that muddy middle. It makes sense that she'd deny everything."

"So what now?" Jessie asked.

"We charge her," Ryan said more definitively than she'd expected. "She has no alibi and she lied about her whereabouts. In fact, she constructed an entire fake alibi to hide the fact that she was in L.A. She was having an affair with the victim's husband so there's motive. She had access to the house. She knew about the nook in the pool house where the poisoning happened. She knew where the vacuum cleaner was to eliminate any footprints in the room. She knew Victoria was diabetic and probably saw her administer the injections many times."

"She was pretty adamant in her denials," Jessie said. "You don't find her credible?"

"You're the profiler, Jessie, not me. So I won't pretend to be an expert on her credibility," he said. "But going based on the evidence, I say we don't need a confession. I have to confer with the D.A., but I think we've got enough circumstantial evidence right there to take this to a grand jury at the very least. And don't forget about the stuff that's not admissible from your incarcerated friend in Norwalk. Lady Justice, unhappy with her lot in life. That stuff fits too."

"I guess," Jessie said reluctantly. "I still wonder whether this was her doing alone. Are you comfortable ruling out Michael Missinger completely?"

"He alibied out. Mina Knullsen confirmed she was with him and we have video backing that up."

"He could have put Marisol up to it," she suggested.

"He could have. And if he did, you can bet she'll turn on him to get a better deal."

"When would that happen?"

"Maybe the minute she's charged. Maybe after a night in jail. Maybe never if she's in love," he said. "Listen, I've got to go do the charging paperwork. But I say take the win. We don't always get them. I think this time we did."

Jessie nodded and Ryan headed back to his desk. She decided to step outside to get a little fresh air and clear her head and went out to the station's adjacent courtyard, where she took a deep breath. The cold air was bracing. Suddenly her phone buzzed.

It was text from Pa. It read: *Got your message. Good memories. We should try the bunny slopes again sometime. Only this time you'd be picking me up. P.S. Ma had a good chemo session today. Very little vomit.* ☺

Jessie chucked slightly to herself. That was about as sentimental as the old codger got. She started to text him back as she returned inside. Her head was down and she almost knocked over an older man exiting the building.

"Sorry," she muttered as she looked up.

It was Garland Moses, the celebrated profiler she had still never formally gotten the chance to meet, even after all these weeks on the job. This was the closest she'd ever gotten to him. He looked distracted, as if lost deep in thought. He took a long drag on the cigarette he'd just lit and blew it out slowly.

"No sweat," he replied, his voice low and raspy. His white hair was disheveled, as if he'd just gotten out of bed. He was dressed in rumpled tan slacks, a gray sweater vest two sizes too large, and a sports jacket that hung off him like he was a coat rack. His skin was leathery and wrinkled. And his bifocals teetered at the end of his nose. But behind them, the eyes were sharp.

Jessie wanted to say something quippy but couldn't think of anything. Besides, he looked like he was busy with his own thoughts. She knew he was working on some serial killer case. That was what had Captain Decker so distracted earlier, uninterested in some high society poisoning.

"I hear you nailed someone in the Hancock Park murder," he said gruffly as she started for the door.

She turned around. He was looking directly at her so she figured she had permission to reply.

"Maybe. It's no serial killer case though," she said sheepishly.

"Every solved case is a worthwhile case," he growled. "Besides, I hear you spend more than enough time in the company of serial killers down in Norwalk."

Jessie couldn't help but look surprised. Bolton Crutchfield's location was supposed to be a well-guarded secret. But apparently Garland Moses knew not just where he was but who was visiting him.

"How's the hunt going for yours?" Jessie asked, changing the subject despite her desire to get his take on Crutchfield.

"Slowly," Moses admitted. "Nine dead in the last year. Three in the last month alone. But almost nothing to work with."

"I'm sorry to hear that," Jessie said, not sure what she could say that wouldn't make her sound like a rube. "Nice talking to you."

She turned and opened the door to go back in.

"Why maybe?" he called after her.

"Excuse me?" she said, turning around.

"When I said you nailed someone for the murder, you said 'maybe,'" he reminded her. "Why?"

"Oh. Something just doesn't feel quite right. It's my first real case and I guess I thought it would be tied up in a nice bow at the end. It's not. I suppose I should get used to that."

"They almost never get that perfect bow," he said. "I've been doing this a long time. For every case I get where the puzzle pieces fit, there are ten where I have to jam them together. On the other hand..." His voice trailed off.

"What?" Jessie pressed.

"Sometimes when it doesn't feel right it means you missed something and that's your brain not letting you off the hook. Of course, other times it's just indigestion."

With that, he stubbed out his cigarette with his shoe and walked back inside, leaving Jessie alone with her troubled thoughts.

CHAPTER THIRTY

A day and a half later, Marisol Mendez still hadn't flipped. Ryan considered that a sign that Michael Missinger wasn't involved. Jessie thought he was probably right. But she couldn't shake the apprehension that, despite all the evidence, they were railroading an innocent woman. She told him so.

She even went back to the media room to review footage of the interview with Missinger that Ryan and Trembley had conducted. She hadn't found anything new or revealing in the interrogation itself. But she did notice that after he was left alone to write up his statement—away from the pressure of hovering detectives—Missinger seemed surprisingly sanguine.

He pushed the blond hair out of his blue eyes and settled comfortably into his chair. It was as if all the tension from the interview had drained away. Jessie couldn't decide why.

Was it because he had been playing the role of grieving husband and was now free of it? Or was he simply relieved not to be peppered with constant intrusive questions? Maybe writing out a statement was relaxing by comparison.

With that image still fresh in her memory, Jessie left the station that evening to meet Andi Robinson for a much needed Friday night drink—the one she'd promised to get when the case was finally over. She was in the parking lot when Ryan caught up to her.

"Hey," he said, jogging to catch up. "I couldn't let you go without addressing what you said in there earlier."

"What's that?" she asked. She had said a lot of things.

"It's just…you keep beating yourself up over this case," he said, sounding genuinely concerned. "You have to cut yourself some slack. If you're this hard on yourself after every case wraps, you're going to burn out quicker than Josh Caster, the profiler who moved to Santa Barbara."

"I'm doing okay. I just have doubts."

"Of course you do," he acknowledged. "It's natural. You feel responsible for someone possibly going away for the rest of her life. I feel that way all the time too. It's a major burden to carry. And if you have even a sliver of doubt, the guilt eats at you. It's not like with your husband. I'd imagine a guy trying to stab you with a fireplace poker wipes away most of that doubt."

"Most?" she asked, raising her eyebrows.

"You know what I mean," he said, smiling goofily. "Just don't be so hard on yourself is all I'm saying. Self-doubt comes with the territory in this business. It's good that you're meeting that rich gal for drinks. You deserve it. And she's probably got really expensive liquor."

"I've got to go," Jessie said, trying not to laugh.

"Oh, now you're too good to hang with the rabble," he teased.

She turned away quickly and headed for car, fairly sure he hadn't caught the big grin on her face.

*

The traffic from DTLA to Hancock Park was as bad as usual but Jessie didn't mind as much this time. Something about navigating the mess for leisure made it infinitely less painful.

Despite her misgivings about the case, she decided to let it go. She wasn't the district attorney tasked with convicting Marisol Mendez. She was just part of the team who provided the evidence for that task. The D.A. would present the case. A jury would decide guilt or innocence. It was out of her hands.

She forced herself to focus on the positives instead. There were lots of them right now. Her ma was apparently feeling pretty decent, even going out to dinner and a movie last night. It was a long way from remission. But any improvement was good news.

Jessie was reconsidering whether to join the upcoming FBI Training Academy for this session after all and if she did, thought she might stop through Las Cruces on the way to Virginia. She still had a couple of days left to make a final decision.

She'd also found a new place to live, assuming her offer was accepted. There were two other bids and she was on pins and needles waiting to find out if she'd get it. She was trying, mostly futilely, not to get too excited so there wouldn't be too big a letdown if it didn't pan out. But it was difficult because the apartment was just about perfect.

Ultimately, she had chosen not to go with any of the Realtor's recommendations. Instead, she had picked a modest studio apartment on South Olive, just off Olympic. But in light of how easily Crutchfield had found her last place, she planned to take some extra precautions.

Like her adoptive father had done when he bought the senior living condo, she would rent the place through a company name and have an attorney sign the paperwork. Her name would be found nowhere on the lease.

The unit had secure underground parking. But it was below the retail center next to the apartment complex, not under the complex itself, so anyone following her might be confused about where she was driving.

In addition, the building had a doorman *and* a security guard. Having even one of those was unusual in L.A. Having both was a black swan situation. In addition, none of the units were actually numbered. As part of some cool, hipster thing she didn't understand, residents just had to know which door was theirs from memory. It was weird but it served her purposes.

And even though all the mail went to a central location in the lobby, Jessie still planned to set up a P.O. box address so that all hers went off-site. She would then have a courier service bring it to the station so that no one could link her to it.

Finally, she had hired a security company recommended by Ryan, which would come by right after she officially got the place and install an alarm with motion sensors and multiple cameras. They weren't quite NRD-level precautions, but they would give her a sense that she had at least some control over her life.

She hadn't yet broken the news to Kat that they likely wouldn't be roommates. But she was pretty sure that if anyone would understand, it was the head of security at the lockdown facility holding the man who'd ordered her home broken into.

She'd let Kat know tomorrow when she went to see Crutchfield, who had apparently specifically requested to meet with her. He'd never initiated a visit before and Jessie had to admit she was curious about what he wanted.

And now she was headed over to Andi's, to have her first leisurely evening in forever. She felt a hint of remorse that it wasn't with Lacy, whom she hadn't spoken with since moving out. But she pushed the thought away, trying to allow herself to look forward to an evening at the mansion of a chill, pleasantly sarcastic, non-racist socialite. That didn't happen to her every day.

As she drove up Rossmore Avenue, following the directions Andi had given to her house, Jessie made a last-minute change of plans and turned onto Lucerne, the Missingers' street. She pulled over in front of the house and parked, still keeping the car running.

Somewhere in there Michael Missinger was living his life. Jessie wondered if he was overcome with grief or if he'd already put all that behind him. How long would he wait before resuming his activities? Most importantly, had he manipulated Marisol into taking the fall for him?

She felt herself starting to seethe and decided it was time to move on. She put the car in gear and drove the last stretch to Andi's. The place was even more massive than the Missinger house. From what Jessie could tell, it was three stories and stretched almost a third of the way down the block. But unlike most other homes on the street, it didn't have a security gate. Something about that made Jessie like her even more.

When she arrived at the front door she pressed the doorbell, uncertain if anyone would even hear her knocking. Andi opened it within seconds and extended the drink she was holding in her other hand.

"I took a chance and figured you might be a mojito girl," she said.

"I'm a 'just about anything' girl tonight," Jessie replied, taking the glass. "Thanks."

"Welcome to my not so humble abode," Andi said, waving her inside.

Jessie noticed her host was barefoot and happily slid off her own shoes too.

"I bet that felt good," Andi said, apparently noticing the relief Jessie felt as her feet escaped the confines of her professional footwear. "Come on in and make yourself comfortable."

Jessie peeled off her coat as she followed her through the massive foyer and down a long marble-floored hallway filled with sculptures and paintings. It seemed endless, finally opening onto a carpeted den that was as casual as the rest of the house was formal.

The room was dominated by two huge, comfy-looking couches. In between them was a rustic wood coffee table covered with magazines, and not stuff like *The New Yorker* and *The Economist* but *Cosmo* and *People*—another check in her favor. A wet bar stood in one corner. Directly opposite it was a TV screen that extended almost from floor to ceiling.

"I like a pretty picture when I watch my stories," Andi said in a vaguely Southern accent, noting Jessie's eyes widen at the sheer massiveness of the thing.

"It's like a home theater," she marveled.

"That's the idea," Andi replied. "I'd offer you the whole home tour but that would take up most of the evening and personally, I'd just rather hang in here."

"That sounds good to me."

"Great," Andi said, collapsing onto one of the couches. "I was also thinking of ordering pizza in a bit. You in?"

"I am totally and completely in," Jessie said, tossing her coat and purse down beside her as she plopped onto the other couch. "Do you ever invite the country club gals for any of these mojito and movie nights?"

Andi laughed at the prospect.

"Not so much," she said. "The ones you met, Marlene and Cady, are pretty representative of what the Beverly Country Club has to offer. They're not exactly the 'kick off your shoes and veg out' crowd. They're more the 'judge every possession in your home' types."

"That sounds super fun. Speaking of Marlene, she must have had a field day when the Missingers' maid was arrested."

"That's an understatement. She would not let it go; kept saying it confirmed all her suspicions. The phrase 'I hope this teaches your migrant-loving ass a lesson' was uttered. It was delightful."

"I'm sorry to have played a role in reinforcing her stereotypes," Jessie said, forcing herself not to bring up her doubts about Marisol's guilt with a civilian.

"No chance it was a mistake or there was someone else involved?" Andi asked before quickly adding, "Not that I'm questioning your work. I just don't love the message it sends."

"That's okay." Jessie said despite herself. "Believe me— I've had my own reservations. But the evidence led to her. It'll all come out in the next few months. It's pretty definitive."

Andi leaned in conspiratorially despite the fact that they were on couches six feet from each other.

"Tell me if this is inappropriate to ask," she said quietly. "But there's talk around the club that Marlene's crazy 'affair-with-the-boss' theory wasn't that far off."

"I can't really get into the specifics," Jessie said, finishing the last of her mojito. "But let's just say that Marlene's superiority complex isn't getting undermined anytime soon."

171

"Man, that is a serious bummer," Andi said and then pointed at the empty glass. "Want a refill?"

"Sure," Jessie replied, handing it over and curling her legs underneath her.

This couch is more comfortable than my bed.

Andi went back to the wet bar and started tossing ice cubes in the glass.

"I guess you never know what's really going on in someone else's house," she said. I wouldn't have pegged Michael for the type to shtup the maid at the Bonaventure. It's such a cliché. But like I said the other day, I wasn't that close to them. I guess I bought into the image they were putting out there, just like everyone else."

"Yeah," Jessie agreed. "You never really know what's in someone's heart. I used to live with someone for years, thinking we were birds of a feather. Then he pushed me out of the nest."

"But I thought that was your job," Andi said, pouring various ingredients into Jessie's drink. "Isn't that what a profiler does—look into people's hearts?"

"First of all, I'm new to the gig, so I'm still in 'trial and error' mode. There's a reason I was assigned this case and not the one where a serial killer is currently terrorizing the city. Second, profilers don't look into people's hearts. They look at the crime and the evidence to create a picture of what kind of characteristics the perpetrator might have. I leave hearts to the clergy."

"Fair enough," Andi said, handing her a new drink. "You see what happens when a person who bailed on her education starts making assumptions. Do we want to order that pizza and pick a movie?"

"Actually, before that, do you mind if I borrow your bathroom?" Jessie asked, taking a sip. "It was a long drive over."

"Of course," Andi said. "It's right off this room to the left there."

Jessie put her mojito down and stood up.

"You know," Andi said, "you can take your drink with you. I don't want it to get too watery. Besides, we don't stand on ceremony here at the Robinson abode. If you have one too many, you can take a Lyft home or just crash here if you like."

"Don't mind if I do," Jessie said, grabbing the drink and heading for the bathroom.

"Any pizza preference?" Andi called after her.

"I'm pretty easy," Jessie answered. "Just no anchovies please."

"Dear god, no!" Andi agreed, laughing.

Jessie could still hear her chuckling after she closed the bathroom door. The scent of potpourri wafted over her. She looked at herself in the mirror and smiled.

Look at you, having a girls' night.

She took a big glug of her drink, tied her hair in a ponytail, and threw some cold water on her face. She noticed her cheeks were a little ruddier than usual, probably a result of the alcohol.

Despite her best efforts, Jessie couldn't help but let her thoughts wander back to Michael Missinger. She kept returning to the same questions in her head: What was he doing in his mansion less than half a mile away? Was he mourning in a candlelit room? Was he even there? Or was he entertaining a new conquest at the Bonaventure Hotel at this very moment? Everyone seemed to know that was his seduction spot of choice, even Andi. Apparently it was an open secret.

Was it though?

The thought popped into her head as if planted there by someone else. She tried to push it away, annoyed with herself for letting her brain work overtime on a night she was supposed to be relaxing. But the question circled in her thoughts.

Were his hotel liaisons common knowledge? Because Michael certainly didn't want them to get out. The whole point was to go somewhere that he wouldn't be found out by Victoria or his employees. And that detail wasn't available to the public yet. The only people who knew about the hotel get-togethers were Missinger and his paramours.

"Just stop," Jessie said aloud, staring angrily at herself in the mirror. She noticed her eyes were watering. She grabbed a tissue and dabbed them.

But despite her entreaty to herself, the thoughts kept coming. If Andi knew about the Bonaventure, was it possible she'd just heard about the hotel through the grapevine?

She would have mentioned it to me.

Jessie grabbed another tissue and coughed into it, trying to get rid of the sudden catch she felt in her throat.

Why wouldn't she tell me?

The possibilities came fast and furious after that. If Andi knew about the Bonaventure Hotel, then the only reason for her not to mention it was because she knew that it would reveal she was sleeping with the man too.

173

And if she was sleeping with him, then she was almost certainly being deceptive about a great deal more. For one, she had said she didn't know the couple well. But it would seem she at least knew Michael quite intimately. For another, it was she who had conveniently reminded Jessie about the "affair with the maid" rumor, sending her down the path of re-investigating Marisol's alibi.

Jessie turned on the faucet, cupped her hands, and slurped a gulp of water, hoping it would clear her throat, which felt tight.

What was it Andi had said about her love life when they met for coffee?

It's only recently that I've allowed myself to become open to actually falling in love. I'm trying to make up for lost time, I guess.

Was it possible that she'd fallen in love with Michael Missinger? And if she had, how far would she go to make that love something more than illicit? She'd already proven she was a smoothly adept liar. What else was she capable of?

Jessie coughed again. She felt like her throat was clenching up. That and the watery eyes made her wonder if she was allergic to the potpourri in the bathroom. She needed a puff from her inhaler, which was still in her purse on the couch.

Deciding to behave as normally as she could, Jessie resolved to beg off on the rest of the evening and leave so she could untangle her suspicions away from the object of them. She grabbed her drink and headed for the door.

She was about to open it when she looked down at the glass. The wheezing and coughing and watery eyes had started soon after she'd sipped her second mojito—the one Andi had poured for her right after mentioning the Bonaventure Hotel.

That couldn't be a coincidence.

CHAPTER THIRTY ONE

Suddenly it all made sense.

Jessie flashed back to their conversation at the Coffee Klatch, where she'd mentioned her violent peanut allergy. It wouldn't be hard to slip peanut oil into an alcoholic drink and have it go unnoticed.

Andi must have realized she screwed up by mentioning the hotel and assumed I'd figure it out.

And now, just as she'd eliminated Victoria Missinger and Marisol Mendez as threats, she was taking action once again to remove a person who could get in her way.

Jessie forced herself to breathe in through her nose, which was still clear for now. Even as she did, she felt her skin start to itch and her chest burning with the effort to get air in.

Think, Jessie. Find a way out of this.

She pulled out her phone to call 911 but then thought better of it. She'd be unconscious by the time they answered. She considered calling Ryan but worried that even if he picked up, she wouldn't be able to speak. Even texting the situation might take too long.

Then she remembered the emergency quick-touch code he he'd told her to text if she was ever in imminent danger. She quickly punched in "999" and the message "ASAP" was sent. Hopefully he'd get it and send the cavalry. He knew where she was going tonight. He had access to her phone's GPS and had even used it once before to locate her at the hospital after her husband attacked her. It might work.

But not if she couldn't get away from Andi, who was somewhere on the other side of that door, already committed to making sure she didn't leave the house alive. She had to try to get out without looking vulnerable.

If she could make Andi think the poisoning attempt hadn't worked, maybe she could walk out of the place without a confrontation. She had to fake being fine and not in the middle of a medical emergency. With that goal in mind, she took one more nasal breath, opened the door, and stepped out.

Andi was still in the living room, looking suspiciously casual as she mixed herself a drink at the bar.

"Everything okay?" she called out. "I was starting to get a little worried."

Jessie nodded as she made her way to the couch where her purse rested. She felt a cough coming and forced it down so that it came out like a grunt.

"Where's your drink?" Andi asked.

Jessie pointed back at the bathroom, doing her best not to look directly at her host. She feared that if Andi saw her watery eyes or flushed cheeks, she'd realize that her efforts had worked.

She got to her purse and unzipped the small side pocket where she normally kept the inhaler but it wasn't there. She began rifling through the main pouch, fearing it had fallen in and gotten mixed up with all her other junk. As she did, she felt her throat close almost completely and gasped involuntarily.

"Are you all right?" Andi asked, rushing around the bar with a concerned look on her face. "You don't look so hot."

Jessie felt her vision fade momentarily and dropped to one knee. She gasped again and looked up helplessly at Andi, who was now standing over her.

"How can I help?" she asked urgently as she put her drink down on the table. "Should I call nine-one-one?"

"Puff," Jessie managed to croak, hoping with all her might that she'd misjudged Andi and that her new friend would come to her rescue.

"Puff?" Andi repeated, looking confused. "You mean like an inhaler?"

Jessie nodded vigorously, pointing at her bag.

"You mean like the one I took out of your purse and put on the bar over there?" she asked slowly, her voice turning sickly sweet as she pointed to the red inhaler sitting innocently on the marble bar fifteen feet away. It might as well have been a mile. Andi's lips curled up ever so slightly to form a thin, cruel smile.

Jessie gave a massive hack as she dropped to both knees. She knew she didn't have much longer before her throat closed entirely and she slipped into unconsciousness. As she slumped forward, her upper body crumbling face-first onto the couch cushion, she tried to form a coherent thought in her quickly clouding brain.

Backup plan.

Her backup plan. Her backup inhaler. It was in her inside coat pocket, less than two feet from her—if she could just muster the strength to grab it.

Pushing herself up slightly, Jessie lunged out and managed to clasp the sleeve of the jacket before collapsing back down. She sensed her body slipping from the couch to the carpet and held on to the jacket desperately. She felt it land next to her as she hit the floor and clutched it tightly to her chest as she rolled into the fetal position, now wracked by abdominal pain on top of everything else.

"You may not believe me," Andi said from somewhere above her, "but I really do feel awful about this. It's not how I wanted things to go. I really felt a connection to you, Jessie. I thought we could be pals."

Jessie rolled onto her chest, with her knees curled under her stomach and her coat gripped tightly under her body. As she writhed on the ground, unable to distinguish between the pain in her gut and the burning in her chest, she tried to concentrate on reaching into the jacket pocket for her backup inhaler. She could hear Andi's voice, though it was farther away now.

That bitch has gone back to the bar to get her drink!

"The minute you mentioned that peanut allergy," she heard her hostess say, "I had to go out and buy some peanut oil, purely as a precaution, of course. I never thought I'd need it. But then you made me screw up. I got so comfortable that I let the hotel bit slip out. I knew the second I said it that you'd figure it out, maybe not now but eventually. And since this might be my only opportunity to neutralize you, I had to do it. You understand, right?"

Jessie wriggled her hand deep in the interior pocket and hit something hard and plastic with her knuckle—the inhaler. She grabbed it and pulled it out quickly, doing her best to keep it hidden. She was bent over and facing away from Andi, who was across the room. There'd never be a better chance to do it.

She brought both her hands up to cover her face as a legitimate, rasping cough escaped her throat. As she desperately gasped at whatever air her lungs could suck in, she shoved the inhaler spout into her mouth and sprayed.

"How long should I wait before calling nine-one-one?" she heard Andi ask from somewhere closer than before. "I want to make it seem real. Should I wait until you turn blue to try mouth to mouth?"

Jessie felt a second cough come on and went with it, hacking uncontrollably. On the wheezing inhale, she puffed again, keeping her hands cupped around the inhaler. She felt an ever-so-slight loosening of the tightness in her chest.

Fearing Andi was almost upon her, she took one final puff before slumping on her stomach, hiding the inhaler below her. She was still rasping but could feel oxygen returning to her system. Nonetheless, she played up the breathing troubles, even twitching a bit in the hope that the stalling tactic would give her time to come up with another move. As she contorted, she shoved the inhaler into her pants pocket and out of sight.

As she lay there, the thought of Bolton Crutchfield flashed through her mind briefly. He had hinted that the killer was female. He had suggested she was unhappy with her lot in life. In hindsight, everything that had seemed to match up with Marisol Mendez fit Andi equally well: unable to live up to her father's expectations, a dropout, living a life she knew was empty of meaning, so devoid of love that she would kill to create some spark of it.

"I'm going to call nine-one-one now," Andi said chirpily, from right above her. "I don't want to wait too long and have it look suspicious. It'll take forever for them to answer anyway."

As if on cue, Jessie gave a final wheeze and lay still. She allowed her body to go limp, even as her mind raced.

The pieces all locked into place, like one of those jigsaw puzzles that Garland Moses said so rarely fit together. Andi had the motive to do this and the wherewithal too. Her chemical engineering background would make something as simple as dosing an insulin injection child's play. Sabotaging a neighborhood transformer so that the power—and all the security cameras—went out would be a simple task for someone of her intellect. And given the time and desire, framing her romantic target's employee would be easy and, considering she was a rival, probably very satisfying.

"Hello," she heard Andi's panicked voice shout from the ground beside her. Apparently getting through to 911 hadn't taken so long after all. "Yes, I have an emergency at 2140 South Muirfield Road. My friend has had some kind of allergic reaction. She started coughing and wheezing and now she's passed out. Please send an ambulance right away."

Jessie heard a voice on the other end of the line but couldn't understand the words. A moment later Andi replied, doing an impressive job of sounding like she was just a hair away from completely breaking down.

"Is there something I can do to help her? I found an inhaler in her purse. Should I spray it in her mouth? Should I try to resuscitate her?"

Andi was now crying. Real or fake, it was utterly convincing. Jessie wondered if she would actually pretend to revive her. Would she breathe into her mouth? Do chest compressions? If she did, she'd discover quickly that her victim was far from unconscious. At that point Jessie would have to be ready to react.

Jessie used the sound of Andi's sobbing to hide her own attempts to gulp in as much air as possible. She no longer felt like her chest was going to explode but she wasn't anywhere near full strength either. If there was a physical confrontation, her considerable size advantage would be of no use.

"I'm sorry, say that again," Andi said, perplexed.

The operator said something else unintelligible.

"How could they be pulling up now?" Andi asked. "I called you less than a minute ago."

And then, as if in response to her question, there was a loud knock at the door.

CHAPTER THIRTY TWO

Jessie could feel Andi's eyes on her, boring into her back.

"What did you do?" she heard the woman hiss, her lips only inches away.

There was another loud knock, this time even more urgent.

"Open up!" a male voice shouted. "This is the LAPD. We received an emergency message from this address."

Jessie felt fingers dig into her skin as Andi rolled her over onto her back. She kept her eyes closed and tried not to breathe, hoping she looked like an unconscious person. It didn't work.

"You can stop faking. I know it was you. There's no way they could have responded this quickly. Not that it'll do you any good."

Jessie heard a shattering sound and decided it was time to open her eyes. As she did, the door pounded as if someone was kicking it.

Andi was kneeling directly above her, holding a long piece of her own broken mojito glass in her right hand, which was bleeding profusely. Her eyes were focused in the direction of the banging door.

"Last chance," the male voice yelled. "Open the door or we will break it in."

Andi glanced back down at Jessie and saw that she was awake. Her eyes widened with a crazed glee and she lifted the long glass shard above her head before bringing it down.

Jessie was still clutching at her coat and brought it up to block the blow. The glass tore through the material at first before snagging, losing momentum on the way down and never actually connecting with Jessie's body.

Andi tried to yank the glass free but in the process, managed to pull the ensnared coat as well, tearing it from Jessie's hands. As she forcefully ripped the glass free of the coat, Jessie took in the deepest breath she could muster. Andi fixed her eyes on her again.

Do something now or you'll never do anything ever again.

Still lying on her back, Jessie raised her uncovered right foot in the air and kicked at Andi as she dove forward. Her foot smashed into the other woman's chest, sending her backward before the glass weapon could find its mark.

Andi's back slammed into the coffee table behind her. The force knocked the glass out of her hand. She slumped there briefly, seemingly dazed. The sound of splintering wood from the foyer brought her back to her senses. She began scanning the carpet for the chunk of glass.

Jessie decided not to wait for her to find it. As quickly as she could, she rolled onto her stomach and began crawling away in the direction of the foyer. She heard jostling behind her and suspected Andi had found the glass and was standing up, so she tried to do the same.

She pushed up with the limited strength in her arms and scrambled to her feet, stumbling forward. She could hear several voices in the hallway ahead of her and careened, off-balance, in that direction. She had just crossed the threshold from the carpeted den into the marble hall when she felt a searing pain in her right calf and a hand on her left ankle. She tumbled forward, throwing her arms out to protect her head as she hit the ground.

"Freeze," a voice yelled from somewhere in front of her.

She looked up to see two men in LAPD uniforms, both with guns drawn and pointed in her general direction. Behind her, she heard the distinct sound of glass hitting marble and knew that Andi must have dropped the piece she'd been holding.

"Thank god you're here, Officers," Jessie heard her say. "This woman broke into my home and attacked me. I had to use a chunk of glass to hold her off. I think she's delusional. Please be careful. I think she's armed."

The cops, who had both had their guns trained above Jessie in the direction of the woman behind her, now looked confused. Jessie hadn't been expecting this and wasn't sure how to make the true situation clear. It didn't help that she wasn't even sure she could speak yet. Her throat was no longer closed off but it felt raw and tight. She swallowed hard and croaked out the one word she hoped would let them know the truth.

"Hernandez."

The cops glanced at each other before returning their attention to the women in front of them.

"That's who sent out the alert," the officer in front said to his partner, "Detective Hernandez from Central Station. If she knows that, she must be the one who placed the call."

"Let's cuff them both and sort it out later," the officer in back said.

"Fine by me," the first one said. "Both of you: hands where we can see them. Other than that, don't move."

Jessie nodded, relieved, and spread her arms out on the floor in front of her. As long as Andi was cuffed, she didn't care if she was too. The officer in front holstered his gun and proceeded toward them slowly.

As he did, Jessie heard an almost imperceptible scraping sound behind her. She knew what it was immediately. Andi was picking up the glass again. With every ounce of strength she had left, Jessie yelled as loud as she could.

"Weapon!"

The second officer still had his gun out and didn't hesitate to fire it. Even with the sound of the shot echoing through the hallway, Jessie heard someone hit the floor behind her. Then the screaming began.

Andi was howling an indecipherable mix of unintelligible screams and only occasionally coherent, random words like "bitch," "mine," and "pay." Jessie glanced behind her to see the lady of the house sprawled out on her back several feet away. Her right arm lay immobile at her side. Blood was pouring from that shoulder. Her left hand was flailing about, intermittently trying to stop the bleeding. The piece of glass rested harmlessly on the ground six feet away.

The first officer hurried past Jessie to attend to Andi. The second officer, with his eyes trained solely on Jessie, holstered his gun and pulled out handcuffs.

"You Hunt?" he asked, looking down at her.

Jessie nodded.

"I still need to cuff you until we clear this up."

"I understand," Jessie said, putting her hands behind her back before adding, "Is she going to be okay?"

"She'll recover," the officer said. "I'm a pretty good shot."

CHAPTER THIRTY THREE

The stitches made it hard to drive. It was more painful to brake than to accelerate, as she had to flex her calf muscle harder. As a result, the drive out to Norwalk to see Bolton Crutchfield the next day took even longer than usual. Jessie tried to just accept the delay and appreciate the fact that she was alive.

It could have gone much worse. The cut from Andi's swipe at her leg with the piece of broken glass hadn't gone especially deep. There was no damage to the muscle and no major blood vessels had been affected. But it was still long and deep enough to require seventeen stitches. Luckily, the doctor told her it wouldn't prevent her from going to the FBI Academy.

Jessie wasn't exactly sure when she'd made the decision to change her mind and attend the upcoming session after all. It might have been the previous night in the ambulance on the way to the hospital, when she was lying on a stretcher, dealing with the fact that she'd nearly been outwitted twice in the last few months.

Both times it was because she made assumptions that she could trust people—first her husband, then a seemingly innocuous country club socialite—who ended up wishing her harm. She needed to get better at setting aside her personal feelings if she was going to be a great profiler.

She knew she had solid instincts. But instincts weren't enough, especially if she hoped to catch someone as dangerous as her father before he found her. There were only so many times she could wing it before her luck would run out. She needed more training.

And there didn't seem to be any better time than now. She'd accrued some professional capital now, as she had just uncovered Victoria Missinger's true killer and prevented an innocent woman from going to prison. True, she was partly responsible for Marisol Mendez being under suspicion in the first place. But no one seemed to be holding that against her.

The praise for her work had allowed her to request a sabbatical to go to the National Academy. And since she was technically a consultant, and a junior interim one at that, they couldn't really say no. Ryan said Captain Decker didn't want to look churlish so he didn't have any choice but to sign off on it and hold her position with the department, which would no longer be interim after she returned.

It also made sense from a personal perspective. She'd already signed the paperwork for the divorce. The house was officially sold. And to her delight, this very morning she got the call that her offer on the apartment had been accepted.

Later this week, she would formally move in to her new, highly secure, borderline prison residence. If she had to pick ten weeks in which she could just up and leave town for this program, now was the perfect time to do it.

And since the program didn't begin until after the new year, that gave two weeks for her leg to heal up. She had officially decided to stop in Las Cruces to visit with her folks for a few days before continuing on to Quantico.

She'd already checked with the D.A., who said that she wouldn't be needed to testify against Andrea Robinson for a few months, so there was no conflict there. But her testimony would definitely be necessary as Andi had done a stellar job of covering her tracks.

There wasn't much physical evidence of her crime. The security cameras offered nothing because they were fried. There were no fingerprints or DNA at the Missinger house. Andi must have left her phone at home when she went to kill Victoria because that's where the GPS conveniently showed her during the window in which Victoria was murdered.

There was nothing suspicious in her online search history either. Of course she could have gone to any internet café or public library to check up on how to sabotage transformers or overdose insulin.

Authorities did have Michael's admission that he had been sleeping with Andi and that she'd often talked about them running away together. But other than Jessie's testimony, there was almost nothing to tie Andi to the crime. And even then, Andi hadn't ever actually confessed to killing Victoria, only to poisoning Jessie herself, which she was also being charged with. It was logical to assume she'd done that because she realized Jessie had figured out what she'd done to Victoria.

But Andi was claiming that she'd inadvertently put the peanut oil in the drink, thinking it was liquid sugar. Of course that didn't explain why she was found trying to stab Jessie with a chunk of glass. In the end, the D.A. thought they might have a better chance of convicting her for attempting to murder Jessie than for actually murdering Victoria Missinger.

Ryan had assured her just this morning that now that they knew the culprit, they'd be able to go back through Andrea Robinson's life in recent days and find evidence that they didn't even know to look for before.

"It's been less than eighteen hours since she was arrested," he reminded her. "Give us a little time to do our work. Andrea Robinson may have been smart but I guarantee you she left traces of what she did. We'll find them."

"I really hope so," Jessie had said. "I want her to go down for the actual crime she committed. Victoria Missinger deserves justice."

"That's the kind of attitude that will serve you well at the FBI Academy," Ryan noted. "You'll fit right in with the other straight arrows."

She didn't mention that she planned to anonymously donate half of what she got from the sale of her home to the Downtown Children's Outreach Center or that she had talked to Roberta Watts this morning about becoming a regular volunteer there. It wouldn't make up for the loss of Miss Vicky, but it was something.

"Who are you kidding?" she teased, trying to divert attention from herself. "You're way more of a straight arrow than I am. You follow procedure. I barely know what it is. Maybe you should be applying to enter this program."

"I have actually," he told her, the disappointment in his voice obvious. "I got in twice. But the timing wasn't right in either case. Shelly needed me to stay here. I'll do it at some point."

Jessie didn't press him. He clearly didn't want to get into it. Jessie also realized this was the first time he'd ever actually used his wife's name.

"Are you going to be able to solve any cases without me around?" she asked, trying to lighten the mood.

"I don't know," he said, feigning concern. "Maybe you can get some more tips from your incarcerated buddy that could help me out while you're gone. Is that why you're visiting him today?"

"I actually have no idea," she admitted. "Kat just told me he wanted to speak with me. It's the first time he's initiated a meeting. So I'm more than a little curious."

"Well, I'd say give him my regards, but I don't think he'd appreciate that from the guy who put the cuffs on him."

"Yeah, maybe I'll pass on that that," Jessie had agreed.

But now, as she pulled through the security gate at the Non-Rehabilitative Division of the Department State Hospital-Metropolitan of Norwalk, she knew there was another reason she wouldn't mention Ryan Hernandez to Bolton Crutchfield.

Somehow she sensed that Crutchfield wouldn't be bothered that she knew the man who'd arrested him. Rather, he wouldn't like that she was so friendly with him. She had the weirdest feeling that he would be jealous.

After once again going through the laborious security procedures, she passed through Transitional Prep to the secure hallway where Kat Gentry was waiting for her.

"How are you doing?" Kat asked as they walked down the hall.

"Not too bad, all things considered. I solved a murder and didn't get killed by the murderer myself. And I decided to spend ten weeks in Virginia," she added, explaining her plan and letting Kat know the roommate thing wouldn't work out.

"I understand," Kat assured her. "If you change your mind when you get back to town, let me know."

"I will," Jessie promised, "though I'm not sure you'd want to room with someone who had her place broken into on the orders of one of your inmates, especially one who doesn't like you that much."

"Don't worry about me," Kat assured her as they reached the door to the residential cells unit and she waved for someone to buzz them in. "I can take care of myself."

"Of that, I have no doubt," Jessie said, though she wasn't sure that was the point.

They stepped through the door. Most of the staffers at the security station didn't even glance up. Apparently even Cortez, almost always in playful mode, was too busy to flirt with her. He did manage a quick smile and a wave before returning his attention to the screen in front of him.

"So did Crutchfield tell you anything about why he wanted me to come?" Jessie asked, turning back to Kat.

"Nope," Kat said as she handed over the emergency red-buttoned key fob. "All he said was that it was important that he speak with you. As you know, normally I wouldn't accede to a request like this. But I decided to make an exception in this case."

"Well," Jessie said, with a hint of resignation, "let's go find out what fresh hell he's prepared for me now."

CHAPTER THIRTY FOUR

When they entered the room, Jessie sensed immediately that something was off.

Crutchfield was already standing up, almost as if at attention. He followed her with his eyes as she sat in the chair behind the desk on the other side of the partition.

"I'm glad to see that you're doing well, Miss Jessie," he noted.

"What do you mean?"

"The news said that a woman was arrested for the murder of Victoria Missinger and that the LAPD consultant who caught her was injured in the incident. No name was given but in light of your slight limp, I feel safe drawing the conclusion."

"What did you ask me here for?" Jessie asked, trying to move past the gamesmanship, though she suspected it was a futile effort.

"Patience, my dear," he said, sounding slightly peeved. "Please, I have so little to look forward to in here most days. Won't you allow me this little respite from the drudgery for a little fun?"

"You consider this fun?" she asked.

"I do," he admitted. "Tell me, was my assistance useful? Were my clues on point?"

"They were," Jessie told him. "The killer was a 'lady' who was unhappy with her lot in life. Although, by the time I made those connections, she was already taking steps to get rid of me."

"I'm glad she wasn't successful," Crutchfield replied, sounding something close to sincere. "Although for a time there it looked like you'd pegged the wrong 'lady.' I have to admit I was disappointed in you."

"Yeah, well, we sorted that out in the end," Jessie retorted, more defensively than she intended.

"And it's a good thing you did too," Crutchfield said. "Had you not, I might have been forced to chastise you."

"I feel like you do that all the time anyway, Mr. Crutchfield."

"Oh, not verbally, Miss Jessie," he corrected. "I would have had to teach you a lesson, to *show* you that you were wrong."

"How would you have done that?" she asked uneasily.

"Most likely by having your friend Lacy, the one you're currently slightly estranged from, gutted like a pig."

Jessie's jaw dropped open despite her effort to hide her shock. She couldn't speak. Behind her, Kat shifted uncomfortably in the corner where she stood but said nothing. Crutchfield was more than happy to continue.

"It would have been a hard lesson, I admit," he continued mildly, as if he were discussing restaurant menu options. "But you needed to be made aware that you were on the wrong track with that whole maid business. And sometimes lessons are difficult."

"But you changed your mind?" Jessie asked, finally finding her voice again.

"Yes. I'd say you were about twenty-four hours from losing Ms. Cartwright. But you righted the ship and as a result, her innards are intact. By solving the case, you saved your friend's life. Well done!"

Jessie sat quietly for a moment with her head down. When she raised it to look at him, she fixed him with a hard stare.

"How are you getting your information, Mr. Crutchfield? I can't help but feel like you're cheating."

"Cheating, my dear Miss Jessie? How could I possibly be cheating? You are the one who can walk out into the big bright world when you leave this cell. I'm the one trapped here, with cameras monitoring my every move, microphones recording every word I say, every snore, every gaseous exhalation. And all of it set up by your best buddy over there in the corner. I'm at a tremendous disadvantage in our interactions, don't you agree?"

"And yet," Jessie noted, "I feel like you're about to reveal that's not the case. It's quite clear that you're holding something back. Whatever it is you're dying to tell me, it's taking everything in your power not to shout it out right this second."

"Oh my dear Miss Jessie," Crutchfield said, chuckling softly to himself. "I do have such affection for you. It's true, of course. I do have a tidbit to share. I just wanted to remind you how far my reach extends before I shared it with you, so you wouldn't doubt my words when I say them. Please remember, I'm the one who ordered the apartment break-in. I'm the one who knew the exact time you'd be in danger from Josiah Burress, the vagrant in that abandoned apartment building.

Please keep those facts in mind when I share my next revelation with you."

"Noted," Jessie said, certain from the gleam in Crutchfield's eyes that he couldn't hold off much longer. "You've proven that what you say isn't to be taken lightly."

"Thank you for acknowledging that," he replied. "Then let's get to it. You recall, of course, that I met with your father a few years ago, in this very facility, for a conversation that proved most enlightening."

"I recall vividly," Jessie said, thinking back to the video of the two men talking.

"Well, Miss Jessie, I just wanted you to be the first to know that we've scheduled a follow-up."

"What?"

"I'll be having a little chat with your father," he repeated. "I won't spoil things by saying when. But it's going to be lovely, I'm quite certain."

"How?" Jessie croaked, her throat suddenly dry.

"Oh, don't you worry about that, Miss Jessie. Just know that when we do talk, I'll be sure to give him your regards."

THE PERFECT HOUSE
(A Jessie Hunt Psychological Suspense Thriller—Book Three)

In THE PERFECT HOUSE (Book #3), criminal profiler Jessie Hunt, 29, fresh from the FBI Academy, returns to find herself hunted by her murderous father, locked in a dangerous game of cat and mouse. Meanwhile, she must race to stop a killer in a new case that leads her deep into suburbia—and to the brink of her own psyche. The key to her survival, she realizes, lies in deciphering her past—a past she never wanted to face again.

A fast-paced psychological suspense thriller with unforgettable characters and heart-pounding suspense, THE PERFECT HOUSE is book #3 in a riveting new series that will leave you turning pages late into the night.

Book #4 in the Jessie Hunt series will be available soon.

BOOKS BY BLAKE PIERCE

A JESSIE HUNT PSYCHOLOGICAL SUSPENSE SERIES
THE PERFECT WIFE (Book #1)
THE PERFECT BLOCK (Book #2)
THE PERFECT HOUSE (Book #3)

CHLOE FINE PSYCHOLOGICAL SUSPENSE SERIES
NEXT DOOR (Book #1)
A NEIGHBOR'S LIE (Book #2)
CUL DE SAC (Book #3)

KATE WISE MYSTERY SERIES
IF SHE KNEW (Book #1)
IF SHE SAW (Book #2)
IF SHE RAN (Book #3)

THE MAKING OF RILEY PAIGE SERIES
WATCHING (Book #1)
WAITING (Book #2)
LURING (Book #3)

RILEY PAIGE MYSTERY SERIES
ONCE GONE (Book #1)
ONCE TAKEN (Book #2)
ONCE CRAVED (Book #3)
ONCE LURED (Book #4)
ONCE HUNTED (Book #5)
ONCE PINED (Book #6)
ONCE FORSAKEN (Book #7)
ONCE COLD (Book #8)
ONCE STALKED (Book #9)
ONCE LOST (Book #10)
ONCE BURIED (Book #11)
ONCE BOUND (Book #12)
ONCE TRAPPED (Book #13)
ONCE DORMANT (book #14)
ONCE SHUNNED (Book #15)

MACKENZIE WHITE MYSTERY SERIES
BEFORE HE KILLS (Book #1)

BEFORE HE SEES (Book #2)
BEFORE HE COVETS (Book #3)
BEFORE HE TAKES (Book #4)
BEFORE HE NEEDS (Book #5)
BEFORE HE FEELS (Book #6)
BEFORE HE SINS (Book #7)
BEFORE HE HUNTS (Book #8)
BEFORE HE PREYS (Book #9)
BEFORE HE LONGS (Book #10)
BEFORE HE LAPSES (Book #11)

AVERY BLACK MYSTERY SERIES
CAUSE TO KILL (Book #1)
CAUSE TO RUN (Book #2)
CAUSE TO HIDE (Book #3)
CAUSE TO FEAR (Book #4)
CAUSE TO SAVE (Book #5)
CAUSE TO DREAD (Book #6)

KERI LOCKE MYSTERY SERIES
A TRACE OF DEATH (Book #1)
A TRACE OF MUDER (Book #2)
A TRACE OF VICE (Book #3)
A TRACE OF CRIME (Book #4)
A TRACE OF HOPE (Book #5)

Printed in the USA
CPSIA information can be obtained
at www.ICGtesting.com
LVHW050951211223
766685LV00053B/302

9 781640 296978